PRAISE FOR

All the Winters That Have Been

"At last a love story that is truly from
a man's point of view—terrific! I loved it!"
—Jayne Anne Krentz

"Poignant and emotionally satisfying. . . . Delivers an
impact that will not easily be forgotten."
—*Library Journal*

"A moving, bittersweet novel. . . .
A wonderful read."
—*Romantic Times*

Books by Evan Maxwell

All the Winters That Have Been
Season of the Swan

Published by HarperPaperbacks

ATTENTION: ORGANIZATIONS AND CORPORATIONS

Most HarperPaperbacks are available at special quantity discounts
for bulk purchases for sales promotions, premiums, or fund-raising.
For information, please call or write:
Special Markets Department, HarperCollins Publishers,
10 East 53rd Street, New York, N.Y. 10022.
Telephone: (212) 207-7528. Fax: (212) 207-7222.

HarperChoice

Season of the Swan

Evan Maxwell

HarperPaperbacks
A Division of HarperCollinsPublishers

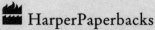 **HarperPaperbacks**
A Division of HarperCollinsPublishers
10 East 53rd Street, New York, N.Y. 10022-5299

If you purchased this book without a cover, you should be aware that this book is stolen property. It was reported as "unsold and destroyed" to the publisher and neither the author nor the publisher has received any payment for this "stripped book."

This is a work of fiction. The characters, incidents, and dialogues are products of the author's imagination and are not to be construed as real. Any resemblance to actual events or persons, living or dead, is entirely coincidental.

Copyright © 1997 by Two of A Kind, Inc.
All rights reserved. No part of this book may be used or reproduced in any manner whatsoever without written permission of the publisher, except in the case of brief quotations embodied in critical articles and reviews.
For information address HarperCollinsPublishers,
10 East 53rd Street, New York, N.Y. 10022-5299.

ISBN 0-06-109975-9

HarperCollins®, ®, HarperChoice™, and HarperPaperbacks™ are trademarks of HarperCollinsPublishers, Inc.

Cover photograph © 1997 by Uniphoto

A hardcover edition of this book was published in 1997 by HarperCollinsPublishers.

First HarperPaperbacks printing: April 1998

Printed in the United States of America

Visit HarperPaperbacks on the World Wide Web at
http://www.harpercollins.com

❖ 10 9 8 7 6 5 4 3 2 1

Season
of the
Swan

One

The cellist was a madman. He sweated and puffed his cheeks and writhed in agony. Then he lay his cheek on his fingerboard like a sleepy child. His antics would have been hilarious but for the magnificence of the music he made.

Kate Saarinan sat on the stage, her instrument on her lap, watching the performance. She was the principal violinist in the string quartet, a striking feminine presence in a forest-green velvet gown, yet for the moment she was invisible. The two hundred people in Weill Recital Hall were focused on Piotr Dubrovnik. The flamboyant Russian cellist was giving the most important performance of his career in front of the most exacting audience in the world.

Kate was at home on the low stage of the Weill, one of the small recital venues within the confines of Carnegie Hall. The arched and draped room, with its three glistening chandeliers and its elaborately molded walls and ceiling, was a launching pad, a critical rung on the career ladder of young classical music performers. It could be a wonderful and promising place.

Only two months had passed since Kate's solo debut in the hall. She had been brilliant—and lovely in the bargain. Everyone had said so, even Grace Willingham, the usually acerbic reviewer from the *New York Times*.

But Kate had no illusions about the Weill. It could also be a killing ground and a graveyard. Promising careers had died on that small stage. Decades of practice and performance could collapse into shambles.

The Weill's two hundred seats were usually occupied by real fans of music, people who knew and cared passionately about music. Weill regulars would pounce on fudged phrases or slurred notes like vultures on a carcass. If a musician were unlucky or unwise, he or she could be destroyed in a single night.

Kate wondered how the man who had been her friend and confidant for fourteen years would fare. They had arrived in New York at about the same time, but from different directions—she from the Pacific Northwest and he from Moscow.

Born in St. Petersburg when it was called Leningrad and trained in Moscow, Piotr had fled the Soviet Union when defection still had real meaning. He had been successful in New York, and now made a good living as principal cellist with the New York Philharmonic, but he longed for a bigger career. Tonight's concert was just the beginning.

The Dubrovnik Quartet—Piotr, a violist-violinist couple named Alan and Helga Green, and a temperamental first violinist named John Dorling—was Piotr's creation. He had worked for five years to secure the private sponsorship necessary for a Weill Recital and then, two weeks before the date, Dorling had quit.

Ordinarily, the petulant resignation would have forced cancellation of the recital, but Kate had volunteered to fill in. She and Piotr had played together for years, as students at the Curtis Institute, as street buskers, in off-Broadway pit orchestras, and in pickup chamber groups. They knew one another instinctively, from friendship and affection.

During two weeks of almost continuous practice, Kate had relearned the skills of playing in an ensemble. She had tempered her own style and melded it with the others. In the future, she would be replaced by a regular violinist, if indeed there was a future for the Dubrovnik Quartet. But for the past two weeks and this concert, Kate had allowed herself to become a brilliant support player.

Until this moment, the concert had been a triumph. The Mozart had sung itself through the strings, and a quirky Mendelssohn quartet had become sinuous and vivid. The first two movements of the Brahms had been lucid and calm. Then Piotr had made a critical artistic decision, launching into a solo that was a reinvention of the theme.

The new solo was Piotr's creation. He intended it, and others like it, to become the trademark of his quartet. He was as ambitious as he was brilliant. He wanted to impose himself and his own personality upon string quartets.

Piotr and Kate had discussed the improvisation again and again at practice. She liked the solo. She thought it was an intriguing, exhilarating new interpretation, but she had warned him of the risks. No matter how brilliant the passage, no matter how well he played, a critical recital was not the place to experiment.

Piotr had agreed to reconsider, to make his choice based on the feeling of the moment, but Kate had suspected he would succumb to the temptation. He was too proud to back away from the challenge, too full of his own ambition.

The decision had not been merely musical. There were pragmatic considerations, as well. The Brahms had been selected with a particular member of the audience in mind. Grace Willingham, the *Times* critic who usually reviewed Weill recitals, loved Brahms and doted on daring young performers. If ever there was a critic in New

York who was sympathetic to Piotr's choices, it would be her.

Kate listened to the solo carefully. Its opening passage was brilliant, full of contained energy. Then, a minute and a half into the solo, she saw her own worst fears take shape. A bulky figure rose from a seat at the end of one of the middle rows and stared up at the stage for a moment.

In the reflected spotlights, Kate caught a familiar glint of thick eyeglasses and recognized George Mayhew, a freelance critic who sometimes filled in for Grace Willingham. Kate felt her heart stop. She glanced unhappily toward Piotr, trying to catch his eye, but it was too late. The cellist was caught up in his work.

Hell, thought Kate. What rotten luck.

Mayhew was a dyspeptic young man, a clarinetist of small note, a failed musician who turned to criticism as a vent. He wrote beautifully when he liked a concert and savagely when he did not. Worse, Mayhew was known for his dislike of Brahms and his slavish dedication to classical scores as written. He regarded improvisation as an insult to his ear.

Kate held her breath as she watched the critic turn and stalk up the aisle. Perhaps he's just leaving a little early to make a deadline, she tried to tell herself. Perhaps I'm reading too much into this.

But that vain hope vanished when Mayhew reached the door. He turned for one last look at the stage and Kate caught a flicker of stage light on his thick glasses as he shook his head in what could only be disgust. Then he stalked out.

Piotr was still caught up in his own reinvention of the classics, oblivious to everything but his instrument and the music in his mind. The Greens watched his performance closely. The audience seemed riveted on the stage.

So far as Kate could tell, she was the only person in

the room who had seen Mayhew's departure. She was the only one who sensed disaster in the making. For a moment, Kate felt hollow and old. She had worked almost as hard as Piotr had, preparing for this night. She had little to gain, because her own solo career was well launched and because this program was designed to showcase the Russian. But Piotr? Well, Piotr, old friend, she thought, you may have just shot yourself in the foot. God, but this thing called life can be cruel. One misstep can turn promise into pessimism. One bad review in the *New York Times* can set a career back a decade, or kill it altogether.

At that moment, Piotr opened his eyes and glanced in her direction. In mid-phrase, he came out of his self-induced trance, grinned faintly, and winked at her, full of the joy of performing and living.

Kate smiled back out of reflex. Her affection for this big, mercurial man was deep and abiding. She loved to see him perform.

She drew a slow deep breath and straightened her shoulders, bringing herself back to the moment and the one thing that truly counted, the music itself. Why ruin the moment, she thought? Perhaps Mayhew wouldn't bother to write a review. Or perhaps his screed will be squeezed out of the paper by something that was truly important.

She turned her head subtly, stretching the long, tight muscles of her neck. Her dark hair, loose and free, brushed across her bare shoulders lightly. In that instant, she felt relaxed, oddly free considering the moment.

To hell with ambition, to hell with critical reviews, she thought. She and Piotr and the others were doing what they wanted to do, playing music they loved and helping to please audiences in the process. She would survive, no matter what, and so would Piotr. No one lived and died by what happened here in the recital hall tonight.

Her decision took her outside of herself, to the place where music was born. She felt the knots in her shoulders begin to untie. Suddenly, she could breathe deeply again.

She listened more carefully to the involuted and spiraling improvisation that spilled from Piotr's darkly burnished cello. Here in the bright spotlight, she could almost see the vibrations from the taut strings shimmer down the hard maple bridge and spread across the soft pinewood of the cello's belly.

The instrument was a priceless seventeenth-century Italian Guarneri, and its rounded thickness had always seemed pregnant. Piotr's passionate intensity with the bow might have made Kate uneasy, except for the tenderness of his strength. He lavished the same intensity on his wife and two children.

Kate sensed a change in the music. She glanced over at Piotr. He opened his eyes again for an instant and nodded slightly toward Kate, inviting her and the others back into the song.

Piotr drew the last long solo note from his cello, and Kate smoothly lifted her own violin to pick up the thread. The second violin and viola gathered their own portions of the tapestry and wove in between Kate's soaring air and Piotr's dark and brooding undercurrent.

That was brilliant, Piotr, but this is the music Brahms wrote, this is our inspiration, Kate's fiddle seemed to say. Piotr's cello grumbled a bit, as though acknowledging the limits of its own efforts. Then the other two instruments joined in, a final affirmation of harmony and an acknowledgment that the original work had not been bettered in a hundred and fifty years.

Kate was lost in the last bars and the blend of strings. She drew out the last phrase, and together the four musicians let the piece end itself as easily as a summer's day turned to night.

The audience's response caught the quartet by surprise. Kate looked out past the footlights and was astonished to see two hundred people on their feet, applauding as though they, too, had finally understood the ultimate unity of past and present, music and silence.

Piotr came out of the music more slowly. He set the cello aside, wiped the streaming sweat from his eyes and his forehead with a clean white handkerchief, and then looked around as though he had just awakened. Only then did he hear the cheers.

Kate and the other two were already on their feet. She reached out for Piotr's hand. Slowly he stood, the bear awakening, a faintly foolish half-grin on his face.

"They love you, madman," she said quietly, squeezing his hand.

"Of course they love me," Piotr said. "I'm brilliant."

"Then show them you love them back." She dropped his hand and stepped back, drawing the other musicians with her, leaving the cellist alone at center stage.

The applause swelled, and Piotr acknowledged it with a smile. He raised his hand and waved, letting the energy of the audience animate him. His smile spread, his joy apparent. Kate felt as though she had just sat down before a warm fire.

There would have been an encore, but as the applause swelled, two children broke away from their seats in the front row and climbed up the broad steps onto the stage with squeals of delight.

Sasha and Igor, or, as Kate knew them, Sassy and Ig, five and three years old, dashed across the stage. Piotr looked dismayed at such a breach of recital-hall decorum. Then he surrendered to a stronger impulse and swept his children up in his arms. In that instant, he was not a musician but a father.

Both children kissed their father wetly. Iggy wrapped his arms around his father's neck and burrowed in like a happy pup.

Piotr threw his head back and laughed grandly. He gestured to his wife, Dina, who still stood by her seat. Reluctantly, she joined them, her face burning with a mixture of embarrassment and delight.

The family stood together as the applause and the laughter swelled. Then Sassy turned in her father's arms and reached out for Kate, her godmother.

Kate hung back, not wishing to intrude on the triumph, but the little girl clapped her hands together and reached out again.

"Kate, too," she said.

Dina heard the child's voice above the applause and turned, opening the circle. Piotr roared his approval, and suddenly Kate was swallowed up in the embrace of the entire Dubrovnik family.

"Thank you, my big sister," Piotr said softly over the cheers of the audience. "That last passage was magnificent."

"You were the star," Kate replied uneasily, as if worried that her performance had somehow overshadowed his.

"The music was the star," he said. "Thank you."

When they turned again to face the audience, Kate found herself holding her violin and bow in one hand and Sasha with her other arm. The applause doubled. Cheers and whistles sounded against the acoustically perfect walls.

For that moment, Kate felt as much a part of a family as she had been in fourteen years. It was a wrenching, bittersweet sensation that told her what she already feared: She had left too much of herself in the past.

A half hour later, the crowd of well-wishers backstage had begun to thin out. Kate surrendered Sasha to her father, kissed Igor one last time, and turned to go.

"So soon?" Dina protested. "Please stay."

"I can't. I have a seven A.M. plane. Langley, Washington, remember?"

Dina remembered. Then she looked worried.

"Oh, Kate, you are pushing too hard. First tonight, with all it has meant, and then you commit yourself to a week of free lessons and concerts in some far-off place. You must take more care for yourself."

"I look at it as a healthy inoculation," Kate replied with a smile that was a little forced. "A week with a bunch of ungrateful little fiddlers in a small town and I'll be reminded of why I came to New York in the first place."

Dina examined Kate through squinted eyes. "You don't fool me, Kate."

"What makes you think I'm trying to fool you?" Kate asked quickly.

"Maybe you're trying to fool yourself," Dina said. Her smile softened. "I've seen you with Sasha and Igor. You hunger for children."

"That's the old country talking," Kate said. "I love being with Sasha and Igor because they don't belong to me. When they turn into little terrors, I can give them right back to their mother."

Dina shook her head and laughed. Then she pointed to her children. "Sasha and Igor know you better than you know yourself," she said.

Kate watched the two children for a moment. Each held onto one tail of their father's cutaway coat for balance. The excitement had begun to wear off. They both looked hollow-eyed.

"They'll be asleep before you get them home," Kate said. "Do you need some help?"

"Ah ha, see?" Dina said. "You can't wait to hold them."

"All right, I love the little monsters," Kate admitted with a wry smile. "And I care about the kids I'm going to see in that closed little town out in Washington, where new ideas are fought like a disease."

"Why are you going?" Dina asked. "Is this Langley your hometown?"

"No, but I was raised in one like it." She shrugged. "I suppose that's why I'm going. I was once a wretched little fiddler in a narrow little town on the Washington coast. It cost me a lot to get out. If I can help some of those kids get out with their souls intact . . ." She shrugged again.

"You're very tired, aren't you?" Dina asked, putting her arm around Kate's shoulders.

. Unbidden, the words of an old childhood hymn came back to Kate. *I'm tired and so weary, but I must go along . . .*

She squared her shoulders. "Nothing a night's sleep won't cure," she said. "Besides, I'm looking forward to this trip as a triumphant return. It will be fun."

Dina's expression said she didn't believe a word of it.

"Whatever," Kate said. "I'll be back in a week and I want you and Piotr to plan a getaway of your own. I'll take Sassy and Ig off your hands and you can fly away to Florida for a couple of days. How does that sound?"

Dina looked shocked at the suggestion. Then she glanced at her husband, noting that he, too, was beginning to look hollow-eyed with fatigue.

"Would you?" she asked.

"Of course."

The two women embraced and broke apart, both suddenly surprised at the depth of understanding they felt for each other.

"It's not too late, Kate," Dina said. "You could still have some of your own, if that's what you want."

For an instant, Kate's face showed something that might have been pain. She glanced once more at the two children and shook her head. Then, without another word, she touched Dina on the arm and moved away through the crowd toward her dressing room.

Two

*K*ate closed the dressing room door firmly behind her and leaned against it with her back as though to bar a pursuer. She was always most vulnerable in the moments following a concert, particularly a concert that had demanded as much emotionally of her as this one had.

She drew in a deep breath and let it out slowly, calming herself. Drawing another deep breath, she held it for a moment, letting the haunted, hunted feeling pass.

It was fourteen years ago, she thought. A long time.

But not long enough to forget. If anything, the feeling of hollowness was growing.

Perhaps it is this trip, she thought. She had been so focused on the quartet recital that she had not been able to sort through her own feelings about small towns and children and the rest of it. She had accepted the mentoring assignment on an impulse that had surprised her even more than it had her agent.

Maybe Dina was right, Kate thought. Maybe I should cancel, take a few days off for myself.

Nonsense. Don't make more of this than it is, a simple commitment you made some time ago, an adult commitment that you can no more avoid than you can avoid a trip to the dentist.

That analogy calmed her. The trip wasn't penance. It was just a one-week fellowship in Langley, Washington, home of the Island Tulip Festival. You like tulips, you'll love Langley, that's what they say. And who doesn't like tulips?

She put her violin away in its velvet-lined case and gathered her cape and purse. As she turned to pull the cape over her bare shoulders, she caught a glimpse of herself in the big mirror that covered one wall of the dressing room. With the detachment of someone whose profession puts her in the public eye, Kate examined her appearance.

Her long, gypsy-dark hair was a gift from her Hungarian mother, and her pale, fine skin from her northern European father. Her parents had come from a long line of farmers. Not peasants, but not bourgeois, either. Both had died too young to see what their daughter would become.

Kate wondered what they might think of the fashionable, self-possessed urbanite who was staring back at her from the mirror.

They would probably be horrified to see me with bare shoulders in front of two hundred people, she thought. I don't think they would have known what to make of me.

They would probably want grandchildren, too. Expect them, in fact. Well, their happiest dream would have been their worst nightmare, so it's just as well they never knew.

Kate pulled the warm wool cape around her. Seventh Avenue in the middle of the night was no place for a lone woman to parade bare shoulders. That was one of the irritating drawbacks to New York; the gleam of success was always tarnished by having to dodge aggressive panhandlers or catch a cab on a dark street in the middle of the night.

A firm knock on the dressing room door interrupted

her thoughts. Before she could answer, the door opened. Ethan Farr stuck his head in.

"Perfect," he said. "I've never heard you play more wonderfully. And here I thought you disliked Brahms."

Farr, with his thin, chiseled features and a full shock of snowy hair, was Kate's agent. As far as she was concerned, he was arguably the best-looking and certainly the most effective agent in New York. Though he had represented her for a decade, she was surprised to see him anywhere near Carnegie tonight. He had opposed her participation in the quartet from the beginning, fearing that it would detract from her solo career.

"Hello, Ethan," she said cheerfully, settling her cape in place. "Does this mean you've forgiven me?"

A smile passed over Farr's face so quickly that she couldn't read it. He shook his head.

"I was wrong, I admit it," he said. "The fact is, this concert may have been the most important you've ever given. Do you have time for supper?"

"Me? Supper? I didn't know you ever took your clients to supper," she teased, for Ethan was renowned for his discriminating taste in restaurants. "I'd love to any other time, but I have an early morning flight for Seattle, remember?"

"Oh, yes, Seattle." He cleared his throat. "Uh, do you suppose you could cancel this trip of yours to the wilds of Washington state?"

"My God, is there suddenly a conspiracy to keep me away from the San Juans?" Kate asked with a trace of exasperation in her voice.

"I haven't heard," Farr said innocently. "Does sound like an excellent idea, though."

"It probably is, but I'm going anyway."

"Why?"

"I accepted, last year," she said. "Surely you remember."

"You weren't famous then."

"I'm not famous now," she said. "I'm just a small-town girl who takes her word very seriously."

"Some things are more important in the long term than disappointing some young, er, farmers," Farr replied diplomatically. "It is a very long way from New York to this place you're going."

"I know every inch of that way. I was one of those young farmers in a small town in the Northwest. If I can give one kid a glimpse of the wider world, and a belief they can get to it, then it's worth a few days of my time."

Farr held up his hand to turn her irritation aside.

"I didn't mean that as personally as you took it," he said. "Normally I would applaud your generosity, but something unusual has come up. It might be very important. It might be . . ."

He hesitated, a cautious man reluctant to finish his thought.

"I'll let you judge for yourself," he said finally. "Come with me. I want you to meet someone."

"Who?"

Farr started to speak and then stopped himself again. "Don't ask questions. Just be your beautiful and charming self."

"Beautiful? Charming?" she said in disbelief. "Who are we talking about?"

"You. I hope."

He picked up Kate's violin case and offered his arm.

"Ethan, what's—"

"Where is the elevator down to the main level?" he asked before she could finish.

She looked at his diabolically angelic face. Ethan Farr was a shrewd negotiator with a well-deserved reputation for honesty. He was always cautious, about both good news and bad, but she had the clear impression he was about to burst with anticipation.

"This had better be good," she said, taking his arm.

"I do believe it will be."

Kate led the way to a back elevator that took them down two floors. It let them out in a long, deserted hallway that ran down one side of the most famous auditorium in New York's cultural history. Farr looked both directions, orienting himself.

"Perfect," he announced when he saw where they were. "Now come along."

He steered her toward a closed door that would let them into the main auditorium. He stopped at the threshold.

"Though you don't believe it, you have grown from an awkward, determined country girl into a beautiful, cosmopolitan woman," he said, smiling with genuine fondness.

Kate's eyebrows rose.

"Pretend this is a concert," Farr urged. "Leave your irritations and worries here in the corridor and concentrate on the moment. It's one you have worked toward for a very long time."

For an instant, she was speechless. Her relationship with Ethan was close, but not personal. She had never before sensed the depth of his affection for her, principally because he had always kept it so carefully concealed.

"You make me feel like—" She paused, groping. "—like a bride being walked down the aisle to an arranged marriage."

Farr chuckled. "Beautiful, charming, and frighteningly intelligent. Shall we meet the groom."

With a grand gesture, he threw the door open and escorted Kate into the hushed, deserted auditorium of Carnegie Hall.

The Great Hall was dark, except for the hooded, dimmed houselights on the ranks of box seats and the fronts of the upper galleries. Kate looked up the curved wall of boxes. She had never performed on the main stage, but she had attended a hundred concerts here. Each time, the place was new and special.

Carnegie was a holy place of sorts, shrine to a tradition she honored and joined, a tradition that went back to the first musicians in the human race. Now, deserted, it was like an empty cathedral waiting for humans to give life to it.

The stage itself was bathed in spots and fill lights. The frescoes and columns and arches of the backdrop, ornate relics of another century, seemed to glow magically in the silence. On the polished wooden planks of the stage, a grand piano waited, with top raised and bench drawn up to the keyboard. The piano was positioned just off-center, as though to accompany a solo recital.

"Daniel," Farr called out.

A man appeared from offstage and peered out into the dark hall. "Come up, come up. I want you both to take a look at the view."

"This is my intended?" Kate asked, under her breath.

"Don't be smart," Farr whispered. "That's Daniel Heller."

"Daniel Heller? Of Polyphony Records?" Kate hissed back.

"There's only one," Farr assured her, "and he's it."

Premonition prickled over Kate's skin. Polyphony Records was one of most important recording labels in the world, an arm of a Japanese-owned international entertainment company that dominated popular music.

"If I were a pop singer, I'd be orgasmic," she said softly.

"Hush! Come on."

As they moved down the aisle toward the stage, Kate studied this man Heller with more interest than she showed. He was young as executives go—less than forty, trim, athletic, and closely shaved, even at the end of what was probably a sixteen-hour workday.

He was dressed carefully in a beautifully tailored blue

suit with a crisp blue shirt and a rich, perfectly knotted burgundy necktie. The necktie was a brilliant stroke, too bright for a banker, just right for an entertainment executive.

But the whole pattern of the moment was still obscure. Polyphony was a pop label; it had a robust list of rockers and punkers and rappers and alternative bands, but its stable of classical artists was less than illustrious.

When she and Farr reached the short stairway that led onto the stage, Kate hesitated. The stage belonged to performers. Something in her resisted meeting a businessman there.

"Come up, Kate," Heller urged. "The view is grand."

Ethan's hand on her elbow gave her little choice. She was propelled up onto the stage.

The smooth yellow planks of the hall's new floor seemed to give subtly beneath her feet. Carnegie itself was an instrument; its stage resonated like the belly of Piotr's cello. That was part of the magic of the place.

Heller met her halfway across the stage and took her hand in both of his, turning the handshake into something more intimate.

"What a pleasure to finally meet you," Heller said, his smile surprisingly warm and apparently genuine. "Your performance tonight was magnificent."

He glanced sideways at Farr. "You really ought to be ashamed, Ethan. Her publicity photos don't begin to do her justice."

"You were in the audience?" she asked in surprise.

"I certainly was," Heller said, still holding her hand lightly. "I hope you don't mind, but I made Ethan promise not to tell you. I wanted to see the real goods, not some overproduced and self-conscious number."

Kate felt herself go still, as though she had just found ice rather than wood beneath her feet.

"Really?" she said softly.

Farr's hand tightened on her elbow in sudden warning. Then he released her.

"I've been in charge of recruiting new talent at Polyphony for several years, and I prefer to work anonymously. What I saw tonight confirmed everything I had heard about you. You were brilliant."

Heller paused, enjoying himself as powerful men often do when demonstrating their power.

"I admit there was a moment there where I wondered," he said. "You seemed a little distracted part of the way through the Brahms, but then you pulled the group and the piece together. I thought you did a wonderful job of rescuing the cellist from his own foolishness."

Kate started to defend Piotr, but her agent's warning glance stopped her.

"It's true, Kate," Farr said. "The whole audience came alive after Piotr's solo. People were talking all over about it."

Kate shook her head. "It was Piotr's night, not mine."

"Of course, but you made it possible," Heller said. "I've never seen more generosity and at the same time more virtuosity. You broke out like a bird in full flight. The rest of them stayed earthbound."

Suddenly, Heller's expression changed. He let go of her hand and stepped back a foot or two. Then he tipped his head to one side, studying Kate carefully, examining her face and figure with a cool, speculative eye.

Kate returned the look coolly. She disliked being on display, but it was part of her career. She had learned to tolerate it with a kind of regal disregard.

"That's it," Heller said, a self-satisfied smile spreading across his face. "Look at that elegance, Ethan, that remote beauty, the disdainful curve of that long neck. She is a swan.

"The Black Swan. What a perfect cognomen, what a

splendid stage identity." He rubbed his hands together with glee. "Dark dresses, the long, dark hair, the mysterious beauty; those are all things the publicity department can really work with."

Kate gave her agent a sideways look.

"What *is* he talking about?" she asked bluntly.

"You haven't told her?" Heller asked Farr.

The agent shook his head and smiled like a rug salesman. "Last time I checked, there wasn't even an offer on the table."

Heller swept the objection aside.

"Details, Ethan," he said grandly, "and trust me, we can always work out details."

He turned back to Kate as though he thought she would be an easier target. "How does half a million dollars sound to you, Kate?"

Kate bit her tongue.

"That's just a signing bonus," Heller said.

"I'm not an assassin," she said, "nor am I a courtesan. I'm just a violinist."

Heller shook his head. "That was yesterday," he said. "Today you are a rising star of classical music, an international celebrity in the making.

"It will take a lot of work, on your part and on the part of Polyphony, but Sony did it for Cecilia Bartoli, and I'll do it for you."

Kate glanced at Ethan Farr. "Have the two of you been drinking too much champagne?" she asked.

"I'm saving it for later," Farr said. "What Daniel hasn't said is that he isn't alone in wanting to sign you. Ever since your recital last month, I've been fielding phone calls from hopeful recording firms. Daniel is simply the most insistent, although until now he hasn't seen fit to make a concrete offer."

"Concrete offer? Concrete offer?" Heller's laugh was double-edged. "That's a preempt and you know it, Ethan."

"No, Daniel, a preempt offer would be at least a million,"

Farr said calmly. "A million to sign, with fat percentages and a guaranteed promotion budget, a carefully designed concert tour, and a few other odds and ends I have to think about. Anything less suggests a lack of sincerity."

"Details," Heller said impatiently. "Polyphony needs the Black Swan and she needs Polyphony. The rest is for the clerks to work out."

With a gesture that was more commanding than gallant, he reached out and picked up Kate's hand.

"Sign with us and we'll make you an international sensation, the brightest star in the classical sky," he said.

For an instant, Kate felt light-headed, as though a tight steel band had been removed from her chest. She drew a deep breath, as though for the first time in fourteen years.

"What does that mean, to be a star?" she asked quietly. The question seemed directed more to herself than to Heller.

"Being a star means you can have whatever you want, Kate," Heller said. His smile was brilliant as the sun. It was the key to his success.

Kate stared at him in a way that made him realize her eyes were as green as unmelted glacier ice.

"Is that so?" she said softly. "Is that really so?"

"Of course it's so," Heller replied. "Once in a generation, a remarkable talent collides with just the right kind of promotion and a star is born. You are that star, Kate. I'm sure of it. You're a very lucky woman."

Kate did not speak the thought that echoed in her mind. *Fourteen years. Fourteen lonely years. Fourteen years and, presto, life is transformed again.*

She drew a deep breath. Slowly, a smile as beautiful as sunrise spread across her face.

"This will take some time," she said, shaking her head as though she still didn't believe. She looked at Farr. "I think I'm going to leave now, let you two work on details."

"Wait a minute, Kate," Heller said quickly. "We have the rough outlines of a deal here. That calls for a drink, maybe some supper or something. We need to celebrate."

He spoke quickly, like an auto salesman trying to close a sale.

"I think not, Mr. Heller, but thank you anyway. You and Ethan have minutiae to discuss, and I have a plane to catch in seven hours."

"You are still going to the coast?" Farr seemed surprised.

"I gave my word, Ethan," Kate said simply. She looked at Heller. "Even stars are supposed to keep their promises, aren't they?"

"Only if they want to," Heller replied.

Kate started to reply, but stopped herself. "I'll be back in a week," she said. "We can celebrate then."

She picked up her violin from the piano bench where Farr had left it, turned, and walked quickly off the stage. Her cape lifted behind her like the shadow of wings.

"See?" Heller said with satisfaction. "The Black Swan."

Farr smiled, though he felt like frowning. He had an uneasy feeling that his swan was flying away.

Three

Exhausted from a sleepless night, Kate spent the flight in a state somewhere between dazed and dozing. When she looked out the window over Idaho, suddenly she was unsure of what was real and what was dream. The snowy peaks of the Cascades reoriented her and the chill air of the Seattle morning refreshed her, but she still felt unreal as she drove north through the heart of Seattle.

Within an hour, she left the last of the suburbs and passed into open country. The blooming yellow Scotch broom choked the roadside verges, and alder thickets beside the road showed the reddish cast of full bud. She recognized springtime in a way that she never could in Manhattan.

Then she saw a familiar landmark off the highway— a long, low, tin-roofed chicken house beside a moss-covered hip-roof barn on an abandoned farm.

Home. Not quite the place where she had been raised. That was a hundred miles south of Seattle. But like this place, home was near the coast, in the woods and fields that lay between the mountains and the mystic sea.

Home. She had been away for fourteen years, but she

still understood its rhythms, she knew what it felt like, what it smelled like, what it was.

She knew the air outside was chill, but not bitter and acrid like New York in March. She knew the names of the trees without thinking. She recognized the styles of the barns. She knew the farmer in the field was pulling a three-bottom plow and the birds circling in a cloud above him were seagulls looking for worms in the fresh-turned soil.

She had not expected to recognize so much. She had not expected to feel at home in Washington. She had not been there since she was sixteen, yet little had changed, except perhaps herself.

She watched the countryside unreel past her car, wondering what made a barn so familiar and intimate to her. How could a fresh-plowed field look like an old friend, its black dirt turned over in knife-straight rows? The furrows, she thought. Dad had plowed furrows like that the day he died, the day he and Mother died.

In that moment of unexamined memory, Kate felt the orphan's loneliness as though it were brand new.

Her father had been a fine farmer. Jarri Saarinan's spring furrows were competent and efficient, row after row, field after field. He had been a man with imagination; he played Sibelius and Grieg on his violin. But first and foremost, he was a man of the earth with manure on his boots and dirt under his fingernails.

How had he reconciled those two parts of his nature?

Kate's mother was different, impassive. Aniko Saarinan was strong, stout, warm, and devout, but she had little imagination. On the day she died, she had milked the cows by hand, separated the cream, and churned it into butter, all in the span of an hour. Yet not once in that hour had she wondered what forces were at work in the process.

To Aniko, making butter was no more or less magical

than her ability to take a man into her body and make of
the experience a child.

That was a mystery to Kate. She and her mother had
talked about, argued about, that mystery of creating new
life the day her parents had died.

Now, years later, Kate could still replay their last conversation, still hear her mothers calm words.

Magic? Lord, no. That's just the way things are.

Aniko used that phrase to describe everything she
didn't understand or didn't want to explain. Her reticence had always been a wall between herself and her
daughter.

It's the way things are, child. Accept it.

No! There is more to it. There has to be.

Accept it, Kate. That's what life is.

No!

In her mind, Kate had revisited that argument again
and again in the years after she lost her parents. Now she
was no longer bitter about the loss, but she did wish that
she and her mother had been able to climb over the wall
of reticence, to hammer through it or step around it.

In the same way, Kate wished she had been able to
play Grieg for her father.

Just wishes, old wishes, yet they were still as vivid as
the yellow of Scotch broom against the pewter sky.

The interstate traffic thinned out as she drove north.
The afternoon sky was gray, threatening rain. The trees
beside the road bent before the wind. There was something calm, almost cozy, about being in a car on such a
day. For a few hours, Kate had the absolute luxury of
being in transit, passing from one place to another, one
time to another.

She tuned the radio to the Seattle classical station
and listened for a while. The music was modern and
atonal, often annoying, a program director's way of
proving he was cutting-edge and sophisticated even
though he worked in a minor market.

Kate endured it for a while, until natural static began to interfere with the man-made atonality. When a country-and-western station on an adjacent frequency began to bleed over, she turned the radio off. For the next hour she drove in the capsule of silence, absorbing the landscape of her childhood and her abrupt adulthood.

As the car crested a hill, she looked off to the west, to the waters of Puget Sound, steel-gray and cold. It could have been fourteen years ago. The ocean and the sound had changed not at all. She was beginning to wonder if anything truly had, including herself.

She glanced at her watch and sighed, knowing she couldn't put off the call any longer. Reaching into her leather traveling bag, she pulled out a cellular phone, punched in a number from memory, and waited for the ring on the other side of the country.

The instant Farr heard her voice, he asked, "Where are you?"

"I'm not at the edge of the world, but you can see it from here," Kate said, laughing. "I'm looking out on the Skalbeck Valley now."

Her agent sighed, disappointed, as though he had expected her to change her mind at the last moment.

"Are you sure you don't want to get yourself back here?" he asked. "It's a done deal. You can call yourself a millionaire, minus my ten percent, of course."

Kate was silent for a moment, turning that number over in her mind. A million dollars lacked reality. Reality was the two thousand four hundred and ten dollars in her savings account the last time she had checked.

"A done deal," she repeated. "I'm not sure what that means."

"It means the contract is being drawn up now. Heller and I thrashed every detail out last night, right there on the stage at the Carnegie. Strangest negotiation I ever conducted."

"It was pretty strange for me, too."

"That's where they want you to give your first concert," Farr said. "Polyphony has arranged to sponsor a Carnegie series featuring their new artists. You'll be the first."

That had more meaning than a string of zeros after a dollar sign. Kate felt a tingle of excitement, like a charge of electricity.

"I thought the Carnegie stage was booked months in advance," she said.

"It's booked as far as mere mortals are concerned, but not as far as Polyphony Records is concerned. They pumped so much money into the remodeling fund that Sandy Weill gave them pretty much what they wanted."

"The good old golden rule," she said. "The guy with the gold makes the rules."

"This is all part of a major campaign by Polyphony. They know they need to spruce up their classical list. You're just the first step in that process. Heller admitted last night that Tokyo has authorized him to spend twenty-five million acquiring talent and sponsoring concerts."

"So I'm a drop in the bucket, huh?"

"More like a million-dollar cup," Farr retorted.

Somehow that made it more real. Kate felt a shiver pass through her body. "A million dollars," she said, her voice wry and wondering. "My father never earned that much in his entire life."

"If you are as smart as you usually are, you'll never have to worry about money again."

She gave an odd laugh.

"You have a busy schedule ahead of you," Farr continued. "Polyphony wants to start sessions with their publicity and promotions people as soon as possible. Wardrobe and makeup, new photos, a whole new you. At their expense, of course."

"If the old me was that bad, why did they want a contract?"

"Heller has fallen in love with the idea of making you into the Black Swan. He's even talking about buying you a black violin, maybe a Strad. I understand there's a dark one for sale in London."

"A Stradivarius? Good Lord."

"'Can't have our star playing anything less,' as Heller put it," Farr said. "It would belong to the company, of course. They would probably want to name it the 'Polyphony Strad.'"

Kate felt the wind outside buffet the rental car. It made her uneasy. Stradivarius and windstorm, future and past, all of it mixed together with no place to hang on in the present.

"The idea for the Strad came out of their publicity department," Farr continued, "but even the financial people have signed off. They think a Strad would be a defensible investment for the company."

"Money men," she said. "Bean counters."

"Tiresome creatures, but they do pay the bills for high ticket items like you."

She laughed. "From stardust to the bottom line. You have a way of making it all too real."

"It is real. Polyphony's parent company, Ikedo, is committed to vertical integration. They want to control everything, from the consumer electronics hardware to the software—the music. That's where you come in."

"I'm software?"

"You're a corporate asset."

"Funny, I thought I was a person."

"That was yesterday. Today, you're that enviable entity, a megastar in the making."

Kate wasn't certain whether it was anticipation or something less comfortable that tightened her stomach.

"All I really want to do is play music," she said.

"Oh, you'll do a lot of that, too."

She looked at the sky and the water and said nothing.

"When you first came to me ten years ago," Farr said,

"you told me you wanted your music to make a difference, to bring beauty to the world."

"Yes," she said softly. "That hasn't changed."

"You are blessed with talent and looks and everything else that a star needs. I know the past years have not been easy for you, even if I don't know all the details.

"But that's over. The struggle is behind you now. You finally are going to get the recognition you deserve. Enjoy it. You've earned it."

For a moment Kate couldn't speak. Farr's evident affection touched her more deeply than she could ever have imagined, perhaps because he was the only one in the world whose advice she sought or accepted. She felt tears well up in her eyes, relief and something else, a haunting question from the past.

"Okay," she said, her voice edged with emotion.

"Is it?" he asked quickly. "You sound odd."

She turned aside to clear her throat. "I'm fine. It's just that—well, this country is very like the place where I was born. I've been thinking about my parents. It never gets easier, does it?"

Farr's parents were both dead, too. It was one of the few personal things the two of them had ever discussed.

"Nope, kid, it doesn't."

For a moment, both of them were lost in their own thoughts and memories.

"Listen," Farr said, "if you do want out of this thing in Langley, I can certainly call them and handle the cancellation. I've already checked with Piotr. He would be glad to fill in for you. That way you would know the job was being done properly."

Part of Kate found the offer attractive. Another part of her, the part that had urged her to take the assignment in the first place, rebelled. She needed time to examine the two halves of her life, the time before New York and the time after. She had grown as far as she could without integrating past with present.

And if she didn't grow, her music wouldn't grow. Then there would only be an unbearable silence.

A fat raindrop splashed against the glass of the windshield. Another struck beside the first, wet and chill, a reminder that warmth and cold were part of the same continuum, like mountains and sea, past and present.

"Piotr needs time with his family," Kate said. "Besides, I'm looking forward to Langley. Maybe I can finally go back to what I came from."

"You haven't gone back before. Why now?"

"For the same reason I play the violin. Because I must."

Farr hesitated, then said, "Call me as soon as you find out what your local phone number is. Or do you have your cellular along?"

"Yes, but I think I'll just shut the damned thing off and enjoy what may be my last few days as a human being. After that, I'll be a corporate asset, right?"

"You'll be a very well paid performer," Farr countered.

"Whatever. When I get back to Manhattan, I'm going to buy a case of the most expensive champagne I can find. We'll drink it, one bottle at a time. How's that?"

"I'll buy the case, and the caviar to go with it, if you come back right now," Farr said, making one last sortie.

"Good-bye, Ethan, and thank you," Kate said.

She turned off the phone and tossed it into her bag. The gesture gave her a great feeling of freedom. She knew it was an illusion, but she enjoyed it just the same.

For the next half hour, Kate let herself savor the unexpected turn her life had taken. Ethan Farr was a very cautious man. He would not be so excited unless the deal was, indeed, done. For the first time since her parents died, she was financially independent. More important, her future as a musician was secure in a way that few performers except rock stars ever experienced.

Through a twist in life as unexpected as her own success, classical music had become part of the popular culture. The Three Tenors had performed a miracle and gone "mainstream." They were international celebrities drawing larger audiences than rock groups. Cecilia Bartoli had gone from amateur anonymity to cover-girl status in less than five years. Other performers had made the jump, and now Kate had a chance to join them.

She knew her life would never be quite the same, but that was fine with her. She had known enough loneliness and insecurity. Her life was beginning anew by her own choice rather than by circumstances forced on her by life. And death.

Finally she could meet life on her own terms. That meant more to her than the money. Celebrity was a foundation and a platform for her growth as a musician. If the price of that growth was becoming a "corporate asset," she had overcome worse in the past. Much worse.

Kate was so caught up in the possibilities of change that she nearly missed the road sign announcing the turnoff to Langley and the San Juan Islands. As she coasted off the interstate and onto the two-lane highway headed west, the sun broke through beneath the gray clouds, dazzling her and matching her ebullient mood.

The raking light defined the land in a new way—the glum little slough beside the road became a vital marshland dotted with ducks and blackbirds, the pencil-thin, barren stand of poplars beside a distant farmhouse became an element in a broader impressionist landscape. Time and land, sky and change, seasons always becoming other seasons.

Ahead beside the road there was a splash of color, astonishingly large and intense. As Kate drove closer, she recognized a field of tulips, brilliant red in the cold light of the sun.

Ten acres, at least, her farmer's sense told her. Ten acres of tulips in bloom. A commercial bulb farm. It must be.

She pulled to the side of the road and watched the sunlight and shadows of the clouds play across the field. Beyond the tulips there was another field, yellow but too pale to be tulips. Daffodils. She grew her own in a window box in her New York apartment, but a window-box gardener dared not think of bulbs by the hundred thousands, flowers by the millions.

As she sat beside the road, the sunlight shifted again and settled on a white building that stood alone in a grove of large bare trees across the fields. The building had a stout steeple, and it stood on a neatly clipped two-acre lot amid stone blocks, gravestones in an old country churchyard.

There was another white building off to one side, perhaps a school, partly screened by a grove of trees. The church itself would have been lost in the gray shadow, except that the walls of the chancel and steeple caught the golden sunlight like a blessing. The shingles on the roof, wet from a passing squall, gleamed like black slate.

For an instant, Kate was stunned by the simple peace and beauty of the place. She had been raised in a similar country church. Her first memory of music came from the church. She had played her first concert there. But she had not worshiped in fifteen years, and she was not inclined to do so now, even though the white church shone like a benediction in the red and yellow fields.

She turned off the engine and got out of the car. The wind had teeth, like memory. She stood for a while in the faint shelter of the car, her white coat drawn around her, her hands thrust into her pockets. The wind, and the memories, tore tears from her eyes.

Fourteen years and a million dollars, and part of her

was still the sixteen-year-old orphan with a love of mystery and no way to express it except in her music.

Martin Thorson had loved music, too. He had been a better singer than he was a preacher. His sermons always seemed mild and passive compared to his singing of the liturgy and the lusty way he led the old Norwegian and Finnish hymns. At first, music had been the connection between him and Kate.

But Martin had loved mystery, too. He loved mystery even more than he loved music, and Kate had been his mystery. He could not help himself. He needed to know the texture of her skin, even as he prayed to his God for the strength to resist.

Kate had never found his prayers convincing, and neither, apparently, had God.

Nor had God answered her prayers, later, when she missed her period and then another, when she solved the mystery without her mother's assistance.

For five minutes, Kate stood in the cold wind, the tears streaming down her face. She seldom allowed herself to think of the past, of Martin, the tall, gaunt, intense pastor, the shepherd who had betrayed his flock.

She tried not to think of the child they had created together, the child she had carried for nine months and then given away. She tried, but often she failed. Fourteen years wasn't enough to forget a child. She feared that even a lifetime wouldn't be long enough.

During the months in a Lutheran home for unwed mothers, she learned to take solace from her violin. The confinement of pregnancy had given her what Martin had never been able to provide, a sense of herself and an understanding of her own talent.

For that reason, she had never hated Martin, though he had seduced and then abandoned her. He had betrayed himself and his God even more profoundly. She had betrayed herself only out of ignorance.

But she had lost the church. She had not been in one since the day she walked out of the maternity home's chapel, leaving her child behind her. Nor did she intend to enter one now, not even one so beautiful as this one, surrounded by tulips and bathed in mysterious light.

Kate realized that her face had gone numb from the cold wind. She dug a tissue out of her pocket to wipe her eyes. Strangely, or perhaps not so strangely, she felt better, as though her tears had softened some of the scars left by the past.

She was turning to get back into the car when a strange, faint warbling sound caught her ear. She listened, trying to isolate and identify it. The sound was lost in the wind for several seconds. Kate turned her head, listening. She heard it again, louder but still unidentifiable. She looked around, then squinted toward the west.

A ragged chevron of birds came out of the setting sun, flying low and strong and straight for her. The birds saw the car and changed their path, angling to pass thirty yards to one side. They were white, although the slanting sun gave them a golden cast. As they came nearer, Kate heard them talking to one another in rich, resonant voices that were more like a language than any animal sounds she had ever heard.

Swans. Trumpeter swans. She had seen them before, as a girl. Trumpeters wintered regularly in the saltwater flats and marshes around Puget Sound. Jarri Saarinan had planted winter wheat each fall to attract them. Trumpeters, the largest, most noble of God's birds, he called them, and the most musical.

The swans passed so close that Kate could hear the whistle of air in their pinion feathers. Their call was well crafted and resonant, like the sound of a deep wooden flute or the single low pipe of an organ.

Kate counted them.

Seven.

She thought of the fairy tale from her childhood, the

seven brothers transformed into swans, then saved by
their sister, who wove them coats of nettles.

The seven birds flew across the tulips and daffodils,
then broke into two groups that banked and settled on
the ground close beside the church.

That was when Kate realized that some of what she
thought were gravestones were actually swans. She
could see dozens of them scattered across the cemetery.
The transformation of stone into birds was thrilling, like
music where silence had been, a myth brought to life.

Knowing only that she had to get closer to the swans,
Kate climbed back into the car. A quarter mile down the
highway, a gravel road led in the direction of the
church. She hesitated for an instant, not wanting to go
near the church that was so like the one in her memories.

Don't be silly, she told herself. A graveyard isn't a
church. After all, everyone ends up in a graveyard
sooner or later.

Three hundred yards farther along, a one-lane road
broke off and led toward the church. As Kate turned
onto the narrow track, she saw swans scattered across
clean pasture. Several hundred birds were gathered in
clans, grazing together. They were not tame, merely
oblivious.

At this distance, Kate could see some of the birds
were naturally gray, youngsters by their size, capable of
migrating but still growing.

She stopped and rolled down the window. Over the
idling engine, she heard the brassy trumpeting sounds of
conversation among the birds.

One of the adult swans broke away from his group and
danced a few steps along the green grass toward the car.
He trumpeted loudly, a challenge, then arched his back
and flapped his broad white wings as though he were testing his own strength against the spring wind. Then he
danced back to his clan.

Several of the other birds greeted him, arching their long necks and dipping their heads again and again, applauding the big swan's strength and the music of his calls.

Kate lifted her foot from the brake and rolled slowly up the road toward the church. She stopped fifty yards from the white building and watched small family bands of swans and cygnets moving among the markers.

Cemeteries held no special meaning for the birds. They eagerly trimmed the green grass from around family monuments and paddled indifferently over headstones that had been in place for a hundred years.

Kate remembered when she herself had been indifferent to death. She and other youngsters had dared the great unknown of death to play hide-and-seek in the churchyard, using gravestones for cover. For better or for worse, Martin had taken religion from her, but even now she felt an atavistic twinge to see creatures walking on the faces of the dead.

At the edge of the graveyard, close to the road, a family group gathered to graze, two adults and two gray cygnets. The male swan, the cob, and the two youngsters waddled about easily, cropping the new green shoots right and left. The female, the pen, rested on the mowed lawn, reaching out with her long neck like a white giraffe, deftly stripping new grass from around the base of a head-high gravestone.

There was something elegant and at the same time comical about the way the lazy pen stretched out to pinch off a few last stems of new grass and then straightened her long neck to swallow them.

Kate watched for a moment from the car, unwilling to get out and upset the little domestic scene in order to get closer to the magnificent birds.

Then, in the sudden, unexpected way of life, danger came. A knee-high dog with a rough black-and-white coat appeared from the vicinity of the church building.

The animal must have been lying in wait behind a grave-stone. He cut a long arc out and around the four swans, running so fast and so low to the ground that he seemed to move without legs. Never once did the animal take its eyes off the four birds.

The swans instantly sensed the dog's focus and intent. The cob and two cygnets turned and faced the invader. The cob dipped his head and moved to meet the threat. The two youngsters held their ground and dipped their heads nervously.

The pen struggled up from her spot beside the head-stone and lurched awkwardly toward her family, seem-ing to trip over her own feet. When the pen staggered again, Kate saw that her feet were trapped in a tangle of what looked like translucent string.

No wonder the dog was so intent on this group, Kate thought. The predator's logic was unassailable: single out the weak or the lame.

She watched, partly fascinated and partly repelled.

The dog circled wide behind the family group, then slowed, turning and pinching in toward them.

The four swans seemed to discuss the situation among themselves, watching the attacker and gauging distances.

Slowly, tentatively, the dog closed in. The cob and cygnets retreated toward the pen, then turned to face the attacker again.

Other swans in the cemetery had scattered during the dog's first rush. Now they stood by passively, watching and commenting among themselves on their own good luck to have escaped the dog's attention.

Kate studied the black-and-white dog carefully. Country dogs were two-faced creatures. When trained and controlled, they were man's helper and friend, but loose and feral, they could turn marauder in a moment. At least the swans were big enough to drive off a dog of this size.

Then the pen stumbled and staggered again, flopping about. Kate realized the bird was helpless. She opened the door and stepped out of the car.

"Hey!" she called out, trying to distract the dog. "Leave them alone!"

The dog paid her no attention. Instead, he advanced again on the birds.

Kate searched the ground for a weapon. Dogs, even dogs of this size, could be vicious. The winter wind had broken a two-foot stub of branch off an aging elm tree beside the road. Kate picked up the stick and circled around the car so the dog could see her and her cudgel.

The animal cast one quick glance in her direction and then went back to the swans. Cannily, the dog pressed in, like a stalking lion, then flattened out again to wait for the right moment to attack.

The farm girl in Kate told her that she shouldn't intervene; death from the quick snap of a dog's jaws was preferable to the slow, lingering death that came to a maimed wild bird.

Then the pen called her fear and alarm, and Kate started for the dog.

Four

Brian Corry's ambush had been carefully laid. The family of swans was well separated from the rest of the flock. He had focused Campbell on them as though they were sheep. The dog was ready to do his job. It wouldn't be the first time Campbell had rounded up injured birds. Herding was a passion bred into the dog's bones.

Then, the unexpected, always the unexpected.

"Damn," Corry muttered.

The blue car came wandering down the lane like a lost soul looking for the solace of the church, and Corry's whole plan started to unravel.

Corry reached out and took hold of Campbell's collar. The whip-tough Border collie trembled beneath his master's touch, but he didn't take his eyes from the swans. They were big birds, not nearly as big as woollies nor as nimble on dry ground, but Campbell had lost an encounter with a barnyard goose as a puppy. It had made him wary of such creatures.

"Steady, lad," Corry whispered. "Let's see what happens. Maybe this idiot will go away."

The car halted halfway down the lane. Corry could see through the windshield now. The driver was a woman with long dark hair. She was alone. He didn't recognize her or the car.

"Steady," Corry cautioned. "Keep them in your eye, but steady."

Campbell held, an eager rock. Then Corry felt the dog shift uneasily beneath his hands. There was a limit, even for Campbell. Corry was either going to have to loose him or call him off.

The pen got up and moved a few feet.

Corry saw that she was still tangled, as she had been for the past two days, in the ball of discarded gill net. He had come to dislike gill nets on principle; he hated careless gillnetters.

The car rolled forward a few feet, then stopped again. It was obvious the driver intended to come into the churchyard, if only to turn around. That would put the finish to Corry's plan, and probably to the pen's life as well. He had to move.

"Okay, Campbell," Corry said, loosing his hold on the dog's collar. "Quickly, now. Drive!"

Campbell sped away as though he were on a rocket sled. His outrun was perfectly oblique. He scattered other swans like bowling pins across the cemetery, but the family group of four stood frozen in place, unthreatened by the path of the dog.

Corry edged out of the shelter of the rectory door to see more clearly. Campbell was so damned smart that most of the time he hardly needed directions once the target had been chosen.

The dog began to curl in, letting the swans see his intent now. The cob and the cygnets watched the collie warily. The pen hobbled toward the shelter of the family circle.

Corry gave a short, flat whistle.

The dog stopped and sank down to his belly in the cold grass. Then he seemed to disagree with the whistled command. He rose up slowly and came forward a foot.

"Campbell! Lie down!" Corry's command was like a whip.

Campbell sank down on his belly instantly, but without apology. He still watched the birds as though they were the most fascinating creatures in the universe. At the moment, they were.

The car edged forward, distracting the swans. Corry could sense the woman's disapproval from fifty yards away. He wasn't surprised when she stopped and stepped out of the car. She waved her hand, trying to break the dog's concentration.

Campbell shifted an inch or two but didn't look at the woman.

Corry could see the intruder now, a cascade of black hair and pale features that would have held his eye at any time except now. She wasn't a local. No local woman wore a white coat into the fields on a muddy spring day.

Damnation, he thought. A local girl might recognize a dog at work and have the sense to stay clear.

The woman stood behind the open door of the car, looking about. Corry took advantage of her hesitation. He gave a long, sharp whistle, freeing Campbell to start his drive again.

The dog lifted and came forward ten yards. The movement startled the cygnets. They dashed away, headed straight for the gap between the Engebretson and Wells family markers. The adult swans tried to follow, but the pen was so badly hobbled that she fell over herself. The cob left his mate's side and turned back toward the dog, who was now fifteen yards away.

Corry stood stock still in the doorway, unable to move for fear of adding another element to an equation that was already unstable. The dog, the birds, and the woman were locked on one another—controlled predator, flighty prey, and unpredictable spectator.

The cygnets milled about, gabbling worriedly to each

other and asking advice from their parents. The cob stood his ground, facing the dog, his head up and his wings spread, greatly magnifying his size.

The woman must have realized what Corry already knew: The dog wouldn't listen to her. She went to the windrow of trees along the drive and picked up a stick the size of her wrist. She tested its heft, then marched resolutely up the road toward Campbell.

Corry swore and measured the distances and angles and times. He had only one option. The cygnets had moved to one side, away from the mist-net trap.

The contest was now between Campbell and the two adults. The moment the woman intervened, the swans would fly, the pen included. Her feet were tangled, but not her wings. Once that happened, Corry doubted he could locate them again before the gill net cut into the pen's legs, crippling her.

Corry whistled, raising Campbell, hoping to drive the swans straight ahead through the invisible gate and into the trap. The dog came forward five yards and stopped, waiting for the swans to react. The pen withdrew, but the cob, all forty pounds of him, held ground, his beak opened to show its blood-red outline. The bird dipped his head and advanced, dwarfing the black-and-white dog.

"Go home!" the woman shouted at Campbell. Her voice was sharp and commanding in the wind.

Campbell stopped and crouched. He had a clear idea of what his master wanted, but here was this other human advancing on him with a stick.

"Get out, dog, get out! Go home, go home!"

Corry whistled again, urging the dog forward. The pen staggered ahead. She was close to the net. One more move would put her into it. Corry whistled again, a warble of commands that told Campbell to shed the pen away from the cob and drive her to the trap.

The warbling whistle pierced the wind. The woman

with the stick heard it, but couldn't locate its source. Yet she hesitated as though suspecting that the dog wasn't running loose.

Corry took heart. Maybe she wasn't such a fool after all. His chances improved—and so did the female swan's.

Drive the pen, he commanded Campbell silently. Drive her, don't pay any attention to that big cob, just take the pen. Push her toward the mist net.

Campbell did as he was commanded, but the cob moved to put himself between the dog and his mate. The big bird sounded a battle call. Swans had been fighting foxes and coyotes and dogs for thousands of generations. The cob spread its wings and waited for a chance to break the dog's back.

Campbell stopped, his path blocked by the cob. He edged to one side, trying to slip past. He was more agile than the swan, and he was fearless, but Corry knew the danger his dog faced.

The woman shifted the stick to her right hand and darted forward, obviously intent on getting between the ancient adversaries.

"No! Go home!" she shouted, advancing toward the dog and raising her stick.

Campbell shifted to one side and plastered his belly into the grass again, focused on the pen, ignoring both the cob and the woman.

Once she got close, Kate was astonished at the size of the swan. His angry head was almost level with her own. He swept his powerful wings back and forth. She could feel the force of their strokes against the air.

He was a wild creature in the grip of instincts far older than man. Kate knew she wouldn't be able to intimidate him. The dog was another matter. Even if he was behaving badly, he and his kind had been bred to respond to man for thousands of years.

"Go home," she shouted, swinging the club through the air in front of the dog. "Go home!"

Suddenly, she was struck from behind with stunning force. The black-and-white dog danced to one side like a leaf driven by the wind. Then Kate hit the ground and lost all sense of time or direction.

"Jesus God," Corry snarled as he saw his careful plan explode into chaos. "The elegant little fool is going to get herself killed."

He broke from the shelter of the doorway and ran across the cemetery.

The woman was trying to get to her knees when the enraged cob attacked again, lashing out with all his strength at the closest of what suddenly seemed like a world full of enemies.

When the swan struck, the dog's instincts took over. Humans might be confusing, but he was always on.their side. He leaped across the fallen woman and at the cob, snarling and barking. The big bird's wing caught him in midair and sent him flying.

Corry saw his dog strike the corner of the Engebretson monument and roll, yelping in pain. Swearing, Corry leaped in front of the attacking swan and roared like a madman. His primitive bellow stopped the big swan.

He threw his arms in the air, mimicking the attacking cob, swelling himself up like a giant, sandy-bearded monster.

The swan hesitated. This new creature was even bigger than himself, and just as fearless.

"Get back, you feathered devil!" Corry roared.

Kate was still on the ground, stunned and unsure of what had happened. She stared at the man dressed in rough clothing and howling of devils. He had appeared from nowhere, like a specter in the graveyard.

She wasn't sure whether he or the swan had attacked her.

"Back," the man commanded, waving his arms again at the swan. "Get back!"

The cob brandished his wings once more and turned to look at his mate.

Corry glanced over his shoulder, too.

"Get up," he ordered.

Kate shook her head, still dazed and confused.

Suddenly the madman jerked her to her feet and shoved her in the direction of her car.

"Go before you get your foolish self killed."

Kate still held her club in one hand. Instinctively, she whirled and raised it. She didn't like being shoved about.

For an instant, Corry was surprised. His eyes widened. He seemed to look into her with one glance. He held up a hand, staying her blow. He hadn't realized how frightened she was.

"Are you all right?" he asked. "Did the swan hurt you?"

She shook her head numbly.

"Then get out of here before he gets another chance," he said, pointing toward her car.

Slowly, she lowered the club and stepped away from the man. When she was beyond his reach, she turned and walked toward her car.

Corry had already swung around to look to his dog and the swans. Campbell had been stunned by the blow from the cob's wing and from striking the stone marker. The dog staggered to his feet and shook himself, trying to orient all four feet at the same time.

"Good boy," Corry said. "Just got the wind knocked out of you."

He watched the dog for a moment longer, reassuring himself. Then he turned to the swans.

To his surprise, the pen was neatly trapped in the fine monofilament mist net that he had strung between the gravestones. The cob was at her side, ruffled and urgent and mostly confused that his mate wouldn't flee with him.

"Why, bless me," Corry said, laughing. "And bless you, my feathered beauty. Your problems are over."

He reached into his pocket and brought out a well-worn stainless-steel pocket knife that had an odd, hump-backed blade. With a practiced motion, he used his thumb to pick the blade open. It locked into place with a metallic sound.

Corry started toward the helpless swan.

Kate was right on his heels. "No, wait! That swan isn't injured, just tangled up!"

Corry turned and looked at her blankly. Then he understood. "What do you think I'm going to do?" he demanded. "Cut her throat?"

"I . . ." For the first time Kate realized how badly she had misread the entire situation. "I don't know."

"Then stay the hell out of the way. Your meddling nearly killed Campbell and the swan in the bargain."

Before Kate could tell the stranger what a rude bastard she thought he was, he turned his back on her and headed for his dog.

Five

Corry whistled to the black-and-white Border collie, watched him move, and then knelt down to check him. He didn't appear injured, but Border collies had been known to herd sheep on compound fractures.

Corry ran his hands over the dog's rough winter coat, watching for a reaction that signaled pain.

"Took a little flying lesson, did you?" Corry said gently. "How'd you like to make that big white bastard's life miserable in return?"

The dog looked up at his master, reassured by the human's tone, but utterly baffled by the words.

"Okay, then," Corry said, straightening up and gesturing toward the big cob. "Let's get him out of here."

Campbell understood the hand signal and the tone. He charged the big bird straight on. The swan dipped his head and flared his wings, but held his position.

"Come by with him," Corry whistled in the special language of herd dog and herder.

Campbell had worked swans before. Unlike sheep, a swan would not be driven. They could be lured, however. It was just a matter of the right bait.

The dog approached the swan, then danced away, lunging and harrying, staying just out of the range of the hard beak and the dangerous wings. Each time the swan reached out for him, the dog retreated just a bit.

Slowly, Campbell lured the big bird away from his mate. Corry stood motionless as the dog drew the swan past him. The two cygnets tagged along behind their father.

Corry waited until Campbell led the swans into a tight file of family headstones that served as a convenient barrier. Then he whistled the dog into a flanking run that cut the birds off from the pen.

The swans realized they had been cozened. They tried to return to the pen, but Campbell became a dervish, barking and snarling and nipping.

Standing beside her car, Kate watched. She was amazed at the wiry dog's stamina, bravery, and intelligence.

Corry went to the mist net and the flopping, frightened pen. He knelt beside her, laying the open knife on the ground. Then he stripped off his flannel-lined canvas vest. Holding it in one hand, he tried to capture the swan's head and neck with the other.

The pen thrashed and bleated, but more in terror than pain. The mist net was made of light mesh. The swan's struggles threatened to break it, freeing her wings to fly but leaving her legs tangled in the much heavier filament of the gill net.

Corry moved slowly and spoke softly, soothingly. "Here, here, girl," he said. "This will all be over in a minute, silly thing. It's better not to watch."

The pen ducked and avoided his grasp once more. She managed to free one wing and lashed out with it, rapping Corry on the side of the forehead. He took the blow without flinching, for it was the price of getting in close. He caught the swan's wing and folded it back as gently as he could. Then he tried to gather the flapping bird into his arms.

Suddenly, he and the bird were eye to eye. The swan

instinctively pecked at the most vulnerable part of her attacker—the eyes. It was the opening Corry had waited for. He threw the vest over her head like a blanket, trapping her.

A voice came from behind him. "Can I help?" the woman asked.

"Yes," Corry panted. "Stay out of the way. I have her now."

Kate watched as he grappled with the frightened pen. Instead of panicking at the sudden blindness, the bird seemed to calm now that she couldn't see her attacker.

Corry looped his arm around her, holding his vest in place with the crook of his elbow and stilling her wings with his hands. When he had her pinioned, he reached out his left hand blindly, feeling the ground beside him for his knife.

It was just beyond his reach.

Kate moved in quietly, picked up the knife by its handle, and reversed it so that she held it by the back of the blade.

"Here," she said.

She held the knife out in front of his face so he could see it.

Corry looked at the knife and realized that it was being presented perfectly. Without a word, he took it by the handle and went to work.

Kate realized with mild shock that his left hand was missing a portion of its index finger and most of its middle finger. The excision seemed not to bother him. He worked over the bird with great deftness.

"Can I do anything else?" she asked.

"Just get back," Corry growled. "And watch that cob. Devil will break your arm in a minute."

Despite the warning, Kate lingered. She was a farm girl, after all. She had held her share of flailing, frightened animals for her father and the vet.

Besides, she had decided long ago that she would not

take orders from arrogant men, though this seemed a bad time to press that point.

The locked blade of the knife flashed like a small scythe, tearing away at the gill netting that was wrapped around the swan's black, webbed feet. The plastic monofilament was sun-rotted and dirty. It stripped away quickly.

Finally, only one strand remained, but that strand was still strong, intact. It was wrapped around the bird's leathery black leg so tightly that it had begun to bite through the tough webbing between two of her toes.

"Here, here, girl," Corry called softly, stilling the bird.

Skillfully, he slid the tip of the blade between the bird's leg and the line. The blade tugged upward gently.

The swan kicked out, misunderstanding the pressure. Her webbed foot raked across the back of Corry's hand.

He cooed softly to her as he caught the line on the tip of the blade. This time he cut all the way through it. He laid the blade aside and inspected the net cuts in the leathery black webbing of the swan's foot. He turned the foot over and probed the leg itself.

"A few days more, my lady, and you would have lost that foot and probably your life as well. But you'll be fine now. You're strong enough to heal."

Kate watched, intrigued by the unselfconscious way the man handled the bird, talking to her as though he believed she understood.

Maybe the swan did. She was certainly calmer as he went to work untangling her wings and head from the mist net. The process was speeded by the fact that the bird's struggles had torn rents in the flimsy mesh.

When Corry had her free, he picked her up and stepped out of the tangle of ruined net. He set the swan down on the ground, pointed her in the direction of her family, and lifted the hood from her head.

The freed pen squawked once, more in irritation than

in fear. She lumbered toward her family, pausing only
long enough to take a nip at Campbell as she passed
him. The dog danced out of the pen's reach. The four
swans milled about for a moment, assessing the terrain
and the opposition.

Corry whistled Campbell off guard, and the dog
came back to his master and sat, still watching the big,
unpredictable bird. The cob and the pen checked their
youngsters and then faced each other in what seemed
like a formal pose, trumpeting sharply and puffing
themselves up. They dipped and bobbed like mechanical toys, bowing and flapping their wings and shifting
from one foot to the other. Their strong, resonant
voices were like martial horns at a victory dance.

The young cygnets stood by, yodeling and congratu-
lating themselves and each other.

"You're entirely welcome," Corry called out wryly.
He touched the spot on the side of his forehead where
he had been rapped by the pen's wing. "It was nothing
at all."

Gradually, the dance subsided and the swans went
back to grazing, confident and content.

Corry picked up the shreds of the mist net and
inspected it sadly. The capture device had never been
intended for swans in the first place. He pulled two
long, white primary feathers out of the fine netting and
walked to where Kate stood.

"Are you all right?" he asked when he saw her pale-
ness.

"Fine," she said tersely, meeting his gaze with
sparkling green eyes.

Corry suddenly suspected her pallor had less to do
with pain than with anger. He glanced at the sleeves of
her white down coat. They were dirty and stained green
from her fall onto the new grass.

"You've ruined your pretty white coat," he said.
There was a trace of mockery in his voice.

"When I picked it out, I wasn't expecting to be knocked down from behind in a graveyard," Kate shot back, obviously angry.

Corry squinted at her, confused. Then he realized she hadn't seen the attack that knocked her down.

"It was the swan who clobbered you, not me," Corry said.

Now it was Kate's turn to be confused. She recovered quickly. "Your dog was the cause of the whole thing," she said. "I thought he was attacking the swans. And you didn't help. You might have warned me."

Corry rubbed his sandy beard, using his maimed fingers as a rough comb. He scowled, searching for a reply. He started to say something, then stopped and thought again.

Kate recognized his type. She had been raised among rustic males, men who hated explaining themselves, particularly to women. She let him sputter some more.

At the same time, she found herself staring at his mutilated hand. The scars were old and white. The fingers had been lost long ago. But there were fresh scratches on the hand now, from the hooked claws in the pen's webbed foot. Blood welled up in the scratches, dark, almost black in the fading daylight.

"How would I have warned you without stampeding those swans all over the landscape?" Corry finally said. "I've been laying for them since day before yesterday, when I first saw the pen tripping all over herself." He made an expansive gesture with his hand, almost an apology. "I suppose I did cut it a little close," he added. "I didn't mean for that cob to knock you on your . . . to knock you down like that, but I didn't want to frighten the pen. I didn't know whether I'd get another chance at her before it was too late."

Kate crossed her arms in front of her, rejecting the oblique apology. "Is this what you do for a living?" she asked. "Chase swans?"

"I do lots of things for a living. I only chase swans for fun."

He glanced at the back of his hand, noticing the scratches for the first time. He wiped his hand on his worn work pants. Blood left a dark stain on the butternut-brown cloth.

The pants were designed for a working man. They had a loop on the left hip for a hammer and a cloth holster on the right thigh for a wrench. Kate noticed that the rough cotton, more like canvas than denim, was worn through at the knees. Beneath the cloth, she caught a glimpse of a strong leg dressed in tight forest green.

Long underwear? she thought, but no underwear comes in forest green. Tights? she wondered. That would explain it. A man who wore tights beneath his work pants. What an oddity, even in cold country.

Corry seemed unaware of her inspection. He examined the feathers in his hand carefully, as though they held the answer to some question he was pondering.

"Will the swan be all right?" Kate asked.

"The monofilament would have cut through her leg in a day or two, but there seems no permanent damage now," Corry said.

"Shouldn't you have called a vet or something? I mean, trumpeter swans are endangered, aren't they?"

Corry made a show of looking around the graveyard and out across the fields.

"Do they look endangered?" he asked with a small grin.

Kate followed his gaze. There were perhaps two hundred swans in sight.

"I don't know," she said. "I'm not an expert. I was just trying to help, that's all. They're such beautiful birds, and beauty is so rare . . ."

Both of them were silent for a moment, watching the swans scattered across the graveyard and the field. The birds had begun to gather up into small bands. Suddenly, a group of eight turned into the wind, ran a few yards, and spread their wings. All at once, they were airborne.

The eight powerful creatures stroked against the wind, gaining altitude. They turned overhead and passed so close Kate could hear their intricate, musical conversation and the dry rustling sound of their wings in the air.

From the corner of his eye, Corry studied her in profile. To his eye, she was beautiful, a bit like a swan herself with her long, elegant neck and that white coat.

Expensive, though, he decided. A hundred-dollar haircut and a four-hundred-dollar coat. Slender legs clothed in stirrup pants that were tight enough to show her shape.

It was worth showing.

"If they aren't endangered, why did you go to so much trouble for a single bird?" she said without looking at him. "Most farmers I know would have wrung her neck and been done with it, if they even took that much trouble over a wild creature."

Corry got the impression she was trying to bait him. She was still ruffled from being knocked down and was looking for a target.

"I guess I'm not a farmer, then," he said. "It seemed a waste to let a good bird die a slow death because of some careless gillnetter."

She glanced toward him. In the last light of day, her eyes looked like green glass, cool, striking.

"I take it you're not a gillnetter, either," she said.

"Once I was," he said simply. "Once every man around here was a gillnetter. If fact, if you believe the bumper stickers, Jesus was a gillnetter, too. But not anymore. The fish are gone."

Frowning, she looked back at the swans.

Then he added, "I wouldn't expect you to know about such things as farmers and gillnetters."

"Really?" she said, glancing at him and arching a dark eyebrow. "Why not?"

He looked her up and down as an answer. Then he nodded toward the thin leather flats on her feet.

"Those are for sidewalks," he said.

"Don't they have sidewalks here in . . ." She stopped and looked around. "What do they call this place anyway?"

"Skalbeck. Skalbeck Valley. Are you lost?"

She shook her head. "No. When I realized that some of the headstones were swans, I wanted to get closer."

Corry smiled. "I guess they do look like headstones from the highway."

Campbell, like all herding dogs that had nothing to do, quickly became bored. None of the many words being spoken were directed toward him. He walked around his master and looked curiously at the woman who had yelled at him.

Kate took the advance as an overture. She dropped down on her heels to the dog's level. He looked at her, then past her, as though he weren't sure whether to trust her.

"Hello, boy," she said gently, holding out her hand, inviting him to sniff it.

"His name is Campbell," Corry said. "He's not real sociable. He'd rather be at work."

"Oh," Kate said. "Is that so? Hello, Campbell."

She made a soft whispering sound with her lips. Campbell looked at her quickly, intrigued. Then he looked past her again. She made the sound again and he succumbed, edging forward a step to sniff her fingers delicately.

The dog had seemed fierce and formidable when he faced the swans, but now Kate could see that his muzzle was small and delicate and his body light-boned.

His whiskers brushed her fingers. He drank her scent like water. Finally, he allowed her to touch his rumpled ear. The long dark fur was like silk. Kate stroked it with one finger, then with her whole hand.

Campbell suffered the attention for a moment, then moved away ever so slightly, just out of her reach.

Corry watched but said nothing.

"He hasn't quite forgiven me," she said.

"You were pretty fierce," Corry said. "I'm surprised he let you touch him at all."

"I was hardly more fierce than the swan."

"Swans are silly creatures," Corry said. "Humans are another matter altogether."

Kate thought she detected a trace of bitterness in his tone. "Would he let me pat him if you told him to hold still?" she asked, surprised at her own question.

"He's his own creature," Corry said. He looked over his shoulder toward the church. "I'd better get back to work."

For an instant, Kate felt uneasy. She looked at the church. It was older than it had seemed from the highway. It looked run-down, abandoned but for the swans keeping the graveyard tidy.

Yet there was still beauty in the building, echoes of former power. The last sunshine was striking the west side of the building, streaming through to the stained-glass wheels and arches of the chancel windows on the east side.

"Are you the minister?" she asked quickly.

Corry laughed. "No," he said. "I'm here to tear the place down. Good day, miss."

He turned and started to leave, but found his way subtly blocked. He looked down. Campbell was at his knee.

The dog sat on his haunches and looked up at his master earnestly. Something passed between them, almost like an unspoken message.

Puzzled, Kate saw the man turn and walk back to her as abruptly as he had left. He came within reach of her.

For the first time, she was aware of his size. She was five feet eight inches in flat shoes and he was half a foot taller. His shoulders were like some kind of sturdy tree, an oak.

She found herself thinking again of his green tights. They both reassured and intrigued her, like the contrast between his strength and the gentleness with which he handled the frightened swan. She found herself wondering what he would be like as a lover.

The line of her own thoughts startled her. It showed in the flush of her cheeks.

He stared down at her for what seemed like a long time. Then he smiled faintly and offered her one of the two long, white feathers he had taken from the net.

"Campbell says you earned a trophy, even if you started off on the wrong side," he said.

He turned and walked back toward the church. The dog looked back at Kate for just a moment, wagged his tail, then turned and trotted after his master.

Kate stood alone in the failing light, wondering if Druids ever wore green tights.

Six

The sky in the west still glowed a wintry lemon yellow as Kate turned off the state highway onto the main street of Langley. Any hope she might have had that Langley would be different than the small towns of her youth was quickly dampened.

Lights were coming on—neon signs in front of the Friendly Tavern and the Hometown Lumber Yard, the distorting brown mercury-vapor streetlights along North and South Main, the clear-glass vanity bulbs that outlined the mirror in the window of the Shear Delight Beauty Salon. But all those lights seemed wan and thin, like birthday candles flickering against the falling darkness.

Three thousand miles from the Great White Way, she thought. Five hours by air and forty years by calendar.

The buildings themselves were worn out or merely utilitarian—single-story Victorians with display windows so old the glass had sagged, garages and storage buildings with white paint slapped over cinder block, commercial storefronts made of plywood and plate glass. They looked as if they had been punched out with the same cookie cutter and then frosted with different colors of stucco. Even the supermarket managed to look old and out of touch.

Kate drove the entire mile-and-a-half length of Main Street, looking for a sign of individuality or hope. If there was one, the lights hadn't come on yet.

An old-fashioned drugstore stood vacant. The marble countertop and chrome faucets of its fountain were visible through windows that had been soaped opaque so long ago they were nearly transparent again.

Someone had painted "We Quit. All Clothing Must Go" across the front window of the shop next to the drugstore. Down the street, several taverns presented blanked-out windows adorned with neon brewery logos. A pawnshop advertised half-time hours. Two cafes offered breakfast and lunch, as though no proper person would think of eating dinner anywhere except at home.

It was after six P.M. The town's five traffic lights had become flashers, red to stop traffic from the side streets, yellow to warn cars on the main drag. Not that there was much need; the streets were all but deserted, the sidewalks empty.

It wasn't merely that downtown Langley was sleepy. The little commercial district seemed spent. It radiated a weariness, as well as a wariness, that was as thick as the fog beginning to roll in off the saltwater at the foot of Main.

Kate chose a side street off the thoroughfare and found herself in a turn-of-the-century residential area. Bungalows with sagging porches and weather-beaten steps gave way to a scattering of once grand stone Victorians, four to the block. A few of the big, old houses had been converted to professional offices. The rest were boarded shut.

A sadness grew in Kate that was worse than the pain she had felt in remembering her own dead parents. The land itself had changed very little. The process of growing and fruiting, dying and resting before rebirth still flourished. The tulips and the swans and the geese were strong and healthy and alive.

Langley wasn't. Nothing had changed in forty years, except to decay and settle. The town had turned its back on the rest of the world, whether from anger at being passed by or from grief at the loss of the golden old days or from the simple, inexorable weariness of age.

Depression settled around Kate. She told herself she was being unfair. Sections of Manhattan were wretched, too, streets lined with buildings refurbished so often that their layers of paint were a fire hazard. On warm nights, the city smelled of garbage and auto exhaust. But Manhattan was still alive, still fighting, still creating, still looking toward the future with confidence.

Langley wasn't. There was little sign of life, less imagination, such a quietly overwhelming poverty of spirit. Too many of its inhabitants had been beaten by life; too many others, the energetic ones, had moved on to places that looked forward rather than backward.

No wonder people drank behind closed doors in small towns, Kate thought. No wonder the most destructive citizens picked domestic fights and the most self-destructive hanged themselves from rafters in the garage behind the house. If I were trapped here, I'd do one or the other myself.

No, I'd leave, just as I already have. Life is too grand a place, too thrilling and too intoxicating, to spend in the rolling spiritual brownout of a small town like this.

She blew out a deep breath, as though trying to dispel the stifling air. Then she drove back along the moribund main street to the town's largest motel, where the welcoming committee was waiting to greet her.

Kate longed for a chance to wash away the grime of a transcontinental flight, but her hostesses, a dozen well-meaning and earnest women, descended upon her like a flock of hungry crows on a cornfield.

Before she could catch her breath, she was intro-

duced all around—a minister's wife, the high school
music teacher, the owner of a real estate firm, and nine
mothers of members of the youth orchestra. All of them
told her they were charmed to meet her, and every one
of them silently noted the grass stains on the sleeves of
her white down coat.

Kate started to explain the stains, but didn't.
Although she was accustomed to being a public person,
she found herself annoyed by the way the women scruti-
nized everything from the cut of her hair to the slim line
of her woolen slacks.

She was an outsider, a foreigner from Manhattan, as
alien as a French whore or a Martian saucer pilot.

It was already shaping up to be a long week.

For the next hour, Kate made conversation as politely
as she could and ate as lightly as possible of the deep-
fried chicken with mashed potatoes and country gravy.
She was exhausted, but no one seemed to notice or to
care.

Then the little speeches began, defensive and boastful
by turn. Kate could hear her own mother apologizing
unnecessarily for being a country woman. The daughter
in her wanted to scream.

"I know this is not New York, Miss Saarinan, but I
think you'll find yourself pleasantly surprised at how
progressive this little town of ours is," said the wife of
the Presbyterian minister and cochairwoman of the
organizers in her welcoming speech.

"We try real hard to give our children what they'll
need to compete in the world," added the realtor's wife.
"We think we do a pretty good job, but we always
appreciate the help of worldly people like yourself."

Kate smiled until her face ached and hoped she was
hiding her growing impatience. Beneath their self-
deprecating speeches, the women were comfortable
and self-satisfied. Kate could do little one way or the
other to affect their lives. She could only hope that

their children hadn't lost all their curiosity and hunger for beauty.

As the welcoming speeches stretched out over the faint sound of dishes being cleared, Kate watched the two waitresses who served the group. Both were in their twenties. Both wore plain gold wedding rings on their right hands, not their left. They had little time to inspect the fancy guest from New York. They were intent on cleaning up and getting home, as though they had young children waiting.

Both waitress were caught in the dilemma of working women earning dirt wages. Kate felt no kinship with the local mavens of society, yet her heart was with those two tired young women. If she hadn't left, she could have been one of them.

Kate had made the wrenching decision to give up her child, but she, too, had waited tables late at night. She, too, had struggled for enough space to grow and thrive, to *live*. She could have been as trapped as these two young women.

She looked at them and wished she had never come back. Surely she already knew the futility of such a narrow existence. It wasn't necessary to have a refresher course. Yet something in herself had driven her back to the very kind of place she once had fled.

Exhausted and restless by turns, Kate waited for the formalities to wind down. Finally, she left the table as though to go to the restroom. Passing the waitress' station, she dropped two fifty-dollar bills into the tip bucket she knew would be there.

The two waitresses were standing nearby. When they saw the bills, both of them looked stunned.

"Geez, thanks," one of them said.

The other said, "What's that for?"

"A bus ticket out," Kate said.

"Oh, Langley's okay," the first waitress said. "I've seen Seattle. This is a much better place to raise my daughter."

"Then take her to Seattle for her birthday," Kate said. "There's a big world out there. Every daughter should get a look at it."

When Kate returned to her seat, the minister's wife and the doctor's wife appeared at either elbow to outline their personal plans for her upcoming week. If Kate had not already been numbed by fatigue, she might have objected. The two women seemed intent on dividing her evenly between them like a prize, tying up her every waking hour in Langley.

Her savior turned out to be Verna Stayton, the music teacher. A sharp-eyed woman with steel-gray hair and half-glasses perched on the end of her nose, Verna announced that their guest was exhausted and needed to see her quarters. Then she proceeded to disentangle Kate from the welcoming committee.

When the two of them were outside in the parking lot, Verna gave Kate a wink.

"Those two will pick you clean if you let them," Verna said. "I'll get a schedule tomorrow and we can go over it. Anything you want to skip, just let me know."

Kate was caught off guard.

"I'd hate to disappoint anyone," she said, realizing as she spoke that she sounded like her own mother.

"Let me worry about their disappointment," Verna said. "I've got broad shoulders. I can take it."

Gratefully, Kate followed Verna's car back through town and beyond, to a road that led along the waterfront out onto a rocky point at the edge of town.

"This house belongs to a local man, but he's away," the teacher said as she unlocked the front door and handed the key to Kate. "It's yours for a week."

The house was a surprising departure from what Kate had seen in the rest of Langley. It was laid out on three levels that marched down a rocky point to Langley Cove and offered a moonlit view of the San Juan Islands and the snowy peaks of Hurricane Ridge.

The entrance level consisted of a magnificent great room with a two-story domed redwood ceiling and massive, oiled fir beams. There was already a fire burning in a stone fireplace that was large enough to roast an ox.

The second level consisted of a kitchen with a pantry and a well-stocked refrigerator and two bedrooms that were closed off. The lower level was a master bedroom with a glass wall that looked out onto the water. A separate bathing area included an oversized whirlpool bathtub set in a corner that was formed by two walls of sliding glass windows.

Kate took one look at the tub and groaned softly with pleasure at the prospect of using it.

"Long trip?" the teacher asked.

"Very long. My body still thinks it's in New York, long past midnight," Kate said. She didn't add that her shoulder had stiffened after the blow from the swan's wing.

"Well, I'll get out of here and let you relax, then," Verna said.

Kate could have kissed her on both cheeks.

In the end, Kate chose a hot shower over the tub. Then she fell into the big soft bed and slept. She awoke only once, just before dawn.

Through the glass wall, the setting moon had turned the night sky to silver. The path of its light on the water glittered like a hammered mercury roadway to heaven.

She lay there half awake for a time listening to the sounds of sea meeting land. Then she drifted off again and awoke in the morning to the keening sound of gulls circling over the water in front of her bedroom.

The house and the setting lost little of their magic in the daylight. There was an energy and wildness about the place that was startling and invigorating. She had a hard time believing that the house was only a few miles from the listless town of Langley.

Fourteen years hadn't changed much, she thought. Small towns are still terribly isolated and out of touch, perhaps more by choice than by necessity, considering the speed of communication and travel. Everyone seems trapped in the fifties.

She was amused and dismayed that the women were still in charge of organizing the cultural and social life of the community. It was as though the men in places like Langley were uninterested in matters as insubstantial as music and art.

The past three decades had seen a cultural revolution in the roles of women. Surely men in places like Langley would have been sensitized, just a little. Surely they would have begun to change with the times.

But no, apparently not. They were still as ruddy and tongue-tied and impatient with female things as ever.

The image of the big man with maimed fingers and powerful arms popped into Kate's mind. She had thought about him several times during the night. Then she had been too tired to wonder why. Now she wasn't. She was face-to-face with the surprising realization that she had found him attractive—torn work clothes, green leggings, and all.

It was the way he handled the swan, she decided.

In her own childhood, that type of bluff, hearty outdoors man would have noticed migratory waterfowl only over the bead sight on the end of a shotgun barrel. She couldn't think of a man from her hometown who would have laid an elaborate trap and risked a good whacking just to rescue a swan tangled in fishing line.

The man at the church was good-looking, too, once she thought about it. His way of moving, with head up and eyes alert, suggested a powerful animal, a bear, even a grizzly, self-sufficient and confident in his strength.

Or maybe it was his green tights.

Kate laughed out loud even as she wondered why she was giving the man a second thought. She had taken lovers in the past, but she had never been attracted to a man solely on a physical basis. Her first sexual experience had been with the minister called Martin Thorson. She had worshiped him. He had seduced her, then abandoned her when she was pregnant. The experience had left her bitter about men, looking over her shoulder at all the wrong times. None of her relationships had survived that strain.

Maybe things would change, she thought, now that her career seemed truly launched. She might have the confidence now to fall in love as an adult, to have a personal life as well as a professional one.

Even if it's finally time, she thought, looking out the windows, I wouldn't choose some powerfully built and physically active workingman like the one at the church, even if he did show an unusual kindness toward swans.

A flock of bright white birds flew past, just out over the saltwater, headed north. Kate rolled out from under the comforter, went to the door, and stepped out on the cedar deck.

The birds were climbing, spreading in a widening vee. At first she thought they were swans. Then she listened more carefully to their call. The birds' voices were thin and reedy, almost shrill, much less resonant than the trumpeter swans she had heard in the tulip fields on the Skalbeck flats.

The formation turned. She could see dark patches on the trailing edges of the birds' wings. Snow geese. Another bird from her childhood, when they had been numerous in the fields.

There was something focused and purposeful about their flight, she thought. South to North. Migration. Time to move on. The swans would go, too, in the next few weeks. They always did. North to the Arctic to nest.

She thought about the little family group she had tried to save yesterday. She wondered if the young would stay with their parents one more year or would set out on their own to find mates and brood clutches of eggs somewhere on the tundra of the far north.

Odd, she thought, how the entire family moved without awareness through the churchyard, free to nibble the grass off graves and from around headstones. God's wild creatures were free in ways that humans never could be.

Creatures moved through the eternal now, without thought or memory. They responded to forces older and more powerful than themselves and they did so without the slightest self-consciousness. They did not need to invoke God as inspiration for their transcendence. They were ungodly, yet they possessed an almost godlike freedom. They were alive, and complete in that life.

Humans seldom had the luxury of wild freedom, and if they had it, they seldom used it. Thought and memory, the human blessings, were also the human curse. Thought looked forward, memory looked back, and together they could freeze a man or a woman in place.

Kate knew all about the wild kind of freedom. She had escaped the small town of her youth because there was no memory to bind her, no prospect to entice her. She had been as free as a swan and, in retrospect, she had made the most of that freedom. But she also knew freedom had a terrible cost. Loneliness.

The singularity of her own life suddenly chilled her in a way that the morning air could not. She stood barefoot a moment longer, listening to the fading calls of the geese. Then she stepped back inside and moved quickly to the bathroom for a hot shower.

After she dressed and made coffee in the French press she found in the kitchen, Kate set about ordering her day. She had committed herself to several tutoring sessions at the high school late in the morning and a short performance that evening at a music society fund-raiser.

The fund-raiser sounded like an exquisite bore, but she needed to repay her hosts somehow. Playing a few short solo pieces for a crowd of fifty or a hundred wouldn't sap her energy too much.

She went to the closet where she had hung her clothes and made sure that the press on her wool blazer and skirt had survived the trip. Then she opened her violin case for the first time in a day.

A thin wire waited, coiled in smug surprise on the black fingerboard.

"Crumb," she said. "You're jet-lagged, too, huh?"

She reached down to fix the E string on her violin that had come undone. Then she looked more closely. The string had come undone because the tuning peg that held it in place was broken.

"Oh, shit, oh, dear," Kate said, an epithet from her childhood.

A loose string could be tightened. A broken peg had to be replaced.

Gently, Kate lifted the violin from its case and inspected the ruined peg. The string normally passed through a hole drilled in the center of the peg and was knotted in place, but the hole in this peg had been drilled off-center. The tensioned string had pulled through the thin side of the peg.

She searched in the case until she found the sliver of wood that had broken away. Too thin to glue. She turned the peg in the scrolled box and reluctantly admitted it was now useless. Violinists had a variety of temporary measures to deal with broken instruments, but none would replace a broken peg.

She muttered several quiet epithets, then gently disentangled the loose string from the tailpiece. She held the violin almost awkwardly, as though suddenly unfamiliar with it. In Manhattan, she could think of a dozen shops and studios that could handle such a repair in half an hour, but here, at the far end of the Earth, she was lost.

I wonder if somebody is trying to tell me I should have stayed at home, she thought, running an index finger over the taut strings that remained. Then again, maybe nobody in Langley would notice I was missing an E string.

Immediately, Kate felt ashamed of her sour thoughts.

The people of Langley are earnest, decent folks, she reminded herself. They might not be cosmopolitan concert-goers, but neither were you fifteen years ago. Your tastes have changed, but you were once a small-town girl with lots to learn, so lighten up.

She put the violin back into its case and buttoned it up.

Maybe I can borrow a violin, she thought. Or maybe someone will know a repairman.

Of the two, she thought it more likely that she would be playing on a borrowed, decidedly ordinary violin.

Sighing, she reached for the phone.

Seven

The sullen little darlings had so much to learn. There was no other way to put it.

Two of the six violinists and one of the two viola players couldn't even hold the bow correctly. The rest of the twenty-three students in the Langley High School Orchestra string section showed signs of better training, but they were nervous. They didn't quite know how to react to this sleek new teacher from New York City.

"Think of the instrument as a friend," Kate suggested after listening to a series of scales that made her wince. "Make the bowing motion smooth and *don't break those wrists.*"

She added the last part with what she thought was a firm, encouraging tone, but the students looked startled, as though the basic tenet of classical violin technique was a new and alarming idea.

"Wait a minute," Kate said. "I didn't mean to make that sound so serious."

She drew a deep breath and started again. "How many of you have ever watched a classical violinist at work?" she asked.

There was no response.

Wrong question, she told herself dryly. Try again.

"How many of you have been to a concert? Maybe in Seattle or Vancouver?" she asked.

Two hands came up.

"Good," she said. "And how many have ever watched the string section in a good orchestra on television? Maybe PBS?"

No hands.

"You do get PBS up here, don't you?"

There were solemn nods, but no responses. Kate got the impression that the students had never seen a relationship between what they did and what they saw on television.

For a moment, she studied the members of the orchestra, trying to figure out how to get through to them. They looked like typical high school students, less flashy in dress but otherwise the same as kids she saw in New York.

Somehow these teenagers were subdued, though. They seemed as cautious as the town itself. She had sensed their diffidence the moment she walked into the auditorium.

"Okay," Kate said, "let's go back to some basics, then. How many of you know the difference, the *real* difference, between a violin and a viola?"

The youngsters looked at one another uneasily. They knew it was a trick question and they didn't want to be caught in it.

"No one?" Kate said with an exaggerated look of surprise and disappointment. "Actually, it's quite simple. The viola burns longer."

The students were silent, still confused. Then a blond girl with California hair falling over her viola tittered. The laughter slowly spread to the rest of the class.

Kate nodded, but kept a stern face. "That's right, both are made of wood and they'll burn quite handily, so keep that in mind when you get frustrated with yours."

The laughter grew, a mixture of relief and amusement. It spread out through students who had slipped into the auditorium for a glimpse of the visiting teacher.

"Right now, I've got a violin that I'd trade for a load of firewood," Kate added. "They really can be annoying beasts."

The orchestra students laughed out loud and looked at their instruments with new eyes. They were beginning to relax.

"Actually, I have to admit I stole that line from a very funny man named Victor Borge," she said. "He is also a fine musician. He takes music of all kinds very seriously. He just doesn't take himself too seriously."

Several students laughed again.

"That's what I'd like to do here today," Kate said. "Have some fun. Music is demanding, but it shouldn't be hard work. It should be a joy and a pleasure. Even if none of you becomes a professional musician, each one of you can learn to take real pleasure in what you play and how you play it.

"And if you don't, you might as well use those wooden boxes in your hands for kindling," she added with a wry smile.

"Now, let's do the scale again, trying for a pure, clean tone from each string. Ready. Begin."

The scraping sounds resumed, still not very musical but at least less strident than they had been.

"Think of the difference between a swan and a goose as you play," she suggested over the din. "Both fly and both sing, but the swan has music. The goose is, well, the goose is just a squawk."

She passed among the young string players, adjusting hand positions and shifting instruments to more comfortable spots. She was secretly amused as she studied the players. Their bodies were so different, some still childish and others already taking adult form, with breasts and chests and shoulders that had started to thicken.

One boy had the bulky, corded neck of an athlete—a weight lifter, perhaps, or a football lineman. His wide fingers were slow and stumbling on the fingerboard. He looked like he was trying to push the strings through the ebony neck of the violin.

"A little more gently," Kate counseled. "Treat your violin like it was your favorite girl."

The boy flushed crimson and lost his place in the exercise book as his pals snickered.

Girls and boys. A tender, sensitive subject. Kate felt a sudden rich sadness for these youngsters and all they had to learn about themselves and one another. Most of them never would learn, she suspected, not because they lived in Langley, but because they were merely human.

"Okay, forget the girl idea," Kate suggested. She cast about, looking for a less loaded analogy. "Do you fish?"

The football player looked at her in disbelief.

"Of course I fish," he said. "Doesn't everybody?"

"Then think of the violin like a line with a nice, fat chinook salmon on it. Your job is to keep the proper tension, not too much, not too little. Don't try to drive the strings through the fingerboard, but don't let them get away from you, either."

The boy thought about that for a moment, then lifted his violin to his shoulder and tested the strings with his fingers. Kate could see a light in his eyes that had not been there a moment before. She moved on to the next student and began the sensitizing process all over again.

The minutes passed quickly. Kate felt a surprising sense of pleasure from the experience. The youngsters were less defensive and self-congratulatory than the women she had met the night before. She felt a small glow of satisfaction as the period drew to a close.

Just before the bell rang, Kate noticed there was something else going on in the auditorium. There were thirty or forty students scattered in small groups throughout the big room. The audience had become increasingly restive.

Most of the disturbance seemed to come from a cadre of six young males, all in letterman's jackets. Jocks, full of themselves, impatient with anything beyond their experience. Each time she turned her back, she could hear them commenting on her ass, like construction workers on Fifth Avenue.

She ignored them.

There was a similar group of females, well dressed and conventionally pretty in the same way that the athletes were conventionally handsome. The girls were analyzing Kate in their own way, examining her hair and makeup and clothing as thoroughly as the lettermen examined the outlines of her body.

There was a third group as well, one that Kate recognized instinctively. Unlike the other groups, boys and girls sat together in this one. They favored a kind of unisex look—dark clothing; long, straight hair; and heavy black shoes sticking out in the aisle. The girls wore pale makeup and dark lipstick. Lacking the outlet of makeup, the boys sneered, mimicking the James Dean look.

Kate knew them without ever having been introduced. Young bohemians, intellectual and hip and disruptive in their own way. They had to prove they were far too cosmopolitan, bored, and unconventional to submit to the authority of the high school orchestra.

Verna left her position at the back of the orchestra risers and quieted the group with a quick, sharp warning.

Kate watched from the corner of her eye and, for an instant, she found herself back in her own high school again. As a freshman, she, too, had flirted with the disdainful nihilism of small-town bohemia. She had smoked cigarettes and coughed herself sick. She had sneered at conventional social life and had let her hair grow long and stringy.

Most of all, she had even toyed with the idea of aban-

doning the violin in a show of childish independence.
Something had stopped her.

No, some*one* had stopped her. Martin, to be exact.
He had spoken directly to her, treating her as an adult
although she was only fourteen, making her feel for the
first time in her young life that she was or could be part
of something both bigger and more worthwhile than
herself.

In retrospect, Kate realized that it had been the
beginning of Martin's seduction. He had seen in her flir-
tation with nihilism a search for something that would
transcend the mud fields and narrow dirt roads of her
life, the hard oak pews of the church and the scarred
Formica tops of her school desk.

Martin had taken that transcendent impulse and
channeled it into music. In doing so, he had given her
the gift of meaning, of beauty, of joy.

Looking back, Kate still wasn't sure whether Martin's
action had been selfish or altruistic. Perhaps it was both,
a mixture as complex as the human yearning to transcend the physical and touch the intangible.

Whatever Martin's motives, their relationship had
snapped her out of futile rebellion and had shaped her
life.

She knew that those childish bohemians in the auditorium would grow past their rebellion, too, but experience had taught her that few of them would find a path
to the transcendent.

Luck, serendipity, nature, nurture? Kate asked
silently. What was it that allowed intelligent young people to live in the real, mundane, commonplace dirt of
life and still quest for meaning?

She recognized that hunger for meaning in the
straight-haired, dark-lipped girls and the sneering, prematurely bored boys. As though trying to send them a
quiet message of hope, she turned and looked at them . . .
And met herself all those years ago, spiritual hunger and

defiance in the face of a girl who lounged against the back wall of the auditorium, just at the fringe of the bohemian group.

Kate felt a jolt pass through her body like an electric current. Time twisted, turning back on itself and returning again. It wasn't just the girl's age, it was the look of her body in its tight, black leotard top and loose-waisted black jeans. It was the way her breasts had just started to form and to stretch the black fabric. It was the pale angularity of her neck and the faintly defiant expression on her face.

Kate had seen all of it. In a mirror.

And for an instant, she was convinced that she was looking at the daughter she had given up fourteen years ago.

The sensation was not new. She had felt it before, whenever she saw girls the age her lost daughter would have been. It was a haunting, hopeful, harrowing thing to look in the face of a stranger, searching for some sign of yourself.

The girl looked back at her without recognition.

The bell rang, signaling the end of class. The girl turned and left the auditorium, following the insular bohemians.

Kate was overwhelmed with the feeling her trip to Langley had been a cruel, savage mistake. The past couldn't be healed. It could only be ignored as she had ignored it for so many years.

Eight

For five minutes, Brian Corry had been hanging by his safety belt, suspended and helpless, halfway between the old belfry and the floor of the church. The broad leather belt cut into his belly. Every time he moved, he began to spin in slow, dizzying circles. He wasn't in immediate danger, but he had no idea how he was going to get down.

The old bronze bell in the belfry was above him. He had been inspecting the bell, trying to decide whether to sell it off or melt it down, when the fir flooring gave way beneath his feet.

He looked straight down at the main aisle of the church, where he would have landed if the safety line hadn't stopped him. From this point, there was another fifteen feet to fall if he chose to cut the rope himself. But he felt no great urge to test that option. He had already suffered one broken back in his lifetime. If there was any other way out, he wasn't going to risk another. So he hung there, thinking of other ways to get down.

"Of course, I could get you to come over and stand beneath me to cushion the fall, couldn't I, Campbell?" he said to the Border collie who was sitting on his haunches in the aisle, staring up curiously.

Campbell wagged his tail at the mention of his name. He would have done the rest, too, if his master had been serious.

"Stand easy, gillie," Corry said. "That's not even a last resort. Maybe you could go convince a couple of the swans to fly in here and take me away with them."

Corry laughed at his own joke, then twisted his body in the harness, trying to ease the strain on his middle. The motion sent him spinning slowly, like a piece of kinetic art. He grabbed the safety rope and lifted himself by one arm to relieve the pressure on the belt. Then he tried to go hand-over-hand back up the rope.

His right hand was strong, but his maimed left hand betrayed him. Though his palm was covered with healthy pink skin, the muscles below had been burned away by 7600 volts of electricity.

Corry was a strong man. There were few things he couldn't do, but climbing a rope was one of them.

He rolled back onto his stomach in the harness and spread his arms and legs to slow the inevitable spin. The position was uncomfortable, yet it was the only way he could keep his head clear.

After a moment, the spinning slowed, but he felt a sharp knifepoint of pain between his shoulder blades. He knew his body well. Soon the muscles around the weakened, once-broken vertebra would begin to spasm and he would have to drop his arms. Then he would be back to spinning again.

Time to make the best of a bad situation, he thought. *Better a fall now, while I still have the coordination to roll.*

He was fumbling in his hip pocket for the locking knife when he heard the sound of a car's tires crunching on the wet gravel of the driveway.

Hallelujah!

Through the faded and bubbled stained glass of the church's round rose window, Corry could see the outline of a car as it rolled to a stop. He didn't recognize the vehicle.

Enough of his pride was still intact that he didn't care to scream for help from a total stranger, but he wanted to make sure whoever it was didn't leave.

"Campbell," he called out. "Go get 'em. Fetch them in, boy. Go!"

The collie cocked his head, puzzled. There were no sheep around, no swans to herd, not even Corry's daughter, who had often played the herding game with him. He wagged his tail tentatively.

"Fetch them in, Campbell," Corry commanded.

He waved his hand toward the front of the church, indicating a direction. He had propped the doors open to provide light and air while he worked.

Campbell understood that command, and he trusted his master. If Corry said there was something to fetch, Campbell would fetch it. The dog streaked through the doors.

The dark-haired woman who had attacked him the previous afternoon was just getting out of her car. She carried a piece of paper in one hand and a familiar case in the other.

Warily, Campbell hesitated, as though approaching a swan. Then he figured the angles and dangers and ran down the stairs in a flanking move.

Kate was more confused than the dog. She looked at the map in her hand, wondering if she had gotten lost somehow. She hadn't. The directions led straight to this church.

The owner of the Langley music store had told her there was one man in the entire Skalbeck Valley who might be able to fix her violin. He had written the name "Brian Corry" in one corner of a sheet of lined paper, and then had drawn a careful, detailed map to the worksite where Corry could be found.

What the man had not told her, what she had begun

to suspect when the map led her to the church, was that she had already met Brian Corry once, in the graveyard. Now his dog was circling around her as though she were a swan being driven to the net.

The black-and-white collie dropped to the ground ten feet behind her, watching her intently. When she started toward him, he rose up in warning and barked sharply: Dog at work; don't pet.

"So it's like that, is it?" Kate said. "And me without a stick in my hand. So, Campbell, where do you want me to go?"

She stepped to the right. Instantly, Campbell moved to cut her off. She feinted left. The dog scooted over to block her.

"Not toward you, not right, not left," she said. "How about if I turn around and head away from you?"

Campbell watched her with an intensity that vibrated through his light body.

She turned and walked toward the church, half-expecting the dog to run around and confront her. When she looked over her shoulder, Campbell was low to the ground, following her at a distance of about ten feet, ready to leap right or left if she strayed from the church path.

"Forward it is," she said. "But if Brian Corry isn't inside, I'm going to have your furry hide for a wall hanging. I don't have time to play hobbled swan for a bored Border collie."

Kate stuffed the map in her pocket and approached the church with long strides. Campbell followed with unnerving intensity.

Despite her black and white shadow, Kate hesitated at the open front doors. It had been a long time since she had set foot inside a church.

"Hello?" she called out.

Just behind her, Campbell barked, his sharp animal voice out of place in the church.

"Come on in," a man called out. "The door's open."

Kate recognized the voice immediately—the Druid in green leggings, locally known as Brian Corry.

She stepped into the vestibule. She could see the altar and pews, but the stained glass of the windows made the nave dim and shadowed. No one was in sight. She felt a rising tide of uneasiness.

"Mr. Corry?" she called out again.

"In here."

The voice was close, but she couldn't see anyone. Campbell barked again.

Kate moved into the nave and looked around. There was still no one in sight. Then the creaking sound of a rope under strain made her look up. She gasped.

When Corry turned to look in her direction, he immediately began to spin again. He spread his arms and legs to slow the spin and, as he turned past her once more, he saluted her gravely.

"We meet again," he said. "At ease, Campbell. Good work."

The collie wagged his tail and managed to look pleased at the praise and disappointed that the unexpected game was so quickly over.

Slowly, Corry swung by, looking at the woman who was staring up at him with surprise, concern, and dawning amusement. She had changed somehow, he decided. Her dark hair was drawn back and tied with a white ribbon. She had traded her fancy white coat for a green Gore-Tex parka and stone-washed jeans. She had low, rubber boots on her feet.

But she still had a wild look about her eyes, like the female swan trapped in the tangled fishing net.

Tilting her head from side to side, Kate studied the man on the end of the rope. Slowly, a smile passed over her face.

"Are you supposed to be some kind of half-fallen angel?" she asked.

Corry laughed in spite of himself. That started him turning again. "I'm pagan," he said. "I would probably have to be the hanged man."

"From the tarot deck? That's blasphemy, here in a church."

"Lord save me from a pious woman."

"You want me to leave?"

"No!"

The vehemence of Corry's response sent him into another loopy circle. He countered the motion with one leg and one arm.

"No," he repeated more gently. "I just wish you'd brought a tractor with you."

Kate went and stood directly beneath the slowly spinning man.

"Are you hurt?" she asked when she saw how deeply the safety belt cut into his midsection.

"Only in the pride."

"I guess we're about even, then."

"Call it that, if you will," Corry said. "Did you happen to bring a fifteen-foot ladder with you by any chance?"

"Sorry. It didn't fit in my purse."

She was studying the arrangement of belt and rope that suspended Corry in the air. She set the case in her hand down in one of the pews and reached out to pat Campbell. This time the dog accepted her touch, panting with excitement and grinning up at his master.

"He's in a fix, isn't he," Kate said. "What are we going to do?"

"Go for help," Corry said.

"Where?"

"Look around outside. If you see a farmer on a tractor off to the west, in the tulips, it will be Gordon Johnsrud. Go over and fetch him back. Gord is big enough to let me down all by himself."

"There was no one in the field when I arrived," she said, "and I don't hear any tractors."

"Damnation! Then go to town for help."

"What kind of help? The fire department? I have a cell phone. Does 911 work out here?"

Corry groaned. Rescue by a fire crew of local volunteers wasn't much more appealing than a fifteen-foot drop to the floor.

"I'm not that desperate," he said. "Yet."

He looked at Kate again, suddenly studying her from a new perspective. Then he shook his head, as though rejecting an idea.

"What?" she asked, reading his body language as she had read his dog's. "What were you thinking?"

"Well, I was thinking you might . . . Aw, forget it. Go ahead, call out the volunteers. They haven't had a good laugh since two old folks got caught naked when the sofa bed folded up on them."

Kate smiled. "Would they laugh before they let you down or after?"

"Both."

"Seems a small price to me, but I'm not the one hanging by my belt," she said. "Unless you have a better idea?"

Corry looked her over again. There was nothing sexual in his manner. It was as though he was measuring her against a yardstick only he knew.

"What?" she asked.

"I was just trying to figure out whether you had enough meat on your bones to hold onto one end of the rope if it were turned around a pillar."

She looked at a nearby pillar, then back at him.

"That's what I thought," Corry said. "Go ahead and call the fire department."

"Not so fast," Kate said, "I used to help my father tie down three-hundred-pound dairy calves. You aren't *much* bigger than that."

He looked at her again.

"I'm a lot stronger today than I was at thirteen," she

assured him. "I work out five days a week, three on the NordicTrack, two with weights."

"Well, good for you," Corry said. "Shouldn't be any problem at all for you to heft that cell phone of yours and punch in some numbers."

"Suit yourself," Kate said with a shrug. "If you don't trust me enough to tell what needs to be done. . . ."

She turned as though to leave.

"Wait, damn it."

She stopped, but didn't look up.

"Oh, hell," Corry said. "It's only fifteen feet. If I fall, I fall. Guys fall fifteen feet every day and survive."

His voice wasn't as confident as his words.

"Besides, it takes the volunteers half an hour just to muster out, and another fifteen minutes to get here," he continued. "I'll be one sorry puppy by then."

Kate looked up. Her expression was a mixture of concern and amusement. He didn't blame her. He must look ridiculous dangling at the end of the rope like an overgrown spider.

"Over in the corner," he said, gesturing. "I've got the safety line tied off on one of the pillars that support the balcony."

Kate found the line and examined it. The knot that secured it to the wooden pillar was slipped, pulled back through a loop in the standing part of the line. A quick tug from her direction would undo it, but no amount of strain on his end would untie the knot.

"That's the way my father tied off those bull calves," she said.

"Bull calves? What was he doing? Turning them into steers?"

"Are you worried?"

"Shit."

Corry shifted unhappily. The safety belt around his middle was beginning to feel as though it would cut clear through him.

"Listen," he said. "Do you remember enough of your childhood to undo that knot and let me down a few feet at a time?"

"Yes."

There was no hesitation in the answer. "Okay, then, I guess we can try. First, how much free line is left behind the knot?"

"Quite a bit," she said.

"Enough to bring it back to this other pillar?"

"No problem. See?"

Kate brought the rope to the second pillar and wrapped it once around.

"You should take at least two turns, three, if possible," Corry instructed. "Let it act like a windlass. You'll need another fifteen feet of slack after that, to get me to the floor. Looks to me like you're a couple of feet short."

"I can get another foot or two from your knot on the post."

"Just make sure you don't undo the knot until you've got your turns or I'll go right on down to China."

He watched as she pulled a foot of rope out of the slipped knot. She took another wrap around the second pillar and showed him the remnant of the rope.

Corry swallowed hard.

"Close," he said. "Close enough, I guess. Do you have a pair of gloves?"

Kate dug a pair of black leather gloves out of the pocket of her jacket and waved them.

"Put them on," he ordered. "If the rope pulls through your hands, it can cut you like a knife."

"I know, I know," she assured him. "I wasn't always a city girl."

"Forget I ever suggested it," Corry muttered. "Now take two turns around the second pillar and pick up the slack."

Kate did as she was told. "If I pull another three or four inches, that slip knot will come undone."

"You catch on real quick," he said. "When that happens, I'm going to be in your hands, quite literally. I weigh enough that you may not be able to hold me by yourself, even dallied around the post."

She flexed her hands and grasped the rope.

"Wait!" he said. "Let me down as slowly as you can. An inch at a time would be fine but I'll settle for a foot at a time. And don't hang on so hard that your hand gets drawn into the post. Sure as hell you'd break fingers."

Kate looked at her fingers, covered with thin black leather. Corry's warning reminded her that her hands were her livelihood. For a moment she thought about the phone and the firemen. Then she mentally shook herself; 911 was for cities. She had been raised to make do with what was at hand.

"Okay," she said firmly.

"Then let 'er rip."

Kate wrapped the rope around the second pillar twice, then took one turn around her hand for grip. She picked up the slack in the rope and pulled gently, reclaiming the last of the loop in the slipped knot on the first pillar.

"Here it comes," she said.

"Just tug gently. But be ready. When the knot goes, you're the one in charge. I hope."

The loop of the slipped knot disappeared. There was a snag when the knot refused to come apart. Kate gave it a sharp tug.

The knot came undone all at once, and she felt Corry's full weight. The two loops around the second post took some of the stress, but the force of his weight still dragged her toward the dally post like a powerful magnet.

"We're off the knot," she said, gritting her teeth against the tension.

"When you start to let me down, do it easy. Pay the rope out, but be a miser about it."

Kate tried to let a few inches of rope slip through her hands. A foot of rope vanished. She grabbed and pulled back as Corry's weight tried to snatch the rest of the rope from her.

A rasp, a creak, a jerk, a curse; Corry was two feet closer to the floor.

"Sorry," she said.

"Try it again," he said after he got his breath back. "Inches this time, not feet, okay?"

"Easy for you to say."

Kate paid another few inches into the dallies around the post and felt Corry's weight try to take control of the rope again. She held on but it was more difficult this time. From the corner of her eye, she could see Corry turning slowly.

"Can you stop that twirling?" she said through her teeth. "It makes you weigh twice as much."

Slowly, Corry spread his arms and legs against the turn. The motion made him yaw from side to side as well, increasing the tension on Kate. Another few inches slipped through her hands involuntarily.

"Hold on," he snapped.

"I'm holding on," she shot back. "You hold still!"

Six more inches slipped through her hands. She took another quick wrap around the post and stopped the rope's progress. Corry was still twirling on the other end.

Campbell watched his master with increased agitation. He barked once, nervously, then dashed over to Kate and barked again, as though to warn her.

"Hush," she hissed through her teeth. "I'm doing all right here."

The dog barked again.

"Tug-of-war, Campbell," Corry called. "Get your end!"

Delighted at the familiar game, the collie rushed over and grabbed the end of the rope, adding his fragile weight to the equation.

"I'm going to let you down again," Kate called out. "Here goes."

The first six inches went smoothly. So did the next six, and the next.

"Good, good," he said. "Looking good."

The encouragement gave Kate confidence. She continued to feed rope through her hands. Momentum built up quickly. She tried to slow Corry's descent and ended up jerking him to a halt in midair, five feet above the worn flooring of the central aisle.

Corry grunted at the abrupt stop. Campbell barked excitedly around his end of the rope. The dog's tail wagged like a metronome in a frenzy of pleasure. Next to herding, tug-of-war was his favorite game.

"You okay?" Kate called out.

"Fine," he grunted. "Get on with it."

She paid out more and more rope. Suddenly, she realized she was running out. The three turns around the post had used up much of her slack. Now the collie's grip on the rope had begun to interfere with her own.

"Let go, Campbell," she said. "I need every inch I can get."

Campbell growled in his chest and hiked up the rope a few inches with his teeth.

Corry jerked toward a hard landing.

"Call off your dog!" she said.

"Drop, Campbell," he ordered. "The game's over."

The dog's tail switched into high gear. He growled again, enjoying the contest with the humans.

Rope slipped until Kate's hands were right against Campbell's muzzle. She braced herself, trying to stop Corry's rapid descent. She had paid through all of the slack now. She was being drawn into the post.

But Corry was still alarmingly high above the floor.

"Campbell, you idiot," Corry shouted.

The dog's tail wagged more vigorously. He growled and bared his teeth. There was a difference between herding, which was serious, and tug-of-war, which wasn't. In tug-of-war, orders didn't count.

Corry watched the floor rise up to meet him too quickly for comfort. He was swinging wildly now. He caught a flashing image of himself crashing down onto the pews instead of the floor. The thought wasn't comforting.

"Campbell! *Drop!*" Corry roared.

The tone of voice told Campbell that the game was over. He let go and jumped up to nudge Kate's cheek with his cold nose—no hard feelings.

She made a startled sound. The last few feet slid through her hands. She tightened her grip and was jerked into the pillar. As she fell, she tried to hang onto the rope. It whipped through her hands. She lunged at it, missed, and went sprawling.

Behind her, in the aisle, came a roaring curse that ended in a loud crash.

Then the old church was as silent as a tomb.

Nine

Groans and muttered curses welled up in the hallowed silence of the old country church. For an instant, Kate felt something like fear, as though she expected God's wrath to rain down on such blasphemy.

"Are you all right?" she cried, trying to get to her feet.

Campbell barked happily and danced around in her path, delighted at the unexpected turn to the game. Kate tried to step over the dog, but he darted under her feet and sent her crashing to the floor again, this time between two pews.

The collie yelped and scooted away beneath another pew. Then he ventured back carefully and touched her cheek with his nose.

"You devil." She groaned. "Somebody ought to skin you and make you into a muff."

The dog gave her a quick kiss on the lips with his tongue to show her he didn't believe her.

"Bleck," Kate said.

She pushed Campbell to one side and looked beneath the pews. Corry was on the floor ten feet away beneath a sizable tangle of rope. He was watching her with eyes that were alive with a startling fire.

"Are you all right?" she asked again.

"It's you I'm worried about," he said. "It sounds like a murder going on over there, or worse."

"It's your idiot dog. He tripped me and beat me to the floor."

Corry laughed with what little breath he had left. "Campbell has great instincts."

Kate rolled over and scrambled into the aisle, where Corry was trying to untangle himself from the rope that had run through the pulley and fallen onto him.

"Here, let me help," Kate said, moving to his side.

He grunted and groaned and fought with the safety line like a roped bull. Finally, he threw the rope off and tried to roll over. His back reminded him that he had just fallen onto a hard floor.

"Wait, don't hurt yourself more," she said. "Did you break something?"

"A long time ago," Corry growled, tearing at the rope.

"What?"

"A long time ago," he said distinctly. "I have a couple of fused vertebrae. I can't reach around behind myself very well."

"You do this dangle-and-fall sort of thing often, then," Kate said with relief. "I'd hate to think you arranged it just for my entertainment."

"The only entertainment will come when I catch that dog," Corry said, rolling over into a sitting position. There was irritation in his voice, and some pain as well.

"Where do you hurt?" Kate asked. "Should I call a doctor?"

"No." Corry's voice was gruffly final. "I'll be all right."

Campbell bounced into his master's lap with his front feet and washed the sandy beard with his tongue.

"I should have traded you for something useful long ago," Corry muttered.

The collie paid no attention. He glanced over at Kate, as though inviting her to join the floor games. She knelt down and looked at Corry's face intently.

"How far did you fall, anyway?" she asked.

"Not far enough to break anything. Just give me a minute to line things up and get them marching in the same direction."

He twisted his neck from side to side, then shrugged his shoulders, trying to loosen the knot between his shoulder blades.

It was a gesture Kate understood, tension against tension, stretching muscles against themselves. He rolled to one knee, then stood up slowly, testing his balance and strength.

She stood with him. She had forgotten he was a full head taller than she was, and much bigger all over. She was astonished that she had been able to hold him suspended in midair.

Corry stretched his arms above his head, teasing the knotted muscles in his back into motion. He drew a deep breath and blew it out. Then he looked at Kate. Slowly, his expression changed. His smile made her heart stop for a beat or two, as though she had just seen the sun break through afternoon clouds.

"Thank you," Corry said. "I almost forgot to say that. You're a game one, aren't you?"

Kate didn't know what to say. "I never thought of it one way or another. I'm glad you're not hurt. I'd have felt awful."

"Why? You did your best with a bad situation. Even if I'd broken my neck, you'd have had nothing to feel awful about."

She shook her head. "I don't think of things that way. I was raised to do the best I could, and if that's not enough, you dig down deeper for more."

Corry's smile faded. He looked at her again, measuring her as he had while he dangled from the rope, but this time his yardstick was different. He nodded once, slowly.

A charged silence grew between them, as though they were both surprised by this turn in the conversation.

"What brought you out here, anyway?" he asked. "Going to chase more swans?"

Kate glanced toward the opaque window to avoid the intensity in his eyes. She could see the distinctive shapes of swans against the darkness of the green grass in the graveyard.

"No," she said, "no, I wasn't chasing swans. I saw some snow geese this morning, though. They were headed north, as though they had a purpose."

"Migration. Moving on, free as birds."

There was a faint bitterness in his tone that startled her.

"The way you handled that swan, I thought you liked birds," she said.

"I love them. That's why I hate to see them go. Selfish of me, but the valley's not the same without them."

"It's their nature," Kate said, struck by the bluntness of the big man's confession.

"I know. And they always come back," he added, "but I still miss them."

Corry stretched his arms and shoulders again. "Good thing you left your white coat at home," he said. "It would have been ruined for sure."

Kate stuffed her fists into the pockets of the Gore-Tex.

"It may be ruined anyway," she said. "I doubt if the cleaner will be able to get out the stains. You were right. It was foolish to wear it in the first place."

"I didn't say that," Corry said.

"Maybe you didn't say it, but you sure thought it. It was written all over your face."

"I hope the coat cleans up. It was nice, made you look like a bit of a swan."

"Feathers don't get grass stains."

"But they sure get muddy," he said. "You saw the swans yesterday with red bibs?"

She nodded.

"Some of this flock stops up in the Fraser River valley, below Vancouver, for the first part of the season," he said. "There's a lot of iron oxide in the mud. They get stained digging for cattail tubers. It doesn't seem to bother them, though. For all their rituals, they don't have our vanity."

"You talk about them like they were friends of yours."

Corry nodded. "I admire them. They're very thrifty birds. They live on the spillage of modern agriculture, the leftover spuds, cucumber and pumpkin seeds, the green barley grass the farmers plant for winter cover."

He looked around the church. "We're kindred souls in that. I'm a gleaner, too."

She followed his gaze. For the first time, she realized that the building was being dismantled. The altar and pulpit were still in place, but they had been stripped of their liturgical trappings. The organ on the other side of the chancel had been removed, and the walls around the stained-glass windows had been ripped out.

Corry's enigmatic remark from the previous afternoon came back to her.

"You really are tearing the place down," Kate said.

"Just the choice parts," he said. "That's why I was checking the bell. It's at least a century old and pretty good brass."

She looked up at the heavy bell.

"And the belfry supports are some of the nicest twelve-by-twelve red maple beams you ever did see," he said.

"That makes them special?"

He laughed at the question. "Have you ever seen the sunbursts and rays in a good piece of red maple?" he asked, gesturing toward the belfry. Then he swept his hand around the church. "There's a lot more good wood here, too."

He walked over to the pulpit and tapped the densely grained wood panels of the raised box.

"This is yew," he said. "So is the altar. It has a grain like smoke in still air. Spectacular. You can't find yew anymore, since drug companies found out about taxol."

Then Corry went to where the organ had once stood and pointed to the skeleton of the building that was revealed.

"These timbers are some of the best clear, vertical-grain fir I've ever seen," he said. "Forty feet long, twelve-by-twelves. They were cut in the days when that meant one foot by one foot, and not a single knot in it."

He touched the straight old post with his maimed hand. The gesture was gentle. Kate was reminded of the way he had handled the tangled, frightened swan.

"They cut some wondrous old trees when they built this place," he said. "The wood has been standing here, seasoning, for the last ninety-seven years."

She looked around the old church once more, still skeptical. "Isn't it just used lumber?"

"Used lumber?" he repeated, shocked. "I suppose that's what most people see."

"What do you see?"

"I see about a hundred thousand board feet of the finest wood God ever made," he said with a touch of a dreamy smile on his face. "Of course, it will all have to be resawed, but that's easy."

"What about all the nail holes? Won't that spoil the wood?"

"I've already got buyers for the fir. It will be trim and flooring for a house one of those Microsoft millionaires is building down on Lake Washington."

"What's wrong with new lumber? He can certainly afford it."

"He couldn't bear to think of cutting any more old-growth trees to get the kind of beams and clear-grain flooring he wants," Corry said. "I sold him cedar siding I reclaimed from the timbers of an old railroad bridge up in the North Cascades. There are a few spike holes in it, but he likes it. Says it adds character."

"You do this for a living?" Kate asked.

"I do lots of things, none of them for a living. I gave that up a long time ago."

"I was told you were a violin maker."

He looked at her sharply. "Who told you that?"

"The owner of the music store in town. He said you were the only man in the Skalbeck Valley who might be able to help me. I broke a peg and I have to play tonight."

Corry felt himself go still. For an instant, he tried to tell himself that he was mistaken, but he knew he wasn't.

"Concert? You must be Kate Saarinan, then," he said.

She nodded, not surprised that he knew her name. It was, after all, a very small town.

Damnation! Corry swore silently. Here he was, fascinated with this woman before he found out she was both inappropriate and unattainable.

"Well, then, how do you do, Miss Saarinan."

There was an odd new tone to his voice, distant and disappointed. She didn't know what she had done wrong, but she sensed his withdrawal very clearly.

"Mr. Corry," she replied with a stiff little nod. "But I'd prefer 'Kate.' It doesn't make me feel like your maiden aunt."

He didn't reply for a moment. He was studying her with new eyes, as though trying to get used to relating to her in a different way.

"I should have guessed yesterday," he said, more to himself than to her. "We don't get too many stylish women traveling alone here in the valley. But I understood you weren't due until today."

Corry turned toward the dog, who was sitting in the aisle, watching them.

"Well, isn't that something, Campbell," he said. "You should have been a bit more polite yesterday."

Just beneath the words, there was something of the tone Kate had heard from the women of the welcoming committee.

"My God, does everybody in this place have to act like I'm some kind of foreigner?" she asked impatiently.

Corry's smile flashed, then faded. "We don't get stars from New York here very often."

"I'm a farm girl from a hundred miles south of here who went to New York and got a job that sounds more exotic than it really is," Kate replied.

He didn't look convinced. In fact, he looked skeptical.

"For the love of God," she said, "I never thought I'd feel like an outsider among the kind of people I was raised with."

"Maybe you've left them farther behind than you realize. I don't see any cow manure on those shoes of yours."

"Do I really come on that way?" she asked sharply. "I certainly don't mean to."

He smiled slightly. "Maybe it's just the expectations that get in the way. People around here feel a million miles from New York, for better and for worse."

"New York is a lot closer than they realize," she said. "Even though there are times Langley reminds me of someplace out of the fifties."

Corry looked thoughtful, then nodded.

"It's not a bad place, really," he said. "It's just kind of hanging on. The fishing has gone to hell and the lumber mill shut down fifteen years ago. Losing the mill kind of cut the balls off a lot of the men in town.

They got their buyouts and put the cash into savings accounts that couldn't keep up with inflation."

Kate shook her head. She didn't know much about high finance, but she knew that savings accounts were only a step above shoving currency into a mattress.

"Most of the men have been holding on for dear life ever since," Corry said, "watching their hopes turn to dust. That kind of experience can infect a whole town."

"Haven't they realized that they must change or die?"

"No. They figure change is what got them in trouble in the first place. The ones with their hands on the levers of civic power won't ever let go. They know if they turn loose, even for a minute, they'll never get back to what they had."

"Are you one of them?" she asked. "Is that why you're here?"

He looked at her, trying to decide whether she was ridiculing him. There was nothing in her expression but interest.

"I'm here for my own reasons, and they don't have anything to do with power," Corry said. "I'm the most powerless character you could imagine."

"Like the swans," she said. "Free, after a fashion."

"I'll take freedom any way I can get it. I don't much like what I see in Langley, but mostly I don't pay attention. The town's insularity is hard on the kids." He shrugged. "But the bright ones figure out that they'll have to leave to find what they want."

"And the dim ones stay behind?"

"Sometimes. Sometimes they just want to raise kids in a place where you don't have to have alarm systems on your home and metal detectors at the school door."

"Some kinds of safety can be stifling," Kate said.

Her tone said Langley's safety came at a high price.

"That's why you're here," Corry said. "Maybe you'll give a few of those kids some usefully wild ideas. The town could sure use them."

She thought about the young girl she had seen in the auditorium, the one who so reminded her of herself at that age.

Then Kate wondered if a man like Corry had any idea how dangerous and how liberating wild ideas could be for a girl like that. Freedom was sometimes frightening, sometimes exhilarating, and never without cost.

"The kind of freedom you're talking about is double-edged," she said.

"So is everything that's worth having."

She felt a sudden warmth toward the complex, contradictory man standing in front of her—scarred yet powerful, open yet enigmatic, friendly yet distant. In his own blunt way, he had summed up her half-articulated reasons for coming to Langley.

Without further thought, Kate stripped off her leather glove and offered her hand to Corry, as though they were meeting for the first time.

"It's a pleasure to meet a fellow subversive," she said with a smile. "I was beginning to feel lonesome."

Corry nodded solemnly and took her hand in his.

"It's a feeling you get over, after a while," he said.

"Did you?"

He smiled faintly and ducked the question by asking one of his own. "What can I do to repay you for cutting me down?"

"Fix my violin."

He looked at his scarred hands. "Are you sure you trust me?"

"Like the trapped swan, I don't have much choice," she said.

But she was smiling.

Ten

Corry rubbed his hand lightly across the scuffed leather of the violin case, as though admiring its durability. Then he undid the sturdy catches of the case and opened the lid.

Despite her brave words, Kate watched him anxiously. She felt as protective of her violin as she would have been of a child. It was important to her that Corry be impressed with the instrument. If he wasn't, he didn't know enough about violins to be trusted with hers.

His eyes moved over the violin for a several seconds. He pursed his lips and whistled softly.

"That's quite a fiddle," he said.

"I like it," she said mildly.

Corry took the violin from the case with one hand and turned it so that the light fell across the varnished fir of the belly. He rubbed a rough thumb across the smooth wood, then turned the instrument in his hand and studied the back.

"Maple," he said, looking up at her. "You understand about those beams in the belfry, now?"

"You'll make violins out of them?" she asked, surprised.

"Can't think of a better use."

He tapped the nail of his index finger on the whorled hardwood back and nodded appreciatively at the dry, hollow sound. Then he turned the violin over again. He peered down into its insides through one scrolled sound hole.

"Jacob Stainer, 1659," Corry said quietly, reading the faded old label inside. "We don't see too many of these in the Skalbeck Valley."

Kate relaxed completely.

"Not many people would appreciate a Stainer if they saw it," she said. "Thank God you do."

"I always liked Austrian workmanship," he said. "The masters of Cremona weren't the only ones who could build good fiddles."

"I've had this one for years," she said. "It's like a part of me, now. Somebody's offering me a Stradivarius to replace it, but I'm not sure I want to give the Stainer up."

"Wellll," he said, drawing the word out, "I like the Austrians a lot, but I don't think I would turn down a Strad if someone offered it."

She shook her head a little. "It's not exactly that simple."

"It never is."

He ran his thumb across the strings in a familiar way, then inspected the scrolled peg box at the top of the neck. The broken peg was still in place, although she had removed the string and stored it in the case.

"Who did that to you?" Corry asked gruffly.

"Did what?"

"Fitted your fine instrument with these pegs."

"What's wrong with them?"

"They're some kind of tropical wood. They sure as hell aren't what Jacob Stainer would have used on a fine box like this. He would have used rosewood."

Kate's eyes narrowed. "Rosewood is what I paid for when I had the pegs replaced two years ago, in one of the better violin studios in London."

Corry's grin was wolflike. "Guess they figured you'd never be back to complain. They foxed you good."

"Well, thanks for sharing that with me, Mr. Corry," she said, irritated. "I just play violins. I don't build them. Which brings us back to the main point. Can you fix this by tonight?"

He laid the violin back in its plush-lined case and stood up. He started to say something, then changed his mind. Instead, he walked toward the door that opened into the sacristy.

Kate glared at his back as he disappeared. A moment later she heard an outer door slam.

Campbell seemed unperturbed by his master's exit. The dog sat on his haunches, watching her and grinning, panting lightly, hoping to stir up another romp.

"Your boss is a real bastard," Kate remarked. "Rude, too."

Campbell wagged his tail and came over to be petted. He hopped up onto the pew next to the violin case, sniffed the instrument once, then lay down beside the case.

She stroked the dog's fur absently. Then she heard the sound of the outer door again. Corry came through the sacristy door with a violin case in one hand and several tools in the other. He laid the second violin case next to hers and deposited the tools on the pew beside it.

"As your luck would have it, I picked this up on my way here," he said. "Ronnie McHugh was jamming Sunday night at a country bar over on the mud flats when the ribs came unglued."

She watched as Corry unsnapped the lid of the case.

"He fixed them with Scotch tape for the moment," Corry said, "but I'm going to have to reglue the whole body."

Kate winced in sympathy for the other violinist.

"However, since Ronnie won't be fiddling again until Saturday night," Corry continued, "he won't be needing his pegs. So let's see if one of them will fit your fine Austrian violin, shall we?"

He opened the lid. Inside was a light-blond violin with an elaborately scrolled neck and a checkerboard rib pattern. The varnished body glistened warmly.

It reminded Kate of a Norwegian Hardanger fiddle. The violin was slightly larger than her own and much flashier. She was used to formal symphony instruments, plain and unadorned, yet there was something inviting and playful about this violin.

"May I?" she asked.

Corry looked up at her, surprised or pleased, she could not tell which. He took the violin, handed it to her, and watched intently while she admired it and tested its weight.

"It's heavier than yours," he said, guessing what she was thinking. "Ronnie is hard on his fiddle, so it had to be a little thicker than I wanted."

Her eyes widened. "You made this violin?"

He nodded, but said nothing, waiting for her reaction.

She inspected the ribbing and found the spot where the inlaid checkerboard pattern had begun to lift away. A patch of clear cellophane tape held the thin wooden piece in place. It was an emergency repair she had seen before, one that could hold for hours or days.

She lifted the violin to her shoulder and rested her chin on it. Then she picked the strings, listening. The sound was odd, foreign, intriguing.

"May I play it?" she asked.

Corry shrugged. He picked up the bow from her case, checked its tension, and handed it to her.

Kate put the violin to her shoulder again and drew the bow across it.

The instrument made a sound that was both vibrant and arresting, deeper in pitch than the Stainer, more like a viola or a baroque violin. The note was rough yet pleasing, like the taste of a bold new wine.

She played a scale quickly. The notes rang as clearly as solid silver bells. Then she played a bar from the solo opening of the Beethoven Violin Concerto, her touchstone. The violin responded eagerly, like a horse released from a cramped stall. The notes were vivid and clean.

Suddenly she felt Corry's eyes on her. He was watching her with an intensity that should have disturbed her but did not. She finished the phrase and slowly lowered the violin. Her eyes met his, violinist and violin maker, woman and man; for a moment, both of them hung in the same slice of time and space.

Then Corry turned away.

Kate felt a sagging disappointment. Something had awakened in her for a few instants, something that had been lost or ignored for a long time. She was sure he had sensed it, too, the possibilities like music in the silence.

Yet at the last moment, he pulled back.

Even as she resented the rejection, part of her was relieved. This was not the right time, not the right place, and very likely Corry was not the right man at all, despite his unorthodox charm.

She looked at the violin he had made, then handed it back to him.

"It's lovely," she said. "I've never played a contemporary instrument that is quite as . . ." She grasped for a word. "Lively."

Corry took the violin without meeting her gaze again. "I have a feeling you would make any fiddle-maker sound good."

With that he sat down on the pew and went to work.

She watched while he loosened the peg, then unwound the E string. He carefully fished the knot out of the string. She noticed that he used the fingers of his maimed hand gently and very deftly, as though he sensed things more precisely because of the wounds.

Sometimes he used his ring finger for the missing index finger. The rest of the time, he used the scarred ends of the missing fingers.

Something about the way he handled the violin suggested a familiarity that was more a musician's than a violin maker's. Without thinking, she asked, "Did you play?"

He looked up at her blankly, as though his mind had been far away.

"Before your . . . accident, whatever it was, I mean," she said awkwardly. "You handle the instrument as though you had played it."

He went back to mending the violin.

"I had a good ear and less-than-perfect hands, even before I got cut up," Corry said. "I would never have been a threat to Perlman, or to Johnny Gimble for that matter, but I did play."

Kate sat down beside Campbell, who had laid his head on the pew next to the violin cases.

"What happened?" she asked.

Corry glanced up at her again, trying to detect pity or cruel curiosity in her expression. He was pleased when he found neither.

"I was trying to unload my own fish boat during a longshoreman's strike up in Sitka," he said. "I drove a forklift into some electric transmission lines. I took about eight thousand volts through me, top to bottom."

"Oh, my God," she said, appalled.

"The convulsions snapped a couple of vertebrae in the middle of my back," he continued matter-of-factly, going back to work. "That's why I was having such trouble up there on the rope. The shock also burned off pieces of some fingers."

"How awful," Kate said softly, as she tried to imagine the sensation.

He glanced up and grinned. "Actually, it was quite an illuminating experience, once they got my heart started again."

Kate shuddered. "I've never understood how men can joke about such experiences."

"Who's joking?" he asked, his expression serious. "Haven't you ever heard of the fire in the brain?"

"I read Yeats, if that's what you mean. Are you saying the accident turned you into a shaman?"

"It clarified me, which may or may not be the same thing."

"It cost you the fingers you needed to play the violin," she said.

"And made me learn about making violins," he countered. "I'll take that kind of trade anytime. I guess women have a hard time understanding that, but it's true."

"Women?" she said. "I don't follow."

"My wife couldn't understand, either. When I sold the boat and started messing around in the workshop and in old buildings like this one, she decided my brain had taken a worse burn than my hand."

Wife? Kate thought, feeling a sudden stab of what might have been fear.

The prospect that there was a woman in Corry's life had never entered her mind. Which was stupid. Surely other women found him attractive. No surprise that one had married him.

Yet Kate couldn't help being surprised. She simply hadn't thought of him as married. Off-limits.

"What does your wife think now?" Kate asked carefully.

Corry didn't look up. "I have no idea," he said with crushing finality. "She walked out more than a decade ago."

End of subject.

Kate let the silence spread between them, a wall rebuilt. She wondered if the lesson in distrust he had learned from his ex-wife was the reason Corry had drawn back from the possibility of intimacy just a few minutes ago.

Campbell stirred, lifted his head, and laid it lightly on her thigh, seeking attention. She touched the feathers of fur beside his ears and brushed them gently. He settled in and closed his eyes. She could feel the fragile weight of his head and the warmth of his body. She stroked him, enjoying the sensation of touching warmth that wasn't human.

Corry looked up from trying to remove the peg from its holes in the scroll box of Kate's violin. He glanced over without stopping his work.

"Tell him to shove off," he said. "You don't have to be polite."

"He's no bother."

"Except when he wants something."

Without lifting his head, Campbell flicked his eyes in Corry's direction. The dog wore a worried look, as though he understood his position was tenuous.

"Don't worry," Kate reassured the dog. "I won't make you get down."

She sank her fingers into Campbell's coat and wriggled them. Beneath the fur, the dog's body was smaller than she would have guessed. His bones were light, as though they were made of balsa. She was astonished at how strong he seemed, nonetheless.

"He's just doing what all creatures do," she said to Corry.

He studied the dog with an odd, almost envious expression. "You have that part of it right. Just don't be surprised if he pesters you for more."

"That's fine with me," she said. "I haven't had my hands on a dog in a long time."

Corry continued to work the peg gently in the scroll box.

"Does that mean you aren't one of those Manhattan types who keeps a Great Dane in their apartment?" he asked.

"I love dogs too much to do something like that," she

assured him. Then she added, "How is it that you know so much about Manhattan? You certainly have your mind pretty well made up about the people who live there."

Corry glanced at her with a ready grin. "It's not the people but the place. I spent a week there that seemed like a month. Couldn't get out fast enough."

She tried to picture this rough-edged man in a restaurant like La Scala or a Central Park penthouse.

"Maybe you weren't on the run," she suggested. "Most people I know in New York are escapees from somewhere."

He looked up from the violin, curious. "Is that why you went to New York?"

Kate considered her response. Finally, she nodded. "I needed the freedom that Manhattan had to offer."

He grimaced, but she couldn't tell whether the sour expression was aimed at her or at the stubborn peg.

"You don't think much of freedom, or is it only for men?" she asked.

He twisted the peg again, then glared at it in exasperation.

"I don't think that freedom is ever as simple as it sounds in slogans," he said. "More people talk about freedom than really want to be free. They don't want to pay the price."

Kate picked at a tangle in Campbell's coat, thinking. There was truth in what Corry said. She had gone to New York for freedom, yet she had finally realized that she wasn't free in the way she thought. The land and sky and water of the Pacific Northwest called to her much more deeply than she had wanted to admit. The swans and the tulips and the cold wind were familiar and surprisingly comforting.

There was even an odd joy in seeing that girl in the high school auditorium. She was a reminder to Kate that her unknown child was growing, somewhere, another turn in the cycle of life and death.

But, God, she wished she could hold that daughter if only for a moment. Just once. To feel the separate life, the heartbeat that once had echoed her own.

"Maybe you're right, Mr. Corry," Kate said. "The price is very high."

"Brian," he said without looking up.

"Brian?"

"It's really Bran, the Celtic way, but most people are more comfortable with Brian."

"Bran," she said distinctly. "No one is ever completely free. Not of the important things. The rest . . ." She shrugged. "The rest doesn't matter."

Corry gave the peg one more turn. It came loose. He held it up, showing it to Kate.

"There's your trouble," he said, sinking his thumbnail into the shaft of the peg. "The wood is too soft. Moisture got into the grain, swelled it up. That's why the peg was stuck. Probably why it broke, too."

He tossed the ruined peg into the lid of her violin case, laid down Kate's violin, and picked up the one he had made. He turned the peg that held the E string until it came undone. He pressed with his fingers until the peg slid out of the scroll box.

"You'll need to have all four of the pegs replaced, once you get back to New York," he said. "When you do, make sure you can work them in and out easily."

He picked up the Stainer and tried to insert his peg into the scroll box. As he had expected, the fit was too tight. He laid the violin down and picked up one of the tools he had brought back with him. It looked like a block of wood with two V-shaped grooves cut into it.

Corry laid the peg in one of the grooves and went to work with a sanding block, rolling the peg around in the groove and sanding at the same time.

Once again Kate was struck by the smooth competence of his work, as though the old injury was an aid rather than a handicap.

"I thought rosewood was darker," she said. "Like the bad pegs I got in London."

"I'm not passing this off as rosewood." His voice softened as he looked at the peg. "This is wood from an old Cox's Orange Pippin tree that my grandfather cut down and made into gears for a waterwheel. I salvaged the gears and carved some of them into pegs and the soundboard for this fiddle. That Pippin was like ironwood."

"Cox's Orange Pippin?"

"An apple tree," he replied. "Very powerful, very mysterious."

"Celtic magic again?" she asked lightly.

He looked up. "You don't believe in magic, then? Or is it just too dangerous, like freedom?"

His eyes were unreadable. For a moment she felt as she had a few minutes ago, caught in a space and time that was as full of possibilities as a violin waiting to be played.

"I . . ." She hesitated, unsure how to answer.

"Too long in New York to believe in anything you can't touch?" he asked.

"Maybe," she said, "but what's so magical and dangerous about the wood of an apple tree?"

He went back to work on the peg.

"Apple is the tree of love," he said. "If I were to give you something carved from apple wood, you would have to kiss me."

Kate didn't know what to say.

"You see what I mean about it being dangerous?" he asked, looking up suddenly.

She felt his intensity as though he had touched her. If he had tried to kiss her at that instant, she not only would have let him, she would have met him more than halfway.

"Maybe more dangerous for you," Kate said. "We Manhattan women know how to take care of ourselves."

Corry laughed softly, amused. "That's one of the reasons I don't care much for Manhattan."

"You don't think women should know how to take care of themselves?"

"Just the reverse. Women must take care of themselves. But the cost in Manhattan is awfully high. It tends to make them . . ."

"Brittle," Kate supplied without hesitation.

"Yeah, I guess that covers it," he admitted. "Present company excepted, of course. I certainly don't intend to insult the strength and competence of the woman who just rescued me."

She laughed.

Corry gave the apple wood peg several more strokes with the sanding block. The process generated a thin haze of dust on his hand.

"Won't it be too small for the Bran Corry fiddle now?" she asked.

He looked up, startled. "The Bran Corry fiddle?"

"The one you made. What else would you call it? There are Strads and Stainers and Corrys. Or at least one Corry. Or there was," she added, looking at the sanded-down peg. "Now it's out of commission."

"I still have teeth left from the old gears. If I have to, I can make Ronnie a new one."

He held the new peg next to the others on her violin.

"The color isn't a good match for your others," he said. "Too light."

"I'm not a fanatic."

"That's not the way I heard it."

"Meaning?" Kate asked.

"Meaning no one reaches the level you have in New York music by being anything less than a tough customer."

"You sound as though you've investigated me."

He shrugged. "I read your résumé."

Kate thought about that while Corry gave the peg one

more stroke with the sanding block. Then he wiped the peg carefully with a clean cloth and inserted it into the scroll box of the Stainer violin. It fit smoothly.

With off-handed ease, Corry took the loose E string out of Kate's case and fitted it into the tailpiece. He laid the string across the bridge, threaded it into the center hole in the borrowed peg, and knotted it.

Kate watched the process calmly and with quiet surprise. Normally, she preferred to string her violin herself. Every violinist did, which was something Corry no doubt knew.

He turned the peg, taking up most of the slack in the string. Then he stopped long enough to inspect and adjust the bridge. He looked through the sound hole at the sounder inside. It, too, was a repair, but a good one.

"That's a nice piece of work," he said. "It wasn't done in London, was it?"

She shook her head.

He used his thumb and the stub of his index finger to straighten the bridge a fraction before he took up the rest of the slack in the string with the peg. Gently, he stroked the taut string with his scarred finger, testing the pitch.

Kate found herself wondering if the digit was more sensitive now than it had been when it was whole. In spite of the injury, Corry had pleasing hands, she thought, strong and careful. Even elegant, in a well-worked way, like smooth Spanish leather.

"Here you go," he said, handing her the violin. "I'll let you do the final tuning. Don't be afraid to tighten the E string up properly. That apple tree was a hundred years old when granddad cut it, and that was a hundred years ago. The wood had plenty of time to toughen and cure."

She took the violin, tested the strings, and gave the E string a quarter-turn. The peg was still warm from the sanding or from Corry's touch. She let her fingers linger on the newly sanded wood. Then she picked up her bow and ran it along all four strings to test their pitch.

Campbell lifted his head from the pew and pricked up his ears, watching her attentively.

Kate looked at him and laughed out loud. "He looks like he's expecting a recital."

"He's got a good ear," Corry said, "especially in the higher registers. But you might find his taste in music a little old-fashioned. Downright old country, in fact."

Violin on her shoulder, Kate leaned over and blew a light breath in Campbell's face. He blinked with surprise, then barked softly out of excitement.

"And, kind sir, what would you like to hear?" she asked lightly.

Campbell gave another soft woof.

"Okay, a little Mozart, then," Kate said.

She straightened up, caught Corry watching her with that extraordinary intensity in his eyes again, and felt a flush of warmth spread through her. She liked knowing that he was as aware of her as she was of him.

"Mozart with an old-fashioned twist," Kate amended.

She launched into the opening bars of the young Mozart's first violin concerto. She played two bars with exquisite propriety and then two more with a kind of wobbly syncopation that suggested a country waltz.

"If you ever need a recommendation," she announced, "use my name. As a doctor of sick violins, I doubt if you have a peer between here and New York."

Corry bowed his head formally but said nothing. He was still watching her.

"Thank you," Kate added in a low voice. "I was dreading the recital. A strange violin, strange place . . ."

"Strange people?" he suggested, deadpan.

She smiled. "Will you be there? I'd love to see a friendly face—er, beard—in the audience."

He laughed softly. "I'll be there."

"Good. I'll play something as a special thank-you."

"No need," he said. "As far as I'm concerned, the fact that you came all this way is thanks enough."

There was an earnestness in Corry's voice that surprised her. She started to ask what he meant, but he glanced down at his wristwatch.

"It's getting late," he said. "You better take your new peg home and see how it suits your repertoire."

Kate took his wrist and looked for herself.

"It can't be that late!" she said.

"It is."

Quickly, she put her violin away, snapped the case shut, and patted Campbell. She looked at Corry and wondered what he would do if she patted him, too. But Manhattan-trained or not, she didn't quite have the nerve.

"See you tonight, then," she said, holding out her hand.

He took her hand between his. For just an instant, she felt the restrained power of his grip. Then he released her.

"Tonight," he said.

It had the sound of a promise.

Eleven

$\mathcal{K}$ ate could hear the faint sound of a phone ringing behind the thick front door of the house on the bluff. She fumbled with the key that Verna had given her until she finally got the door unlocked.

But as she walked into the kitchen, the ringing stopped.

"It wasn't for you anyway," she reminded herself.

Her voice sounded odd and hollow in the empty house. She realized she had spoken aloud to herself.

How strange, she thought silently. You've been talking to someone all afternoon. You've talked more to Bran Corry than you've talked to anyone in a long time, and now you're talking out loud, even though there's no one here.

You're lonely.

For the second time in a day, Kate was startled by that realization. She had lived by herself for a long time, but she seldom noticed that she was alone, much less lonely. Now, suddenly, she realized how much of her life was spent in isolation. Even the concert stage was a kind of isolation; the recording studio, where her future with Polyphony lay, was yet more solitary, life lived through earphones, listening to music.

Life as a solo act is free, she thought, but it sure isn't cheap.

The realization unsettled her.

Where did this sudden self-pity come from, she asked herself. Why, on the brink of extraordinary success, should I suddenly feel like a lost child?

The answer came immediately. This valley, these mud flats, this rough gray water, was all part of the past, her own past. The fresh, raw wind of the spring afternoon could have been from her childhood. The feel of it was as immediately familiar as Bran Corry and his dog and his church and swans.

Corry was a complex, enigmatic man, yet for all of that he was . . . familiar. Nothing about him had shocked her, nothing about his manner was alien or distasteful.

True, there was something mysterious about him, something withheld; she had felt it the moment he discovered that she was the visiting violinist. She was also certain that his hidden self was benign rather than destructive. It made his reserve all the more intriguing, rather like the house she was in—strong, open, yet more complex than its deceptively simple lines suggested.

In the brooding dusk of a Pacific Northwest spring, Kate walked around the great room of the empty house looking for a light switch. She glanced out through the tall windows at the last line of light in the west. All color was gone. Black islands rode a gray sea beneath a gray sky.

Kate realized she was cold from her afternoon in the unheated church. She longed to soak in a tub of churning, steaming water, then to lay a fire in the big greenstone fireplace and warm herself by its flames.

Cold and lonely.

The words sounded as clearly in her mind as if she had spoken them aloud. Where in heaven's name is this coming from? Kate wondered unhappily.

She thought about the solitary girl she had seen in the auditorium that morning, the girl who had made her think painfully of the child she gave up fourteen years ago.

That dark-haired girl was remarkably composed for one so young. She had an aura of natural reserve and of fiercely concealed pain that Kate herself had felt as a teenager. The girl was lonely, too, lonely as only a teenage girl can be, lonely in a crowd, lonely as an ugly duckling in a field of swans.

There are people who can be alone in a crowd, Kate thought. That girl. Me. I suspect even Bran Corry is like that. Lonely while surrounded by people.

She didn't have to ask why. She had only to step back and look at herself for the answers to come tumbling into the emptiness she felt.

You're vulnerable to loneliness because you want something more than mere company. You want connections that unsettle most people. You want communion on a level that most others can't sustain. You, and people like you, are blessed in your freedom and cursed because we spend time most of our lives utterly alone.

Kate stood in front of the windows and watched the descending night. At least I have my music, she thought. And Bran seems to have his life, too, his wood and his violins and his dog.

But what of a child like that girl? Where will she find something to challenge and sustain her, particularly in a town like Langley?

Perhaps she won't, Kate thought. Perhaps she'll find drugs instead, or some other dangerous diversion. Or some man to make happy or unhappy as the whim strikes. Or God knows what.

Life. Potential. Hope.

They were the same thing, and all too often they resulted in the same kind of disappointment.

But that dark-haired, cool-eyed girl was someone else's to worry about. Kate might have some small effect on her, or on some other youngster in this town, but in the end, the connections between human beings were too tenuous.

We all make our own way, Kate thought. Often alone and sometimes cold. But we survive and we even enjoy. Sometimes. And sometimes we mourn.

The phone rang again. She followed the sound to a phone in the kitchen. She picked up the receiver.

"Hello," she said.

"Well, finally!"

Ethan Farr's clipped voice was a surprise.

"Ethan? What on Earth? I thought you didn't even know where I was."

"Langley, Washington, is a very small place," Farr said. "It only has one high school, one orchestra society, one newspaper, and one visiting classical violinist."

Kate recognized Farr's tone. It was the one he reserved for moments when he was impatient but trying not to show it.

"Is something wrong?" she asked.

"No, not really. But the longer I thought about it, the less I liked being out of touch. This is a critical moment in your career. I would feel much better if you were in New York to sign papers."

Kate heard the words and something more as well, Farr's innate caution.

"What's going on?" she asked bluntly.

Her agent was silent for a moment. Then he sighed.

"You're too quick for your own good," he said. "I didn't want to bother you."

She heard the implied *yet.*

"The deal memo is drawn up," he said. "I want you to sign it. Tonight would be good. I'll settle for day after tomorrow."

"But—"

"You'll be through with your obligations by then, correct?"

"Yes, but I'd planned on—"

"Good," he interrupted. "Your ticket is waiting at American Airlines in SeaTac. It's not a through flight, but it will get you here."

Kate's chin came up. She didn't like orders, even from someone she trusted as much as she did her agent.

"Fax the deal memo," she said. "If everything is agreeable, I'll sign it and fax it back. That should do it."

"I'd prefer original documents and original signatures."

"Why the sudden rush? I thought we were going to sign the papers next week."

Farr hesitated just long enough to worry Kate.

"I'd just as soon not wait until next week," he said finally. "Nothing concrete, but I'd like to have an original written record of this deal in hand as quickly as possible."

"What's going on?" Kate demanded. "Are we in trouble?"

The hesitation was longer this time.

"I don't think so," Farr said cautiously. "Everyone is still making the right noises and all the papers are marching along at their proper pace."

"Drop the other shoe."

"Well, I did hear something on the grapevine about some squabbling up the ladder in Tokyo. I doubt that it would make the slightest difference in our deal, but I'd just as soon not tempt fate."

Kate sighed and drummed her fingers absently on the kitchen counter. Like everything else in the world, the arts had become hostage to corporate uncertainty. The unspoken reservations she had about the startling Polyphony Records offer grew out of that knowledge.

"Is our new patron getting cold feet?" she asked.

"Heller? Good lord, no. He's almost beside himself

with pleasure. Be careful of him. I think he's smitten with his lovely black swan."

"The only thing he's 'smitten with' are the possibilities for a publicity circus."

Farr laughed out loud.

"You're so wonderfully pragmatic for an artist," he said. "It makes dealing with you . . . piquant."

It was Kate's turn to laugh.

"Stay pragmatic," he said. "And come back. You can take a week or three off after we get this contract nailed down."

"Cautious old Ethan, right?"

"It's what you pay me for. I hadn't intended to mention the rumor because I didn't think it was necessary. You're just too damned perceptive."

"Our relationship has lasted longer than many marriages," Kate said. "It's not surprising I read your silences."

"Then thank God we aren't married," Farr retorted. "You'd make my secret life very difficult."

"You have a secret life?" she said in mock horror. "I'm shocked, Ethan. Just shocked."

"Men must have secrets, too, not just women."

"I'll remember that," she said, almost to herself.

"What's your address?" he asked, all business again. "I might need it."

"I don't know. It's a beautiful house way out in the country overlooking the ocean and surrounded by trees."

"Lovely, I'm sure," he said, yawning. "Don't miss your plane."

"Is there something you aren't telling me?"

"Read my mind," he retorted. "Million-dollar deals don't come along every day. If something happened to this one because you're in East Bumblefart, I'd be unlivable."

"You often are. Good-bye, Ethan."

"Day after tomorrow?"

She sighed. "Day after tomorrow. Damn it."

"It's an early flight. Want me to book you a hotel at that end?"

"I'll take care of it."

As Kate hung up the phone, she wondered if Ethan had really told her everything he knew. After a moment, she decided the question was unimportant. Heller had given his word, and a person's word still counted for something, even in the amoral world of modern corporations.

She felt along the wall, discovered the light switch, and snapped it on. Light flooded the kind of kitchen a cook would have loved.

Sighing for the meal she didn't have time to prepare, Kate went downstairs and dressed for the recital.

Twelve

Corry slipped into the crowded Scandinavia Hall just as the seventh and eighth–grade string ensemble finished. The size and the seriousness of the audience surprised him. The people were dressed as though for a church service or a funeral.

Sunday best, he thought. Well, they can only throw me out. Or try to.

Dressed in a Black Watch plaid tunic and jeans, he lounged against the back wall, scanning the crowd.

Verna Stayton, the high school music director, took possession of the middle of the stage like a Valkyrie. She thanked the crowd for their attendance and enthusiasm, then invited them to a reception for their guest, Kate Saarinan, following the performance.

Corry grumbled silently into his freshly trimmed and well-brushed beard. He wanted to see Kate perform, but he had other plans after the performance. The woman with the dark hair and the clear green eyes had been on his mind since that afternoon.

He needed to talk with her, to explain the miscalculation he had made.

What's the modern jargon? he asked himself. Downstream consequences? Yeah. Well, there's one hell of a downstream consequence I didn't count on when I pushed to get Kate invited here.

As Verna left the stage, Corry caught sight of the embodiment of the complication, his daughter. Alyssa was a member of the volunteer stage crew setting up music stands and arranging chairs for the next group of performers.

Thirteen years old, a child eager and awkward, a woman in her silences. A bafflement to her father. At the moment, Alyssa was frowning seriously while she thumbed through sheet music on the stands and studied the arrangement of chairs. As usual, she was dressed in what Corry thought of as premature black—black sweater over a black turtleneck and a short black skirt over black tights and black gym shoes.

The outfit was her own invention. On her, it looked stylish. Or perhaps she was just growing into the natural, individual style that was hers as a woman.

Corry watched while his daughter ran long fingers through her short, straight dark hair and let it fall back smoothly around her face. The gesture was purely Alyssa. She possessed the magical ability to concentrate without self-consciousness in a crowd.

Stage lights illuminated her face. She focused them like a kind of living prism. Corry saw, all at once, the girl she was and the woman she would someday become.

Someday soon, he thought unhappily, and God help me, I must raise her into that womanhood.

But how?

It was a question that Corry had asked himself from time to time as Alyssa grew. Lately, the question had become a haunting litany.

How does a man alone help a girl grow into her heritage as a woman?

He had a been single parent since Alyssa was an infant and his wife had decided that her quest for motherhood was the worst mistake she had ever made. Soon he was raising the daughter they had fought so hard for.

Caring for an infant and a small child had been a time-consuming chore with startling rewards. After the initial shock of single parenthood, he hadn't felt out of his depth. Then Alyssa had grown. She had come to him with questions a man never faced as a boy. She was subject to moods and feelings he knew only secondhand, if at all.

Corry was well read and widely traveled, but he was old-fashioned in many ways. He refused to buy into the modernist idea that men and women were really the same. As far as he was concerned, men and women were decidedly different. He relished that difference the way some men relish fine whiskey.

He liked women. He enjoyed their company and he valued their presence in ways that other men he knew did not. His appreciation was masculine, but it didn't require sex. He liked pretty women as much as the next man, yet it was female intelligence and sensibility that had the most lasting appeal for him.

Female minds took such surprising turns. Bright women bristled with insights that wouldn't have occurred to him in a lifetime. Women had different ways of looking at the old quandaries of human existence, different ways of solving the problems of living and dying.

Some of those differences were rudimentary. In Corry's experience, men were stronger and women had more staying power. Most men liked toys and tools. Most women's tastes were less practical, more aesthetic.

And most man/woman distinctions were mere matters of degree. Men and women were like two bell-shapes on the same curve of the universe. The two curves overlapped one another, but not completely.

The differences fascinated and pleased Corry. Perhaps it was because he had raised a daughter. Perhaps it was simply the way he was.

His brush with death had taught him the limits of his own physical strength. It had left him more attuned to the female power to create life. But he was no modern apostle of androgyny. His appreciation of women, of their beauty and their intelligence, was frankly male.

And the women he liked most were the ones who possessed the greatest measures of the power he regarded as female. He liked women who had their own sense of completion, women who in other times would have been burned as witches, women aware of their own power and unafraid.

He sensed that power developing in Alyssa, yet he was at a loss to help her channel or control it. That feeling of helplessness was the reason he had become involved with bringing Kate Saarinan to Langley. He wanted to be certain that his daughter was exposed to women who had made it on their own, women who inhabited a bigger world than the one bounded by Main Street and the four walls of a nursery.

This summer, Corry planned to take Alyssa to New York and Washington, D.C., where internationally renowned musicians gave concerts. She had been to such concerts in Seattle, but that city was so close to home that it lacked mystery for Alyssa, the challenge of the unknown. When she was older, he planned to take her to Europe. He had been saving for the trip for years.

Then an idea had come to him from a strange source—strange for the self-declared pagan, that is. A local minister who was a lover of classical music had agitated for Langley to get on the "vacation" concert circuit for professional musicians. He had lobbied Corry especially hard, for Alyssa's sake. It would be a sin for such obvious musical talent to go uneducated. Corry had agreed.

Downstream consequences, he told himself. Educate a child and open up a can of worms I had hoped would remain closed.

Somehow it was both ironic and fitting that man-woman magnetism had taken over the moment he laid eyes on Kate.

If I had known who she was, I would have been on guard. I would have seen her differently. Out of bounds. A teacher, not a lover.

But he had seen her as a woman, and he had wanted her. He still wanted her.

Stupid. Futile. Plain damned dumb.

No matter how many times Corry told himself the truth, it didn't change what he felt. Kate was passing through his life. He wanted her. He suspected she wanted him. If they became lovers, he was afraid of the outcome. Neither one of them was the kind to do things casually.

Damned interfering ministers, he thought. They should stay in their churches and preach to the choir.

But Pastor Thorson had been a good man until his accident, which had left him with his body whole and his mind bruised beyond healing. He certainly had been intent on seeing that Alyssa's talent was nurtured. In fact, he had been so insistent that at first Corry had suspected the minister of other, wholly unappetizing motives.

Pagans could be uncharitable bastards.

The backstage curtain pulled aside. Corry caught a glimpse of Kate. She had set down her violin case and was slipping out of her coat. She wore a long, plaid skirt and a dark sweater with a pleasantly sweeping neckline that started at the points of her collarbones and dipped across the smooth skin above the rise of her breasts.

Her physical beauty made Corry light-headed. In the church and in the graveyard, she had been bundled against the cold. Now he could see the intriguing female curves of her body. For an instant he felt hollow. Then he swallowed hard and drew a deep breath.

He knew then that she would probably break his heart, but he would have her just the same.

If she would have him.

The junior string ensemble trooped onto the stage and sat down raggedly. Verna took her position at the podium and spoke a few words of encouragement to the children that the audience couldn't hear. Then she raised her white baton and carefully set the tempo.

Backstage, the first strokes of bows over violins and viola made Kate flinch as though the false notes were physically painful. Instantly, she composed her face to hide her reaction.

The piece was a Brahms exercise. Once all the players were finally launched, the music smoothed out considerably. Relieved, she picked up her own violin case, set it on a cleared table, and opened the lid.

After she removed her violin, she inspected the scroll box carefully. The new peg was strikingly blond against the dark varnish of the venerable instrument. She held the violin close to her ear so as not to disrupt the players onstage. Softly, she plucked the E string.

The peg had held its pitch perfectly. She drew her thumb softly over the rest of the strings. She had watched Corry check them in the church by ear and make a few tiny adjustments. Now she realized he had tuned them to one another perfectly, almost by the mere touch of his finger.

A shaman indeed. A fire in his brain. Magic in his hands.

With an odd smile, she put the violin back in the open case. When she straightened and turned around, the speculative, very female smile was still on her lips.

She found herself face-to-face with the girl who looked the same age as the daughter she had given away.

The girl's dark hair had glints of red deep within it. She stared down into the violin case for a long, silent moment. Then she glanced at Kate with a penetrating look.

The stage turned to quicksand beneath her feet. The girl's eyes were a silent but unmistakable accusation. Kate felt a momentary panic, a stab of the kind of guilt she thought had passed from her life.

Abandoned, alone, a lost child. And it was her fault.

Kate had felt that dizzying sense of loss when her parents died. She had felt it again when she walked away from the Lutheran home for unwed mothers.

She wondered when this child's pain had begun.

Kate reached out and touched the edge of the table, seeking someplace to ground herself in a world that threatened to come apart.

The girl looked back into the violin case, then reached out with a thin forefinger to touch the scroll box. Suddenly Kate saw nothing more than curiosity in the child's eyes.

I must have been mistaken, she thought. Whatever accusation I saw in those dark, intelligent eyes came from my own mind, not from hers.

Kate glanced over her shoulder. The ensemble was still patiently sawing its way through Brahms. Kate touched her finger to her lips to signify the need for silence. Then she picked up the violin and handed it to the teenager.

The girl took the violin by the neck, handling it in the manner of someone who was fully accustomed to such instruments. She ran her eyes over the dark, varnished belly and touched the strings lightly. She traced the scrolled sound hole and peered inside curiously. Then she held the violin at arm's length and touched the alien peg in the scroll box.

She glanced at Kate in wordless question.

Kate started to say something aloud before she remembered the ensemble. She nodded warily, acknowledging the difference in the pegs, then shrugged as though to say she couldn't explain it in sign language.

The dark-haired girl turned the violin comfortably in

her hands and studied the back. She traced two long marks on the plain maple, scratches that had been there when Kate acquired the fiddle. Then she looked carefully at the edge work and the tailpiece. She seemed genuinely interested in the instrument.

Brahms came to a merciful conclusion. As the audience broke into applause, Kate and the girl were released from their silence.

"How long have you played the violin?" Kate asked, curious about the girl's familiarity with the instrument.

What she really wanted to know was why the girl wasn't out on the stage, but it would have been rude to ask, even for an outsider.

Suddenly the girl turned shy. She shrugged a little, as though she didn't know how to answer.

"Not like that," she said, glancing over at the ensemble on the stage.

The words could be taken several ways. Kate tried to be tactful.

"Maybe practice will help," she said, guessing at the girl's meaning. "Violins do what you tell them to do, not what you want them to do."

The girl nodded, as though agreeing, then touched the inlaid blond peg that held the E string.

"What happened?" she asked with a youngster's bluntness.

"The old peg broke on the plane. A man here in Langley had a spare one that he loaned to me until I can get it fixed in New York."

"It looks—odd."

The faint accusation came back into the girl's expression.

"It plays just fine," Kate said. "Listen and you'll see."

She held out her hands, requesting the violin. The girl surrendered it. Kate picked up her bow from the case.

"Are you in any of the classes I'll be giving?" she asked. "Maybe I could let you try this violin for yourself."

The girl shook her head. "I'm not ready for Brahms," she said, her voice suddenly cool and surprisingly adult.

Kate was bewildered by the girl's response. Before she could reply, she heard Verna announce her to the crowd.

"I'm sure someday you will be," Kate said.

The girl shrugged.

The crowd's applause called Kate away to the loneliness of the stage.

Thirteen

The moment Kate walked onto the stage, she could feel Corry in the crowd. She looked through the audience quickly, but saw no big man with a beard and red lights in his hair. Finally, she spotted him lounging against the back wall of the crowded little hall. He looked like an oversized, aloof, patient cat.

Not surprisingly, he was watching her. She looked directly at him while her stage smile brightened into something more genuine.

After a moment of hesitation, Corry nodded minutely.

"Thank you so much," Kate said as the applause faded away. "I'm delighted to be here and to share my love of music with you. I was born and raised in a place much like Langley. Music has taken me all over the world, but the longer I'm here, the more I realize that roots like mine go deep. It's good to be back, if only for a short time."

The audience was silent for a moment, as though wondering how to respond. Then applause began in the vicinity of the back wall of the auditorium, and quickly spread. When it died away, Kate went on.

"Things haven't changed much here in Langley, and

maybe that's as it ought to be. Everyone needs a quiet place to be himself. Or herself. I feel better knowing Langley is still here, even if I'm stuck way off in that very difficult place called Manhattan."

Light laughter murmured through the crowd. Kate saw several heads nod with agreement.

"In honor of this, my homecoming, I'd like to play something I learned a long time ago and haven't played much since."

The audience stilled as Kate raised her violin and launched into a light Beethoven salon piece, gentle and unchallenging.

The piece was usually played as a piano-cello duet, but it had been transcribed especially for her by Martin, her teacher, minister, and seducer. The selection was known variously as "The Little Maiden" or "The Little Wife."

Kate had not played the piece for years. Now it seemed fitting, both for her mood and for the audience.

Her fingers retraced old phrases like an ice skater retracing school figures. As the music flowed, she reflected on the irony of the music Martin had chosen for her. Now, years afterward, she felt almost able to forgive him, almost able to appreciate the joke, even though it had been on her. The years in New York had taught her that love, even flawed love, was like music. It had a life of its own.

Kate's simple, intricate piece fascinated Corry. He had been prepared for a technically accomplished violinist. He hadn't expected her vivid, deft, hauntingly individual style. She was a gifted musician, and she had cultivated her gift until it became a channel for her soul.

Listening to her music, he was humbled and exhilarated at once. With the violin in her hands, Kate was full of the female power of life. For some reason she reminded him of the trapped swan in the graveyard. It, too, had been caught between pain and creation.

He wondered if that was why Kate had come to the tangled swan, if that unknowable connection of life to life had drawn her off the road and into the deserted churchyard where some headstones were really swans.

He wondered about himself, too, about whether he would have the strength to calm a swan with only the mist net of his yearning to restrain her fear.

The music faded into silence and then swelling applause. Kate bowed slightly in acknowledgment.

"That was Beethoven," she said, glancing over to where the students from the ensembles had gathered on the edge of the stage, "via Mozart's *Silver Flute*, then reworked for me by one of my early violin teachers.

"I know sometimes it's a little hard to see the connection between a German who lived three hundred years ago and a frustrating wooden box in the here and now of Washington state, but the connection is there. The connection is human. If you learn to play Beethoven, you learn about life."

She looked past the students to where she had last seen the dark-haired girl. Though she wasn't there, Kate got the impression she lurked somewhere within earshot.

"Now, for something a little more formal," Kate said.

She played Schubert, choosing a piece that was more intricate and challenging yet still accessible to nonprofessionals. She caught a passing glimpse of Corry as she played. He was watching her intently, his head cocked to one side, an expression on his face that was both approving and oddly challenging.

She finished the Schubert and moved without hesitation into another Mozart. There was an almost female elegance to some passages of Mozart. This was one of them.

Kate let the violin be her voice. Often it spoke more clearly than she could. At this moment, it spoke of the maddening joy of being alive and human.

The crowd broke into enthusiastic applause before

the last note was truly finished. Kate was surprised. She doubted that most of the people here tonight listened to classical music in their own homes.

Kate wondered about Corry's reaction. When she glanced out toward him, his face was carefully composed. The sense of disappointment she felt surprised her as much as the audience's delighted reaction.

The applause grew louder, encouraged by Verna Stayton. They wanted an encore. Kate let the thunder of clapping hands build, then nodded her agreement and moved back to the center of the stage with her violin. While the crowd quieted down again, she looked directly at Corry.

She had never been one to pass up a challenge.

"You may have noticed something a little odd about my old friend here," Kate said, holding up her violin and pointing to the blond peg that held the E string. "I broke a peg this morning. Were it not for a local craftsman, Mr. Corry, I wouldn't have been able to perform tonight.

"But before he could help me, I had to rescue him. I'll let him tell you that part of the story himself. In the meantime, I'd like to dedicate this last piece to him, with my full appreciation."

Smiling slightly, Kate fitted the violin to her shoulder and launched into what sounded like a solo rendition of the opening of Mendelssohn's *In the Hebrides*. After a dozen bars of the rich, mysterious music, Kate improvised a bridge and let the notes slide flawlessly over into "The Man on the Flying Trapeze."

Some of the members of the audience caught the point and turned to look at Corry with speculative grins. He did his best to remain expressionless, but his forehead seemed suddenly to glow with color.

"It's an old song, right straight out of the Golden Book. Sing along if you know the words," Kate urged the audience as she played.

Verna picked up the tune and led the audience in the century-old song.

He flies through the air with the greatest of ease,
That daring young man on his flying trapeze. . . .

Kate finished a verse and the chorus with a flourish while Verna led the sing-along sopranos in the audience into an uneasy harmony on the last notes. The music faded and the applause rose. For a few seconds, Kate let herself be borne along on the elation of being connected with two hundred people.

Then the concert was over and she was surrounded. After half an hour of congratulations and questions, Kate still wasn't given enough room to draw a deep, private breath. First, the youngsters from the string ensembles, then their parents, and finally complete strangers pressed in around her.

The crush had moved from the hall to a reception line in the banquet room next door. Somewhere along the way, Verna had pressed a glass of cold punch into Kate's hand. By the time she got a chance to take a gulp, the cloyingly sweet fruit juice was warm.

The sugar in the punch went directly into her bloodstream. She hadn't realized how thirsty—and hungry—she was. She took another swallow while she chatted with two shy high school cellists. When they finally turned away, she quickly drained the glass while the next contingent of admirers stepped into place.

Five minutes later, Kate began to feel light-headed. She was babbling cheerfully to His Honor, Mayor John Fredrickson, a red-faced insurance broker, when she realized that she was staring at the long, thin lock of hair he had combed from the left side of his head over his bald spot.

She had never seen a left-handed yinkel. When she found herself on the verge of commenting on the ludicrous attempt to comb five strands of hair over a half-acre of bald pate, she realized that the punch had something more powerful than sugar in it.

Verna plucked the empty glass from Kate's hand and replaced it with a full, wonderfully cold glass.

"Did you spike that punch?" Kate demanded under her breath.

"Nope, but somebody did," Verna said cheerfully. "It's from the adult's bowl. But don't worry. It's nothing more than Kool-Aid with a little kick to its gallop."

"A mule should have such a kick."

Verna smiled rather lopsidedly, saluted the guest with another glass of punch, and drank deeply.

Drawing a cautious breath, Kate tried to center herself. The punch was living up to its name. That's how she felt. Punched.

Lord, I'll be lucky not to trip over someone's feet, she thought. My own, for starters.

She deliberately set the second glass aside. A glance down the reception line told her that several dozen more Langley citizens were lined up to meet the star from New York, and said star wanted only to crash and burn somewhere. Alone. In peace.

Suddenly, Kate felt her energy fade. She was exhausted by this farce. It would have been less draining to deal with fans outside Carnegie Hall. She was used to maintaining the appropriate distance from strangers of those sorts.

The people of Langley were different. She wasn't able to maintain effective barriers against them. She knew them at some elemental level and they knew her. That instant intimacy extracted a high price.

She looked around the room for someone who would give as much or more than they took from her. Belatedly, she realized she was looking for Corry. When she didn't find him, she felt very much alone. She drew herself together and went back to work.

Twenty minutes later, the line finally began to shrink, but the stragglers weren't about to let go of her. A realtor with whiskey on his breath rambled on for five minutes about his terrible experiences in New York. Kate listened as patiently as she could, wondering why people went to Manhattan if all they wanted was another version of their own hometown.

A stout, blue-haired matron with a sullen look introduced herself as Athalie Stone, Mrs. Athalie Stone, and launched into a critique of the concert. Kate bit her tongue so as not to point out that she was not much interested in Mrs. Stone's opinions.

"And you didn't play any Christian music," Mrs. Stone concluded. "Are you an atheist."

It was more of a demand than a question.

Kate felt the sweet punch in her stomach turn to acid. She recognized this self-important fishwife from long association and unhappy experience. Every small town had at least one of them. In Manhattan, they wrote columns.

"I'm sure these kids get plenty of hymns in church," Kate said, trying to keep her public smile in place. "I was brought here to give them a taste of the larger cultural world."

Mrs. Stone took the reply as encouragement. "Admirable, I suppose, if one believes that children are capable of making adult choices. But they aren't. They are terribly suggestible, and music is a powerful, primitive force."

Kate got the distinct impression Mrs. Stone had no children of her own and therefore regarded herself as an expert on the children of others. The woman had cold eyes almost the color of her hair.

"Children's musical experiences should be closely supervised," Mrs. Stone continued without a pause. "It would be better if they heard only hymns until they are, say, eighteen. It's for their own good."

Kate felt her public smile slipping. "Hymns and adult supervision can't guarantee God's grace. Not even being an ordained minister can guarantee it."

Mrs. Stone wasn't used to being contradicted. She looked Kate over from head to heels, noting in particular the neckline and the fit of the long skirt.

"I was told you were a serious young woman, that your coming to this town would be an uplifting experience for our young people," she said. "What I've seen so far suggests otherwise. You're as frivolous and godless as the rest of your generation."

"Thank you," Kate said.

Restrained sarcasm had no more effect on Mrs. Stone than politeness had.

"Do all young women in New York wear clothing that accentuates their bosoms?"

Kate returned the woman's glare with a brilliant smile. As a guest, good manners required that she be polite even when she encountered rudeness. She should nod and smile and move on to the next person in line.

She didn't. Narrowness was a powerful, corrosive force. It ate away at the possibilities of children who wanted to grow into a larger world.

"There are plenty of women in New York who wear gunnysacks and preach abstinence," Kate said. "Sadly, denying the existence of sex is useless, or worse. Teenage girls get pregnant in New York, the same as in small towns like Langley."

She felt a firm hand in the small of her back.

"Excuse me, Mrs. Stone, but I think our guest has had enough of your hospitality for one evening."

Corry materialized beside Kate, his hand touching her back in a gesture that was protective rather than possessive. She turned, saw his dark plaid shirt, his neatly clipped beard, and his red-brown hair alive with hidden fire. Drawn up to full height, he was thoroughly intimidating, yet she felt calmed, not frightened.

She smiled mischievously. "Good evening, Bran. You clean up very nicely."

Mrs. Stone glowered at Corry. Then she smiled sourly and pointedly examined the smooth, naked skin above Kate's neckline.

"Well," she said coldly, "I wondered why Mr. Corry suddenly was full of civic spirit. Now I know."

"Our guest has been good-natured with you," Corry said. "But you and I have tangled often enough on school issues that you know what to expect from me."

"I'm glad you mentioned schools," Mrs. Stone said. "I intend to bring this whole unsavory matter to the attention of the board of education as soon as possible."

"Good-bye," he said. Corry's voice was like a dry board snapping.

The old woman took one look at Corry's eyes and decided to find her entertainment elsewhere.

"Heathen," she muttered, turning away.

"Only God knows," Corry said, "and despite your pretensions, He isn't talking directly to you."

Mrs. Stone kept walking.

Suddenly, Kate felt wobbly. Though life had taught her not to back down from confrontations, she had never learned to enjoy public fighting.

"Self-righteous bitch," Corry said distinctly. "She's what gives Christians a bad name."

He looked down at Kate. Her face was white and without expression. Her eyelids flinched as though she were fighting to stay awake or to avoid fainting.

He slid his arm around her shoulders.

"Come on," he said. "You've had enough for one night."

Kate shook her head, trying to clear it.

"Wait," she protested.

"What for?" Corry said fiercely. "These people have had enough of your soul for one night."

"I should thank Verna for—"

"You already did, on the stage," he interrupted.

"My violin and coat—"

"Are in my truck," he finished.

The prospect of freedom from all the needs of the audience was too great to deny.

"Okay," she said. "Okay."

Fourteen

The cold night air was like a splash of water on Kate's face. Corry's arm around her shoulders propelled her gently but unmistakably down the sidewalk.

"Take a deep breath of air Mrs. Stone hasn't polluted," he ordered.

His voice was rich with anger and other emotions.

Kate lifted her face toward the sky and breathed in to the bottom of her lungs.

"Again," Corry said.

"Yes, sir," she said, an edge to her voice.

It was a warning. She never accepted orders easily. She drew another exaggerated breath and stared up at the sky, letting herself expand into the night.

Stars burned white-hot and clean. The Big Dipper leaped out of her childhood lessons, brighter than any memory. The Milky Way was a sparkling scarf flung across the sky. She tilted her head, looking for Orion, her favorite. Instead, she saw Corry's bleak face.

"Are you all right?" he asked.

She nodded. "You needn't have gotten involved. Mrs. Stone isn't the first critic who disliked my music or the cut of my dress."

"That wasn't what the look on your face said."

"Really?" Kate was genuinely surprised. She thought she had covered her reaction to the old battle-ax.

"You looked like she had just stuck a knife into you," Corry said.

"I . . ."

She hesitated, remembering all the savage words and withdrawals she had endured as an unwed, pregnant girl. That, as much as Martin's betrayal of her innocent hunger for transcendence, was what had turned her away from the church.

Kate drew another deep breath. "I guess I have the same feelings about the charity of small-town church-women that you do about the charity of small-town volunteer firemen."

"That bad, huh?" Corry asked, smiling slightly.

"Worse, actually."

Corry stopped beside a black pickup truck parked at the curb. The vehicle had a look of handsome efficiency about it, with deep chromed wheels and oversized tires. It gleamed cleanly in the streetlights. He pulled a ring of keys out of his pocket and unlocked the passenger door.

"Since when did knights give up chargers for Chevrolets?" Kate asked.

Corry chuckled. "St. George favors Fords, and those guys on the Round Table all drive new Dodge diesels, but the rest of us still stick with our Chevy four-fifty-fours and four-wheel drive," he said.

He opened the door and offered his hand.

"M'lady," he said.

Kate took his hand and let herself be guided up onto the running board and then into the seat.

"Where's the faithful Campbell?" she asked.

"He has business of his own to take care of. Why? Do you feel the need of a chaperon?"

"Nope. I just wanted something furry to pet."

"My beard is at your service."

Kate laughed. "Aren't you worried that a godless city hussy like me will ruin your reputation?"

"I give not a damn what Langley thinks."

She had no doubt that Corry meant it.

"Why are you still here, then, in this town?" she asked.

"It's a long story," he said. "I'll tell you about it over a steak, if you're up to it. There's a decent little dinner house at the other end of Main."

She thought a moment, then shook her head. "I've had enough of living in Langley's fishbowl for one night."

Corry tried to hide a flicker of disappointment.

"But there's a whole refrigerator full of food at the place where I'm staying," she added. "I can cook up something."

He looked at her. "Are you sure?"

Kate nodded.

His eyes lost their gentle gleam. For an instant, he let her see his male intensity again.

She felt as though her breath had been squeezed from her body.

"Still sure?" he asked.

"Yes," she said softly.

Corry's slow, patient cat smile reappeared again. Gently, he closed the door of the pickup, put his key in the ignition, and started the engine. He slipped the truck into gear and turned toward her.

"But I'll cook," he said.

"A shaman cutting up veggies in the kitchen," she said, relaxing against the seat. "What a lovely thought. I'll make you an apron out of a dish towel."

Corry was still laughing when he turned onto Main Street.

They spoke little during the ride. As the truck entered the driveway of the big house on the water, Kate realized that he had found the place by himself.

"You *are* a shaman," she said.

"Meaning?"

"This place isn't easy to find. You didn't ask directions. Ergo, you must have read my mind."

Corry stopped in front of the garage and shut off the engine, thinking about how to explain part of the truth without ruining the moment.

"That was one of the things I wanted to clear up when we had a chance to talk privately," he said. "I was the person who arranged this house for you."

"Is that what the old bitch meant about your sudden civic zeal?" Kate asked, yawning.

"That's part of it," he said.

"What's the rest?"

"Later. First, let's get some food into you."

Corry got out of the truck. He came around to her side as she was trying to unload the violin from behind her seat. He took her shoulders and moved her gently to one side.

Kate started to object, but changed her mind. She trusted him with the violin as much as she trusted his arm around her shoulders. The realization both unsettled and intrigued her.

He picked up the violin in one hand and lightly steered her down the steps with the other. The thin edge of the waxing moon hung in the west. Wind lifted lightly off the water. They stopped for a moment on a landing and watched the play of quicksilver waves.

"Darkness and light, all at once," Kate said.

"Sometimes you can see more in the dark than in the light, if you look hard enough."

She turned and found him looking at her. Both of them felt the same elemental pull. Without thinking, she stood on tiptoe and brushed her lips along the line of beard on his cheek. The kiss was a simple gesture of pleasure in his company, and all the more intimate for its lack of seductive intent.

When Corry leaned forward to return the kiss with interest, she planted her hands on his chest and shook her head.

He went still. "I don't take teasing very well."

Kate left her hands on his chest and studied the dark shadow of plaid on his shirt.

"I don't tease," she said. "I was just paying a debt."

"What debt?"

"The apple wood peg. I'm keeping it. I like the new look it gives that old fiddle. One kiss was the price we agreed on, wasn't it?"

She looked up into his eyes. Her expression was guileless until she smiled.

Corry laughed. She could feel the rumble of it deep in his chest.

"You're a quick one," he said. Then he added, "But you'll need to be."

He put his arm around her again, this time resting his hand on the curve of her waist just above the hip. He led her down more stairs and into the house.

In quick order, Corry snapped on lights, turned up heat, and set fire to the wood in the fireplace. As Kate watched, she began to suspect that he was on familiar, even intimate, terms with the owner of the house. No wonder he had been able to arrange for an outsider to use it.

"Are you comfortable?" he asked as he stood up from the hearth. "Folks around here keep their houses colder than city people do."

Kate looked down at her outfit, particularly at the heeled pumps she was wearing.

"I'll be right back," she said.

When she returned ten minutes later, she had exchanged the sweater and skirt for velour sweats with a turtleneck beneath. The heels were now sheepskin slippers. Her dark hair was loose on her shoulders. She looked less tired.

"Off duty, huh?" he asked, smiling.

"Finally."

She looked around. Two glasses of red wine stood side by side on the counter. He was stirring a half-dozen eggs in a bowl and watching an omelet pan warm on the six-burner range at the same time. Sliced French bread waited beside the toaster. Diced peppers and grated cheese made small mounds of color on a cutting board.

"You know how to make yourself at home in this kitchen," Kate said. "The owner must be a really close friend of yours."

"We've known each other for years," Corry said neutrally.

It was clear he didn't want to talk about the relationship.

Kate found herself wanting to push the subject. Telling herself that his sex life was none of her business, she wandered over to the cutting board and stole a few shreds of cheese.

"Does one of those wineglasses have my name on it?" she asked.

"Sure. Bring the other one to me, would you?"

She picked the wineglasses up and came to the stove. Their fingers brushed as Corry took the stem of the glass. He lifted it and touched it to Kate's.

"To the finest classical concert artist this town has ever heard," he said. "Or any town, for that matter. Even when you're making fun of me, you play extraordinarily well."

Smiling, she saluted him with the glass and took a small sip of the wine, letting both it and the compliment linger. The wine had a faint, tannic edge, but Corry's words were entirely pleasurable.

"Thank you," she said. "It's always nice to hear praise that is spoken, rather than applause in the concert hall."

He glanced at her. "You aren't happy in the concert hall?"

Thinking, Kate pinched a few more strands of grated cheese and popped them in her mouth. The cheddar was sharp and rich and her hunger made the flavor all the more intense. She leaned her hip against the counter and watched him cook.

"I enjoyed tonight's music more than usual," she said finally, "because there was a direct connection between me and the audience. Even Carnegie can be sterile, and the recording studio is much worse. It's too easy to get lost in the sounds and forget that the heart of music is communication, not solo fantasies."

Corry picked up the hot omelet pan and dropped a pat of butter into it. He swirled the butter while it bubbled and melted. When he was satisfied, he set the pan back on the burner and adjusted the flame. Then he dumped the glass bowl of beaten eggs into the pan.

"There's something to be said for the pure love of the music," he countered, watching the eggs begin to thicken.

Kate took a few more strands of cheddar. "But great musicians never lose their connection with the audience. Otherwise you might as well stand on the stage and play exercises. Music is a language. Languages are only alive when they're shared."

Corry looked at her, thinking about what she had said. After a moment he nodded, agreeing. Then he rubbed his hands on a towel and came over to where she stood. Slowly, he put one hand on the edge of the counter in front of her.

Surprised, she looked at the hand. It was scarred and confident and strong. His other hand went to the edge of the counter behind her. She was surrounded, hemmed in.

He moved a little closer. She could feel his breath stirring her loose hair.

"I thought we were going to eat," she said without meeting his eyes.

"I intend that," he said softly, "but you make things damned difficult." He inhaled, drinking her scent. "For instance, right now you're standing in front of my peppers."

She glanced at his face, expecting a gentle grin. What she saw made her breath catch in her throat.

"I'm—" Her voice broke and she started again. "I'm really not very good at this sort of thing."

"What sort of thing?"

She looked at him, her eyes as serious as his. Then she looked away.

"I don't do quick flings," she said. "It isn't like me."

"Flings last as long as you want them to last," he said, moving closer.

"I have to go back to New York," she said. "Maybe sooner than I expected."

"Your Strad?"

She nodded.

"Lady Kate," Corry said quietly, "I made up my mind the second time I saw you. I'll take you however I can get you. As long as I do get you."

They stood there, together but not touching. She could feel her heart beating. She could sense his, too, slow and solid. She longed to touch his chest and feel the rhythm there. He was alive, she was alive, they both knew where this would end up, when and if they chose to let it go there.

"Is it fair?" she asked. "To either one of us?"

The question was addressed to herself more than to Corry.

"Haven't you heard?" he asked with gentle bitterness. "Life isn't fair."

Kate turned in the circle of his arms and lifted her hand to touch his cheek. Then she took his wrist and gently tugged on it, opening the gate that penned her.

"I'll get the toast," she said.

Reluctantly, Corry stood aside and watched her

move to the toaster. Then he picked up the cutting board, spread the peppers and cheese across the nearly cooked eggs, and watched the cheese begin to glisten and melt.

"You have wonderful timing," he said gruffly. "The eggs were just about done."

"Good," Kate said cheerfully, trying to break the tension of the moment. "I like my toast light."

She took two more small sips of wine as she watched the white of the bread turn slowly golden under the red glowing coils.

Corry folded the omelet over in the pan and turned the burner down. He picked up his wineglass, looked toward her, and drank half of it in a single gulp. It might just as well have been water.

She felt a stab of guilt. He radiated hunger like fire radiates heat. Her own desire had drawn her as tight as an E string; his need must be like broken crystal, exquisitely sharp and painful.

She hesitated on the edge of rejecting him then and there, freeing both of them from this torment, but she couldn't do it. For the first time since Martin had laid his hand on her young breast and asked her to love him as God meant a woman to love a man, Kate couldn't say the word "no."

But she couldn't find a way to say yes, either.

Corry lifted the omelet pan from the stove and walked over to where Kate stood by the toaster oven. He set the pan on the tile counter and reached around her for the serving platter that had been warming on top of the little oven.

He tested the temperature of the platter, found it satisfactory, and set it down beside the frying pan. With a deft movement of his wrist, he slid the omelet onto the platter and set the pan aside.

Then he turned Kate by the shoulders. His big hands slid down her arms and settled on either side of her waist. His fingers savored the softness of the velour of her shirt, then slipped beneath it to the soft cotton of her turtleneck.

"Swans always fly away," he said, his voice husky. "I can't fly. I'm just a man. But swans return from time to time, if they want . . ."

Kate knew she should refuse. Not only for her own good, but for his. Their natures were too intense to be comfortable with casual sex. She tried to shake her head, to tell him no, but she couldn't force herself to turn away from him.

His simplest touch was magical. Kate felt a gentle movement at her waist and realized that he had pulled the hem of her turtleneck free. His fingers on her skin were callused, hard, gentle. His maimed thumb and forefinger felt soft and intriguing as silk as he traced an invisible pattern on the skin between the arch of her hip bone and her rib cage.

She let Corry gather her to him, slowly, slowly, slowly. He shifted his hands, drawing the back of his fingers across her navel.

"So slender, so elegant," he whispered.

Kate shivered at his touch.

"Are you cold?" he asked.

She couldn't speak. She shook her head instead.

Corry spread his fingers and lifted her gently into his hips. When she felt the strength of his desire, she shivered again. She rested her hands on his chest and lay her cheek against the scratchy wool. She could hear his heart. It beat more quickly now.

There was a shirt button beneath her fingers. Without thinking about it, she undid the button. He wore a singlet beneath the wool. Her fingers found the stiff yet springy hair that covered his chest. She dug through tenderly to the skin beneath.

Corry groaned deep in his chest. The sound was a mixture of his tension and the control he used to restrain that tension. She kissed the hollow of his throat, then lifted her face to his.

This time he didn't ask if she was certain. He simply slipped his arms around her beneath the clothing and drew her hard and close. She sensed his raw strength, but wasn't afraid. She knew his gentleness, too.

Warm fingers stroked the skin of her back, caught the strap of her bra and slipped its catch easily.

"You really are a magician," she whispered. "Or is that practice?"

"Neither. Pure luck. Luck and incentive. I've wanted to touch you since I first saw you."

He eased his thumbs beneath the loosened bra and lifted it from her breasts. The whole thumb and the maimed one found her nipples. He pressed down gently.

At Kate's husky sound of pleasure, his eyes closed and he lifted his head. His mouth was curled in a rich, masculine smile. She lifted her arms to his face and held his bearded cheeks. When his hands moved slowly, she forgot to breathe.

"I've wanted your hands on me since I saw you rescue the swan," she admitted. "I've never felt that with any other man. If I had any sense at all, I'd run like hell."

"So would I."

Corry teased her nipples with his thumbs and watched her pleasure.

"My scars don't bother you," he said.

"Should they?"

"They bothered other women. Or maybe I just didn't want those women enough to risk their refusal. It's been a long time, Kate. If I don't make it good for you the first time, I will the second."

"I'm not worried," she whispered.

She lifted herself under his touch and savored the sensations. He cupped her breasts in his hands and held them. For an instant, she was dizzy with pleasure. Then she kissed him on the mouth for the first time.

The kiss rolled over them like an ocean wave, growing and building with sudden urgency. Corry's hands went to her waist, seeking the loose band of her trousers.

For a moment, Kate almost lost her nerve. It had been a long time for her, too. She stiffened and would have turned away to slow the breaking wave, but Corry held her there between his hands, pinioned in the grip of her surprising lover.

"You only need to say one word," he whispered over her lips, "but you must say that word."

Kate knew the word and she knew Corry would heed it. She trembled in his arms like a child for a long moment, wrestling with doubts and reservations that were real and not at all girlish.

He slid his hands back up the cage of her ribs, waiting. He teased her with his hands on her breasts and his lips on hers. She shifted her body, feeling his rising tension against her belly. There was a vast gulf between the hardness of his body and the teasing gentleness of his lips and hands.

"Yes," she whispered against the bearded corner of his mouth. "It's the only word I can say to you."

Then she opened her mouth and her soul to him, deepening the kiss.

Without a word, Corry lifted Kate and carried her to the bed. He stripped away her clothing and then stood back. For a long moment he simply looked at her, as though he were trying to memorize her body for the time when she would be gone.

Despite the color rising to her cheeks, Kate made no effort to cover herself. Finally, with a smile that matched his own gentleness, she reached to him.

"Come, my bearded shaman," she whispered. "It's cold without you."

Corry took off his wool tunic, but as he stepped out of his jeans, his expression changed. He stood very still.

"What's wrong?" she whispered.

"I'm afraid I might hurt you. That's how badly I want you."

Kate opened her arms. "Swans are stronger than they look."

He lay down beside her and rolled her in his arms. He took her with a strength that would have crushed her had he not been so careful and had she not been so full of power.

Fifteen

When the storm of first passion was spent, Kate pulled the down comforter over them, letting it capture the warmth of their two bodies. She lay inside the circle of Corry's powerful arm, her own arm draped like a protective wing across his belly. Her trip-hammer heart began to slow as she watched the moon in the western sky through the big glass window of the bedroom.

Corry lay propped on a pillow, watching her and the moonset and the cold silver water. His shoulders were bare above the feather comforter. Kate's fingers toyed with the pelt of dark hair on his chest.

"Aren't you cold?" she whispered, touching his bare shoulder.

He laughed softly. "Not likely," he said, slipping his free hand beneath the comforter and letting it rest lightly on Kate's shoulder. "You're frail and slender, woman, but you do keep me warm."

He ran a long finger down her arm and let it stray over to the softness of her breast. He felt a gentle shiver pass through her body.

"It's you that's cold," he said.

She shifted and fit her body more firmly against him.

"Not likely," she whispered, mimicking his rough voice. "You'll keep me warm for lots of nights with love like that."

She lifted her face and the reflected moonlight shone in her eyes. Her arm slid across his chest. She arched gently, reaching up to kiss his lips.

The caress of her breasts made Corry dizzy. His free hand brushed one of her nipples and slid along her rib cage to the softness of her belly. He felt himself stirring again.

"You do know exactly what you're doing to me, don't you?" he whispered.

Kate captured his hand with her own and drew it back, letting the warmth of his palm stir her nipple into a blossoming flower.

"For tonight, I'm yours," she whispered. "As long and as often as you want me."

Corry shifted his body until they lay facing one another. Then he gently rolled her onto her back and kissed her. Their first love had been a flight through a wild storm over gray water. The second was a long, moonlit journey over a silvery sea.

They joined without hesitation and moved together in the slow, rhythmic dance of man and woman, perfectly in tune, perfectly in touch, climbing higher and higher, thigh and belly and breast and lips and breath in unison.

They loved with their eyes open, watching one another in the pale light. A languid smile spread across Kate's face. Corry grounded himself in that expression, letting it guide him in the direction of her pleasure. She came alive in his gaze, as she came alive with a violin in her hands.

Then her lids grew heavy and her eyes lost focus as she fixed herself on their pleasure. Her fingers splayed across the muscular plates of his chest and she held him with her secret, intimate strength as they moved and lay still together and then moved again.

After a long time they slipped over the brink together and fell free for what was a moment and forever. As they reached completion, Kate felt something change in her body and in her mind.

She had never slept with a man she trusted like Corry. He was powerful yet wounded, direct yet gentle. His desire overwhelmed her. Once he had decided to take her, she was powerless to stop him. She didn't even want to. When he entered her, she felt complete. It was as though the two of them, in joining, had found a wholeness that eluded them as individuals.

Within the limits of her rational mind, Kate believed that this was probably their only night together, but even that did not diminish her joy. She spiraled up into the pleasure that was death and life together, drawing him with her. For a moment that lasted until after the moon had set, they remained together.

And when they finally became two people again, Kate was still exhilarated and trembling. Her world had changed. She knew at some elemental level that Corry had drawn her down a path that she had to walk from beginning to end.

If he was aware of what he had done, it didn't show in his expression. He rested on his elbows, catching his breath and looking down into her eyes.

In that moment, Kate got a glimpse of what he must have looked like as a boy, eager, exuberant, untouched by tragedy or death.

"Christ," he whispered. Then he chuckled deep in his body. "That's almost enough to make a man take up prayer."

Kate's smile was calm. For the first time in her life, she touched serenity. "And here I thought you were a pagan," she whispered softly.

His chest rumbled with silent laughter.

"Just one thing wrong," he said.

"What?"

"We didn't die, right there at the end. It would have been okay, you know."

She draped her hands over his shoulders and let her fingernails trail lightly along the bands of muscle on his back.

"I could have kept going, love," she said. "It was you who lost control."

"That's the whole point, isn't it?" he said, kissing the side of her neck and teasing the swell of her breast with his tongue. "I lose control or we'd both die for sure."

Gently, he rolled to one side and drew Kate with him. They lay for several minutes with their heads on one pillow, still breathing brokenly, dreaming, and coming back to Earth.

Then Kate sensed a change in him. She looked up, but the moonlight was gone now. She could no longer read his expression.

"What is it?" she asked.

"Nothing we need worry about now."

"You weren't protected," she said, guessing the source of his unease.

He didn't reply.

"Don't worry," she said.

"You were?"

"Physically, yes," she said. "As for the rest . . ." She laughed oddly. "I doubt that safe sex exists for us. And I'm not talking about microbes."

Corry was silent for a moment, remembering what it had been like to love her. "You're right. It's not a comforting thought. New York is so damned far away."

"I'm right here."

For a while. Though neither said it aloud, both thought it.

They lay in each other's arms, physically together but mentally sliding apart. Finally, Corry propped his head on one hand and freed his other hand. He traced the planes and angles of Kate's face with his amputated finger. Its scar felt velvet-smooth on her skin.

After a moment, she reached up and seized his hand. He let her lift it to her lips and kiss what was left of his index finger.

"Isn't that painful?" she asked, brushing the indented scars just above the first knuckle with her index finger.

"Not anymore."

She kissed the scars, then gently drew the shortened finger into her own mouth and traced the scars again, this time with her tongue.

"Do you still feel the missing part of yourself?"

"Yes," he said, "particularly when you touch it like that. The rest of the time, it isn't really there."

"Should I stop?"

"No."

Kate held Corry's hand carefully for a time, touching it to her lips, thinking about something else that he could not even guess. Then she held the hand against her cheek and lay her head back on the pillow.

Corry felt his own head grow heavy. He watched Kate's eyelids flicker, this time falling toward sleep. He felt his own head grow heavy, hypnotized.

"Nope," he said softly.

Kate's eyelids flicked open. She had almost been asleep. Now, for an instant, she looked confused.

"I can't stay," he explained, "much as I want to, which means I have to get up out of this bed before I let you destroy all my resolve."

"You don't have to go right now, do you?"

"Not just now," he agreed, "but if we stay in this bed, I won't be able to leave at all."

She smiled sleepily and cuddled closer. He kissed her on the forehead and eyelids. Then he slipped out from beneath the comforter.

"Stay warm," he said.

"But—"

"I'll be right back," he interrupted gently, kissing her lips.

Half-asleep, Kate listened as Corry padded off into the darkness. After a moment she heard a sound. By the time she figured out it was running water, she was sliding again toward sleep. Knowing that he wasn't going to leave right away gave her peace. She wasn't ready to say good-bye, even for a night.

The water continued to flow. Other sounds came back to the warm bed, Corry humming some intricate tune and splashing in the water. She had just decided that he was taking a shower when the sound of running water stopped. He came back into the bedroom. He was wearing a bathrobe and holding another for her.

"Come with me, lazy child," he said.

"No," she murmured sleepily. "It's too nice. You come back here."

He walked over and sat on the side of the bed. He slid his hand beneath the comforter and found Kate's smooth arm. He tugged gently.

"Come on," he said.

"Why? It's lovely and warm here, especially now that you're back."

"I told you we had some things to talk about, remember?"

Kate shook her head, but in the end she let herself be drawn out of the warm nest. Corry held the robe for her and kissed her cheek gently as she tied the belt. Then he led her into the big bathroom.

She steeled herself as she stepped from carpet onto quarry-tile floor. She was surprised to find that the tile was warm, as though heated by a fire from beneath.

"How did you do that?" she asked in amazement. "I've almost frozen two mornings in a row taking a shower."

"Magic," Corry replied cryptically.

"Tonight I believe you."

"What about tomorrow?"

"Tomorrow, I'll look for switches and thermostats and other unmagical things."

Smiling, he led her to the sunken bathtub, now full almost to the top. Steam from the hot water had begun to fog the panes of the big windows that were the walls on two sides of the tub.

Kate looked at the steaming water uneasily.

"Not all Finns are crazy about small, enclosed places and steam," she said.

"Tonight is magic. You'll love it."

She looked at him.

"You trusted me inside your body," he said. "After that, what's a bath?"

Kate stepped out of the robe and slid down into the water without another word. The tub was long and wide enough for two. She moved to one side and stretched out, letting the water cover her like a warm, deep blanket.

Corry shed his robe and stepped into the tub beside her. He lay back in the water. His body displaced a great deal more water than hers did. Suddenly, they were both chin-deep in the steaming bath.

Groaning with pleasure, he shifted his head and shoulders, letting the heat of the water sink into tight muscles and old scars. He stretched and rotated his arms and pulled his knees back toward his chest, turning and twisting like a huge otter at play.

Kate knew how he felt. The heat of the water was beginning to penetrate her left shoulder, a violinist's trouble spot because the arm was usually held in a crooked and inflexible position.

But she was still faintly ill at ease. Breathing steam had never been something she enjoyed doing.

"Too much?" he asked.

"The heat feels good. The steam reminds me of when I was a child and had my head held over a kettle to treat pneumonia."

"Sounds unpleasant."

"It was."

"Well, then," he said, "good-bye steam."

He reached behind her and touched a button on the wall. She was startled to hear electric motors snap on. Slowly, the two big windows that formed intersecting walls of the room began to pull away from each other. Without the walls, it was rather like being in a small outdoor pool.

Corry laughed out loud at the look of astonishment on Kate's face.

"Magic," he said.

Then he touched another button and the two of them were suddenly surrounded by bubbles. As the pump picked up momentum, the tub filled with pulsing streams of aerated water.

Kate felt jets at the point of her left shoulder, at her feet, and at the base of her back. Cold air washed over her face like a tonic. She was neck-deep in the tub, but the retracted walls gave her a sensation of freedom. Immediately, she felt herself relaxing into the heat rather than fighting it.

"Magic," she agreed. "Pure, wonderful magic. Your own private hot springs."

"Yeah. Everybody with a broken back ought to have one of these."

The sound of the pump made conversation difficult. For several minutes they simply lay together in the swirling water. Beneath the surface of the water, Kate's hand drifted over Corry's wrist. Her long fingers wrapped around it and she held on, anchoring herself in his solid reality. Faint clouds slid silently across the starry sky, pushed by the same cool wind that bathed her face.

After a while, Corry reached over and shut off the pump. The world went silent. Then the sound of waves lapping on the rocks at the base of the bluff drifted up to the tub. Somewhere off in the trees, an owl hooted softly and then was quiet.

Kate sighed in contentment and closed her eyes.

He looked down at her face and was tempted to say nothing at all. She looked so peaceful.

But if he waited, it would only be more difficult.

"Wake up, my lovely swan," he said, kissing her gently. "We have to talk."

Sixteen

$\mathcal{K}$ate felt the touch of a quick chill on her bare shoulders. She sank deeper into the tub, unhappy with this sudden change. Talking belonged to tomorrow, and it wasn't tomorrow yet. But the tone of Corry's voice and the tension around his eyes told her that for him, tomorrow had come.

"I have a confession to make," he said slowly.

He didn't looked at her. Instead, he studied his nobby toes where they poked just above the surface of the water at the other end of the tub.

"I haven't been entirely honest with you," he admitted.

Kate went cold.

"If you're going to tell me you're married, you'd better step out of the tub first," she said distinctly. "I'm not nearly as vulnerable at the moment as you are."

He turned and stared at her. Then he laughed.

"I've never been a very good liar, particularly without my clothes," he said.

She smiled wanly.

"I wouldn't do that to you," he said, "no matter how much I wanted you."

"That makes you a minority among men," she said with a stiff little smile.

She settled back against the tub and stirred the water with her hand.

"I have deceived you, though," he said.

She looked at him. "How?"

"This is my house."

It was Kate's turn to laugh. The confession was a relief. It explained his familiarity with the house. Not a former lover's house, but his own.

Still, the ownership of the house raised more questions than it answered.

"It's a lovely house," she said, frowning.

"Thank you."

"Why am I staying in it? Besides the obvious, visiting-musician reason, of course."

"It was the only way I could be sure to get you here."

"Are you saying the concert and the rest was all a ploy just to bring me to Langley?"

"In a way, yes," Corry admitted.

"What way? Why?"

He shifted unhappily. Now that he had forced the question, he was wondering if he should have opened his mouth. After all, a lot of what he had on his mind was merely speculation.

"It takes some explaining," he said.

"We've got all night."

"I hope it's enough," he said under his breath. Then he spoke clearly. "Did you hear that Verna had some difficulty at the last minute over money for this week's events?"

"I guessed as much," Kate said. "I overheard something about a potluck fund-raiser."

"It fell fifteen hundred dollars short."

"That's a lot of baked beans and cookies to sell," she said with a flippancy she didn't feel.

"I put up the money and offered this place for you to stay," he said. "That's part of the lure for outside talent; the artist is treated like visiting royalty."

"Royal pain in the ass is more like it. A room in that renovated hotel downtown would have done just as well."

Corry started to tell her about the pastor's accident, the loss of memory, the hospital bills and surgery that had taken all the money that had been set aside for Kate's expenses. Then he decided that was just another way of delaying the truth.

"Well, it was the quickest, handiest solution I could think of on short notice," he said. "It was no problem. I'm bunking aboard a friend's boat in the marina. Even Campbell thinks it's okay."

"Why did you have to do all this anonymously? What's the point of hiding it?"

"I'm a full-fledged, unreconstructed pagan in the eyes of busybodies like Athalie Stone. They see atheists and devil worshipers everywhere they look. Ever since I took them on at a school board meeting a couple of years ago—and won—I've been regarded as Satan Incarnate."

Satan in green leggings, Kate thought, not knowing whether to laugh or cry.

"If Stone and her kind had known I was involved in bringing you here," Corry said, "they would have put pressure on the school board to cancel the concerts and the lessons before you ever hit town."

Kate fluttered her hand beneath the water, fanning the heat over her body to counteract the persistent chill she felt.

"She and her banshees did tumble to the truth, but only after it was too late for them to stop things," Corry said. "Now that you're here, I don't really give a damn what they think."

"You don't care, now that you've got what you wanted?" she asked. She was half-joking, but no more than that.

"I think you know better than that."

"Then you didn't start out to seduce me tonight?" she asked. "You certainly fooled me."

Corry reached over and ran the knuckle of his forefinger down the softness of Kate's arm.

"Tonight?" he said. "Oh, make no mistake, by tonight I had one thing on my mind. You. I wanted you when I saw you take off after Campbell. I wanted you when you stood up to the cob swan.

"Do you have any idea how beautiful you were just then, like some fierce warrior princess with your black hair flowing in the wind and the fire of battle in your eyes?"

Kate felt herself shiver, but not from the cold this time. The intensity was there again in Corry's look. She willed herself not to respond.

"And I wanted you even more today in the church," he said. "There isn't a woman in a hundred who would do what you did, grabbing that rope to keep me from breaking my own damn fool neck. There isn't a woman in the world who would laugh just the way you did when I fell on my face.

"Then you produced that damned broken fiddle and I figured out that you were our guest from New York. I have to tell you, that nearly took the starch out of my shirt."

"Why? Do you dislike New York so much?"

Corry smiled, then shook his head. "I was mostly teasing about New York," he said. "Besides, the more I know of you, the more I realize New York has left fewer marks on you than it does on most people."

He covered her hand with his under the water and gave it a gentle squeeze.

"No, there wasn't anything about you personally that knocked me off my stride. It's just that I had a different role in mind for Kate Saarinan, violinist, than I did for the bewitching swan I found in my bed a few minutes ago."

Beneath the water, Kate turned her hand palm up and laced her fingers through his.

"What role did you have in mind for me?" she asked.

She squeezed his hand gently. He returned the caress and let his hand cover hers.

"I wanted you here because you sounded to me very much like the kind of woman I'd like my daughter to become," he said.

"Your daughter?" Kate laughed uncertainly. "I didn't know you had a daughter."

"No wife," he said, "but a woman who complicates a man's life almost as much. A smart, beautiful daughter with more questions than I can handle."

The clear joy he took in his daughter touched Kate. It helped her understand why she found him so attractive. Men so seldom appreciated women in the way that unlocked women's hearts, but Corry was different. He wasn't afraid of feminine strength.

"Alyssa is as bright as Sirius," he said, pointing toward a sharp, blue-white speck of light in the night sky. "She's startlingly talented and very focused, and she has ambitions and possibilities that most people would never dream of, especially small-town girls."

Kate turned her head and watched Corry as he spoke. The love and pride and worry in his voice made her want to cry for her own dead parents, her own lost child.

"As I've watched my daughter grow," he said, "I've come to realize such talents and ambitions are more difficult for a woman than they are for a man. There are a thousand ways women get diverted from fulfilling their ambition, particularly in a small town like this.

"I suppose every father feels this way, but I genuinely believe that Alyssa has rare gifts. I'd like her to meet people, particularly women, who have similar gifts and who have learned how to use them in a world that's bigger than Langley, Washington."

Corry fell silent, but the smile on his lips suggested he could have talked for hours about his child.

"Alyssa needs something I can't give her. At first I thought it was because she was adopted, that somehow a 'real' father would know what to do," he said. "Then I looked around and saw it wasn't that easy. In every way that matters, she's my daughter and I'm her father. And I'm damned if I know how to help her grow into her womanhood, to become a woman like you, confident in her own strength."

Corry hesitated, trying to read the odd, still expression on Kate's face.

She hardly noticed. She kept hearing one word. Adopted.

Thousands of children are adopted every year, Kate told herself. Thousands and thousands and thousands. She couldn't let her own hunger for knowledge of her daughter overwhelm simple common sense.

"Alyssa?" Kate asked, trying the name tentatively.

Corry nodded, watching her face closely, as though he sensed the sudden, harsh tension in her.

"She's thirteen?" Kate said.

"Yes."

"A slender girl with dark hair cut blunt, so that it frames her face like a well-drawn Flemish portrait?"

"Exactly," he said. He smiled at Kate. "In some ways you remind me of her. Both of you are talented, intense, and intelligent. It shows in your eyes. So clear and direct."

Kate felt light-headed for a moment. She drew a slow, deep breath and tried to center herself.

"Was Alyssa backstage tonight?" she asked.

Corry nodded again. "Did she introduce herself? I thought she might."

"Not exactly," Kate replied slowly. She looked around at the sky and the open walls and the tub itself, as though trying to orient herself. "We exchanged a few words. She seemed fascinated by my violin. I thought she might be a violinist, but she seemed more interested in the new peg than anything else. She must have recognized your handiwork."

He lifted his injured hand out of the water and inspected it as though it were somehow amusing.

"She's a damned fine fiddle player," he said. "I tell myself that it's just a father's pride, but other people say the same thing. She can make that fiddle sing better than I ever did, even when I had all my fingers."

Kate remembered the months she had spent playing and praying and waiting for the birth of her daughter. She had always held a secret hope that her love of music would somehow be passed on to her unborn child.

"Why isn't she in the school orchestra?" Kate asked.

"That's another way a narrow-minded community like Langley can get back at a parent," he said bitterly. "Allie took a big ration of crap from some of the kids after I had my run-in with the school board. She dropped out of everything but her classes."

"Verna seems like a very capable teacher," Kate said. "She would be good for Alyssa. You really ought to get her back into music."

"She's doing fine. She has lots of support and teachers already. A couple of my clients, very fine instrumentalists, have coached her, and then, of course, there's the pastor. Or there was."

Kate's heart stopped. For an instant, it was as though the windows around the tub had been slammed shut and she was trapped in a world full of stifling, swirling steam.

"The pastor?" she asked in a voice that she tried to keep from cracking.

"Pastor Thorson," Corry said, stretching again. "As far as I'm concerned, he's a better musician than he is a God salesman. He's plenty pious, though, for all the good it did him."

"Thorson? Did you say 'Thorson'?"

"That's right, Marty Thorson, well, Martin, really, but I didn't call him that. It's his church I'm tearing down. At least it was his church until the accident."

Kate closed her eyes and tried to comprehend what was happening, her world turned inside out in a heartbeat.

Coincidence, she told herself wildly. It must be.

Corry kept talking, and every word he spoke undermined her attempts to take control of her life again.

"Marty is the one who thought of bringing you here," he said. "From the moment he heard about the Wallace Foundation programs, he wouldn't let go of the idea. Not that I fought it. I was floundering with Alyssa. If I had been a praying kind of man," he added, looking at Kate, "I would have said you were the answer to my prayers."

She couldn't speak.

"Is something wrong?" he asked warily.

Kate's felt smothered in clouds of dense steam. She fought contradictory impulses—to flee and to stay, to scream and to withdraw inside a shell, to laugh wildly and to cry a thousand tears. She stared out into the chill night with eyes that saw no sense, no solution, only further pain.

Corry touched her bare shoulder.

"Kate?" he said gently. "Talk to me. What's wrong?"

He gripped her shoulder and massaged it with his powerful, scarred hand.

Slowly, slowly, Kate came back to him. She looked at the strong hand on her shoulder, then at Corry's worried face. She smiled weakly, then rested her hand on top of his.

"I'm sorry," she said. "I once knew a minister named Thorson. I was just trying to imagine how our paths might have crossed again."

"Maybe he is the same man," Corry said. "I know

Marty's a big music fan, a fan of your work and others, and he's been dedicated to developing Alyssa's talent. When I asked why, he told me he had let down a talented girl long ago. He had vowed to God that he would make it up somehow. He was convinced Alyssa was God's way of giving him a second chance."

Kate felt cold despite the heat of the bath.

"Hey, are you all right?" Corry asked.

She touched Corry's bearded cheek with a trembling hand.

How do you tell a man who had just become your lover that you might possibly be the mother of his thirteen-year-old child?

If there was an answer, Kate didn't know it.

"I'm all right, just tired," she whispered, forcing her stiff lips into a smile. "I'm not used to being overwhelmed by passion and then steamed like a lobster."

Corry frowned and shook his head. "No need to apologize. It's my fault. I knew you were tired. I should have kept my hands off you."

"I'm glad you didn't. Tonight was . . . extraordinary," she said, touching his mouth with her fingertips. "But if I don't get to bed, I'm going to slide down into this hot sea and come unglued."

Water swirled and splashed as he lifted himself out of the tub. In shadowy darkness, he slid the windows closed and latched them, then toweled off and shrugged into his robe, leaving it untied. He reached down with one hand to help her out of the tub.

"Hang on," he said. "I'll have you on dry land before you know it."

He pulled her out of the tub and wrapped the robe around her.

"Sorry," she said in a hoarse voice. "I don't mean to fall apart like this."

"No problem. Alyssa is always toast after a performance, too."

"Toast?"

"As in toasted, finished."

With gently impersonal hands, Corry used the thick terry cloth of the robe to dry Kate's body. Then he took two towels from a cabinet. He wrapped her hair in one and used the other to dry off her feet.

With a hand that trembled, she stroked thick hair back from his forehead.

"You are really something, Bran Corry," she whispered.

"'Something?' That's kind of vague," he said, half-smiling. He stood up and faced her. "Could you be a little more specific?"

In the faint starlight his eyes gleamed, asking Kate to put a name to the feeling that swirled around them. Daring her.

"I shouldn't," she whispered softly. "I'm like the swans, remember? Just passing through."

"Is that the way you want it?"

"It's the way it has to be."

Because if Kate stayed, she was certain she would hurt Corry, wound herself, and scar the daughter she had given away and wanted so much she ached.

Corry looked crestfallen. He started to ask why, to argue, to plead, but the weary, hollow, haunted look in Kate's eyes stopped him.

"We'll talk about it after you've slept," he said.

"Separately," she whispered.

"What?"

"We'll sleep separately. Your daughter has to live in this town."

He hesitated, then shrugged. "For now."

He led her from the heated tiles of the bathroom to the bedroom and peeled back the comforter. Without a word, Kate let him tuck her into the bed. She longed to pull him into bed with her and curl up in his arms and sleep with his heart beneath her cheek.

But that would only make it harder to leave him tomorrow. He had given her more than any other man had. The least she could do was give him an equal gift in return. Her silence.

Through almost closed eyes, Kate watched Corry while he pulled on his clothes. When he turned toward her, she shut her eyes fully. She didn't trust herself not to reach for him.

He bent down and gently kissed her lips.

"Good night, sweet Kate," he whispered. "I'll have someone drop your car by in the morning and I'll call you about ten. I think we need to talk.

"And I'd like you to save tomorrow night for something special."

Kate's eyelids flickered open. "I'm going back tomor—"

He cut her off with another kiss. He didn't release her until her lips softened beneath his. He didn't know what had gone wrong, but he knew that something had.

"Don't leave until after tomorrow night," he said. "Please."

Kate felt pulled apart. The rational part of her told her to abort their relationship at the moment of conception. That would be kinder for everyone, particularly for Bran Corry. All she had to do was say no.

Yet the artist in her, all that was hungry and human and creative, refused to say the word that would destroy so many possibilities. She looked away, unable to meet the gentle, warm eyes of the man she could have loved.

Finally, Corry straightened up.

"Good night, Kate."

She listened to his retreating footsteps and the sound of the front door closing behind him. When she was certain she was alone, great shuddering sobs swept over her like the waves of a storm that would never end.

Seventeen

$\mathcal{K}$ ate awoke at dawn, parched and exhausted from her tears. The sky was clear, but a north wind had sprung up outside. It rattled the sliding windows above the bathtub and churned the waters of the sound into rock-gray swells.

For a while, she lay alone in the bed, outwardly calm in the eye of the storm. Then she got up, dressed warmly against the chill, and made coffee.

As the coffee brewed, she began to pace, exploring the shards of yesterday's world and the shape of the one that had taken its place.

Alyssa. Bran. Martin. Herself.

Kate moved the pieces in her mind, trying to make them fit. No matter how she turned them, they would not go together. Someone was lying, someone mistaken.

Either Alyssa was Kate's daughter, Kate and Martin Thorson's, or she was not. There was no room for both to be true. There was no way of answering the question without destroying someone, perhaps everyone, including herself.

Kate took a mug of the fresh coffee and went to sit in front of the windows that looked out over the water. A sudden hard gust struck the north face of the house. The

joists and beams creaked and snapped dryly, an unsettling
sound from childhood.

Houses were made by man; wooden planks and steel
nails and glass panes. They were weak. They got old.
They collapsed. Nature didn't give a damn. As far as
Kate knew, God didn't care, either.

The wind gusted again, but this time the house was
silent. In the chill of night, its boards had shrunk and
loosened. Now they were settled again by the wind. The
sun had begun to expand them in the new configuration.
They were set for the new day, for a wind from any
direction. The house was sound. It would stand, for the
moment, and the moment was all anyone had.

Corry's house. He had built it, owned it, loved it. The
knowledge made Kate look around with different eyes.
She understood now why the exposed beams were dry
and hard, nearly like stone. They were probably a hundred years old, like the lumber he was reclaiming from
the church. There were patterns of nail holes, dark
against the light, straight-grained wood. To her there
was something clean and honest about wood that had
already lasted a hundred years and was now starting life
over again.

The generous, enduring quality of the house
reminded her of its builder. Bran Corry was like the
wood he worked—strong, honest, surprisingly complex
in his openness.

He was the kind of man who had always frightened
Kate, for she knew that kind of man could change her
life; the only sudden changes that had come to her life
had nearly destroyed her. Corry had ambushed her at a
weak moment or she would never have let him touch
her the way he had, in both body and soul.

Yet he had given her at least as much as he had taken
from her. They had been stronger together than either of
them was alone.

Never again, she thought. I can't allow it.

Frustration tightened through the center of her body. She set the mug aside carefully, suddenly afraid she might hurl it against the window.

Her eyes fell on the violin case that Corry had carried in and laid aside last night. Looking for release, any kind of release, she went to the case and opened it. The violin inside was her only friend now, the one voice that would not betray her. She picked it up, tested the tuning, and adjusted the bow.

The first note she struck was clear and clean. She lowered the bow and twisted her upper body, trying to relax. Then she played a few more notes and found the center of her world again.

She played scales and exercises and snatches of familiar warm-ups over and over, sliding from one to the next, moving over familiar ground. The music sounded good, wonderful, liberating, just as it had always sounded.

Then, suddenly, she stopped, the moment shattered as she wondered which of those scales and exercises and warm-up tunes would be meaningful to Alyssa.

Perhaps none of them would.

Kate was afraid she might never play the violin again without asking herself that question. The instrument suddenly felt heavy in her hands, alien. Her life had changed irrevocably.

She stared out at the cold water and the clear, windswept blue sky and thought for just a second about flying and falling and freedom from pain. It was the first time since the day she found out she was pregnant that she had contemplated, even for a moment, the release of suicide.

Yet she was even more wedded to life now than she had been as a teenager. The ultimate freedom of death wasn't for her.

The telephone rang.

Kate let the first ten rings go unanswered. Corry had said he would call. She was in no shape to talk to him.

The ringing stopped, then started again. That wasn't Corry's style. She went to the phone and picked it up.

"Hello."

"Kate, it's Ethan. I'm glad I caught you. What time is it out there, anyway?"

She glanced distractedly at the clock on the wall. "Seven."

"Oh, dear. I must have awakened you."

"No. But you're up early, considering it's Saturday."

"Well, I just had breakfast with David Heller."

Kate grabbed the name as though it were a life ring in a turbulent ocean. She had not thought about Heller and Polyphony in the past twelve hours. Maybe the encounter with the girl and the heady flight with Corry had been nothing more than catharsis, a way of purging the old to celebrate the new.

Maybe this whole trip to Langley had merely been a way of closing a door on her past forever. She knew she had to do it, one way or another. If she couldn't grow past Martin's betrayal and giving up her child, her music would become as empty and static as she had started to feel in the past few years.

She could fool an audience, but she couldn't fool herself. She was tired of trying. Yet she was terrified of losing even more than she had already lost.

"How are things with David?" she asked.

"A bit frantic at the moment. He's in the office on the weekend, cracking the whip over his contracts people, trying to get our deal down on paper."

Kate detected an unusual, deliberately calm register to her agent's voice. It was the kind of tone he reserved for moments when he was uneasy.

"Weekend, huh?" she said. "Then our David Heller is in trouble. How bad is it?"

"Trouble is a bit too forceful a word, but the situation at Polyphony is a good deal more fluid than we thought."

"What does that mean? In English, please."

"Now, Kate, I don't mean to alarm you. Everything is quite all right. Heller very much wants to do the deal."

"But?" she prodded.

"He has encountered a little trouble at the home office," Farr said reluctantly.

"I thought he was free to make his own decisions. That's what made the package attractive."

"He is, as long as Polyphony remains an independent operation under the broader corporate umbrella. But he would be in a different position if his Japanese parent decided to spin off Polyphony. There's a faction within the corporation that apparently wants to do exactly that."

"They're going to sell Polyphony out from under Heller, is that it?"

"I'm sorry to spring this on you cold. I feel somewhat responsible. After all, that's part of my job, to pay attention to these things. And I don't want to overstate the matter."

"I'm listening."

"There's a meeting of the board on Monday, Tokyo time, and the subject of Polyphony may or may not come up. Heller wants to close this deal with you right now, just in case some change in strategy is in the offing."

"What you're saying is that the deal could be in trouble."

"Heller says it isn't, but I have to think he's working overtime for a reason."

"Shit."

Kate drew a deep breath, thinking. She should have been worried, and she was. However, beneath that worry she was almost relieved. Now, at least, she had an excellent reason to leave Langley, to take flight.

"Don't panic," Farr said. "I think Heller is merely being careful. I don't think his Japanese lords and masters will pull the plug on him overnight."

"Why not? Life is full of unhappy surprises."

Her agent cleared his throat. "On the other hand, I did talk to someone else, a man I know in international banking. He told me that the Japanese have pumped a lot of yen into Heller's division. Some people at the top have begun to lose patience."

"If Heller is in trouble, what's to prevent the rice counters in Tokyo from canceling the contract, regardless?"

"The Japanese are very scrupulous about such things. A contract is a contract, even if it costs them a million bucks. Most courts in the United States would take the same position, as long as the contract had been properly signed and executed. You're quite safe, I think, in that regard."

Thoughtfully, Kate chewed the inside of her lip. The skin there was tender, as though it had been abraded. For an instant, she remembered the power of Corry's kisses and the strength with which she had returned them.

"You're saying that I'd make a million bucks, even if the deal fell through an hour later?" she asked.

"They should be good for at least half a million," Farr said. "But remember, we don't know what's going to happen in Tokyo. There's an excellent probability that Heller will simply carry on, just as he has planned to do. He'll launch you and turn you into the biggest sensation since Anne-Sophie Mutter. Anything's possible. Isn't that what you always say?"

"It's my way of saying that a joyous outcome is not as likely as the other kind," Kate said.

"Um, yes," her agent said uncomfortably. "At any rate, that's why I'm calling. I really would prefer that you come back here immediately."

"I'm not sure I can," she said before she had time to think better of it.

"This is the chance of a lifetime," Farr said. "It may

come down to a matter of hours. That's why both Heller and I feel you should be here and ready to sign by tomorrow at noon, even if you have to disappoint a few folks in the sticks."

A few folks in the sticks.

Farr tossed the words off with perfect New York insouciance. At first Kate didn't react. Then she flashed.

Some of those folks out in the sticks were damned good people. Without expecting to, she had reestablished a connection with them, and with a part of herself that she thought had been lost. Suddenly, that connection was valuable to her, far more valuable than she could have guessed until now.

"There are more than hicks out here," she said. "Some of these people are as interesting as any you would find anywhere."

"Of course," Farr said quickly, too quickly, as though he had detected the anger in Kate's voice. "There are interesting people all over the world. Fascinating people. But very few of them can offer you a million dollars and the chance to become something you've worked all your life to attain."

What he said was true. And yet a part of her simply refused to bow to common sense. She had done too much of that in the past. Perhaps that was the very thing that had stifled her growth as an artist. Perhaps that was why she felt frozen in time, no going back and no going forward and no staying in place, either.

"It's impossible to put a value on some attainments," Kate said finally, softly.

The line was silent for a time. Then Farr cleared his voice.

"Kate, dear heart, you haven't gone and fallen in love or something foolish like that, have you?"

She felt a flush spread over her face. "What on earth makes you say that?"

"You certainly don't sound like the same practical person I put on a plane a few days ago."

"Really?" Her tone suggested disbelief.

"Really," Farr assured her. "You know I care about you a great deal, don't you?"

"Yes," she said quietly.

"Good. You also know I try very, very hard not to get involved in the personal lives of my clients."

"Yes."

"But I'm going to break my rule to say this: If you've gone and found some man who makes you feel good, and I mean really *good*, then I'm profoundly happy for you. Despite your immense self-sufficiency, I've always sensed a kind of loneliness in you. If you have a chance to dispel that loneliness, by all means do it."

Kate didn't know what to say.

Farr did. "But for pity's sake, Kate, get this deal done first! Bring the lucky man back to New York if you have to. Just be here by noon tomorrow."

She listened with only part of her mind. The rest of her was listening to the wind that bent the fir trees and made the house stir as though it were alive.

"Ethan . . ." Kate began.

Then she stopped. There was no way she would be able to explain this to him, not when so much of it was still a mystery to her.

"Ethan, you're very sweet, and if I had half a brain, I'd probably turn and run, right now. But I can't. I simply can't."

"Why?"

"If I could tell you, it wouldn't be complicated."

"As long as your lover is a consenting adult, it's not complicated. Bring him or her or it to Manhattan and sign the damned papers."

"If I can, I'll catch a red-eye out of Seattle and be there by noon."

"And if you can't?" Farr asked.

"Then I can't."

There was a long silence followed by a sigh.

"Okay," he said, disappointed and resigned. "I trust and respect you, even if I don't understand you. Is there anything I can do to help you?"

Kate felt as though she had just betrayed a friendship, yet she couldn't force herself to guarantee that she would be on that plane, no matter what.

"No, but thank you," she said. "This is a box of my own making, even if I didn't know I was making it at the time."

"You're not making sense."

"I know. I'll call you if I miss the plane."

She hung up the phone and stood there, listening to the cold wind and wondering what to do. After a moment she noticed a shelf below the telephone. A phone directory the thickness of a magazine lay on it. Kate picked up the book and looked at the cover.

"Skalbeck County, Skalbeck Valley, and the City of Langley."

The entire county in a single, thin phone book. She fanned the pages, half of which were white alphabetical listings. The other half held yellow commercial listings.

Churches were listed in the Yellow Pages.

Eighteen

Spring was in the air, but in the Skalbeck Valley spring was a raw season. A cold wind bent the tops of the barren poplar trees that lined the intersection of two country roads. Kate stopped and checked her map against the address from the phone book.

She was on a hardtop road a mile east of the old church, between a ten-acre field of fierce red tulips and five acres of daffodils that were already mostly spent. Her map said she needed to go a half mile west.

She hesitated. There was still time to turn the other way. She had lived fourteen years without the truth. She could live without it the rest of her life.

The wind shook the car, taunting her. She felt a spur, anger or pride or both. She had let Martin Thorson take over her life once before. She would not let it happen again.

She turned right and went a half mile down the road.

Thorson. The name on the mailbox was clear enough. The house was a quarter mile across the fields from the church. How odd that he should have been so close without her knowing it. Heart beating helplessly, she turned onto the graveled driveway.

The house and yard were scrupulously neat, but the

faded barn had a drunken lean to it, and the grass in the fence rows around the stock pens hadn't been cropped in years. Kate recognized the signs of a farm that was no longer worked. That wasn't surprising. Martin Thorson was a farm boy, but he had left the plow behind in his youth.

An old yellow dog came stiffly out of his sentry post in the shelter of a loading chute beside the barn. He barked twice, announcing a guest, then stood, waving his flag of a tail slowly.

She stopped the car and waited, half hoping no one was home. As she watched the front windows, a light came on in the parlor. A sturdy, gray-haired woman in a white apron with red flowers on it came and looked out the picture window.

Kate switched off the engine and got out of the car. Between the barn and the church there was a huge flock of snow geese, startling white in the center of a bright green field of winter rye. Kate could hear their high cackling and gabbling even above the wind.

She sat and listened and watched, thinking about geese and swans. Though both types of bird were large and white and migratory, the swans and geese were very different. Swans foraged in clans and family bands. Geese lived like city dwellers in one large, fluid flock.

Kate lacked the sociability of a goose, but despite her nickname, she wasn't a swan, either. She lived alone, cut off from the affection of her own kind.

Feeling a bit unreal, she got out of the car and walked across the graveled yard, up the narrow concrete walkway to the front porch. The gray-haired woman wore a compressed smile as she opened the front door and the glass storm door.

"Good morning," Kate said. "Is Martin Thorson here?"

"The pastor is . . . resting," the woman said. She looked Kate up and down carefully, cataloguing and analyzing. Her smile grew thinner. "Can I help you?"

The woman didn't look familiar, but it had been a long time. She hadn't had many occasions to meet the pastor's wife.

"Are you Mrs. Thorson?" Kate asked bluntly.

The woman's response was mirthless laughter.

"Me? Oh, no, there is no Mrs. Thorson," she said. "Hasn't been for a long time. I'm Emma, Emma Engebretson. I keep the pastor's house."

"I'm . . ." Kate hesitated. "I'm an old friend of Martin's. I was passing through and wanted to pay my respects."

Emma looked the younger woman up and down again, suspicious and curious at the same time. "What's your name? I'll find out if he remembers you."

"I'd rather surprise him," Kate said clearly. "Just tell him I used to be a member of his first congregation, fourteen or fifteen years ago."

Emma did the estimates and calculations in her head. "You must have been a child, then."

"A teenager," she agreed, "but I'd still like to see him."

"He's . . . I'm not sure he'll be able to see you."

"I'm certain he will."

"Wait here."

The storm door swung shut and Emma disappeared into the house.

Kate stood restlessly. She was irritated and apprehensive. Refusing to identify herself had been ill-mannered, but she didn't want to give Martin a chance to compose himself. He had always been too clever at hiding his real self from others.

The old yellow dog came to the foot of the steps and stood, looking up at her plaintively. He waved his tail slowly.

"Come on, boy," she said, welcoming the diversion.

The yellow flag of tail waved more quickly, but the dog stayed put.

"Come on," she coaxed.

The dog looked at the steps and wagged apologetically. Kate realized he was too old to climb the stairs.

Emma threw open the storm door and burst out, looking worried. "He's gone again," she said.

"Gone? Where?"

"Lord knows," Emma said. She stepped out onto the porch and scanned the middle distance. "Sometimes it's the dike, down by the river. That's what worries me."

Kate thought of the old dog who could no longer climb the front steps.

"Is there a special reason to be worried?" Kate asked.

The stout woman chewed her lip and considered a reply. Then she shook her head. "He's just not himself, that's all. Not since the fall."

"Which way is the river?" Kate demanded.

"That way," Emma said, pointing toward a line of trees along a high, grassy bank four hundred yards to the east.

Kate went down the steps and past the old dog. She was halfway to the car when Emma called out.

"No! There he is! See him?"

Kate turned in time to see the snow geese lifting off the green rye in a solid mass of white. The entire flock had risen at once, but individual skeins quickly drew away like strands of white fiber from a ball of cotton lint.

When the cloud of birds unraveled, she saw what had sent them into flight. A thin black figure marched steadfastly across the field, oblivious to the swirling biotic mass that had been disturbed by his passage.

"He's going to the church," Emma said, her hands clasped nervously in her apron. "I've told him and told him, there's no use. It isn't there anymore. They've destroyed it. It's the pressure, you know. Even surgery didn't help him. He'll never get well if he doesn't rest."

She looked as though she were going to cry.

"Is he sick?" Kate demanded.

Emma stared at her numbly, her lips pursed.

"Will I need help getting him in the car?" Kate asked.

The other woman shook her head. "He's not sick. He fell and now he needs rest and he'll heal as good as new, you see if he doesn't."

There was more hope and stubbornness than certainty in Emma's voice.

Kate hurried to the car. She started it, spun it in a quick circle, and headed back to the main road. As she drove the two sides of the square section of land, heading for the church, she kept an eye on the stalwart marcher in the field.

Martin Thorson pressed on without stopping as the geese called and cried and swirled around until they came back down to the field behind him. If he saw them at all, he didn't show it.

Kate pressed down on the accelerator, wanting to arrive at the church ahead of Thorson. She didn't quite make it. He was just coming through a gate in the wrought-iron fence when she pulled into the yard.

She got out of the car and came around the corner of the church. Thorson was fumbling with the sacristy door, trying to open it. She stopped and simply stared.

She had been expecting the man who had seduced her. The man at the door was a shadow, a stranger. Thorson had been handsome, rather vain, his faded red hair carefully groomed and his face close-shaven. He was still fair, but his face was gaunt, almost cadaverous.

This man was neither handsome nor vain. His skin was drawn tight over his cheekbones, and his cheeks and chin were covered with stubble that was more gray than red. Part of his hair was very short, as though it had been shaved off and had only partly regrown.

"Martin?"

Kate's voice registered shock. When she was sixteen,

he had been twice her age. Now he was merely sixteen years older, yet he looked like an aged, frail man.

Thorson looked up from the doorknob and his face suddenly changed.

"Oh, hello," he said, turning around. "I wasn't expecting anyone yet."

For an instant, he smiled and became the man Kate once had thought she loved. Her heart stopped and she knew how Corry had felt, dangling in midair with no hope of rescue.

Abruptly, the shuttered, gaunt look returned to Thorson's face. The light went out of his eyes.

"How are you today?" he asked mechanically, a minister greeting parishioners at the church door after a Sunday service.

Kate sensed the autism in his greeting. A surge of disappointment she had not expected swept over her. The forlorn teenager locked in her memories had hoped that Thorson still loved her. The cosmopolitan woman she had become doubted that Thorson ever loved her in any way but the easy one.

Whatever the truth, this gaunt specter of a man standing before her now was incapable of love. She had no idea what had become of Martin Thorson, but the man who had seduced her and betrayed his God was surely dead.

"I'm fine, Pastor," she said uncertainly. "How are you?"

Another smile, dimmer and more mechanical, passed over the man's face.

"Oh, fine," he said. "It's spring, the tulips are blooming and the church will be full of flowers tomorrow. It's hard not to be fine on a day like that."

He tried the door again. It remained closed.

"I seem to have locked myself out," he said. "You haven't seen the groundskeeper around, have you?"

Kate approached slowly, gathering herself, swaying between past and present.

"Locked out?" she asked automatically. The front doors hadn't been locked when she and Corry left the previous day. She doubted that they were locked now.

Thorson gave the knob one more twist before he stepped back. "Well, I certainly hope he gets here soon. He's got work to do, and one of his jobs is to let me in."

"Did you . . . try the front doors?" Kate asked.

Thorson looked momentarily panicked. "Odd. I never thought of that," he said. "After so many years, you get set in your ways, I guess."

He marched past her and turned two steps past the corner like a man following a trail only he can see.

Kate followed slowly, wishing that she hadn't come. The handsome, compelling seducer she had hoped to confront no longer existed. The confused, skeletal man who had taken Thorson's place made anger and hurt impossible.

Like the old yellow dog, Thorson studied the steps to the front door carefully. He lifted his foot to the first step, then tottered a little. Kate realized he was so weak that walking across the field had worn him out.

"Let me help you," she said, reaching out to steady him.

"I'm fine," he snapped irritably. "I certainly don't need help from you."

His tone was abrupt but familiar. For an instant, Kate felt like a young woman with an aged husband. Whatever illness or injury had come to Thorson had sapped his life. Frailty and proximate death lay in his skin, his eyes, his breath. Whatever he had done to her in the past, he hadn't earned the kind of pain she saw in him now.

"Let me help you," she said quietly.

Thorson looked at her in confusion, trying to comprehend her meaning. Then he let her take his arm and balance him as he started up the stairs. At the top, he stopped to pant.

"I don't know what's wrong with me," he said, frowning. "I go up and down those steps a hundred times a day."

Kate surrendered her hold on his arm and stepped back. "None of us is young anymore, Pastor."

He scowled, pushed open the door, and entered the church. Once inside, he seemed revitalized. His face lost its slackness. His eyes cleared and became like those of a hawk. As he moved through the vestibule and into the nave, his shoulders straightened and his back stiffened. He was back in the place where God's power flowed through him.

"Come in, come in," he called out over his shoulder. "It's smaller than my last church, but it's sturdy and pleasant."

Kate let Thorson lead the way, wondering how he would react to the wreckage inside.

The vacant spot where the organ had been was dusty, and pieces of the altar lay in the sanctuary like disassembled bones, but Thorson seemed hardly to notice. He stepped over the rope that lay in a tangle on the floor where Corry had fallen and mounted the single step to the sanctuary.

"Do you like it?" he asked proudly.

She felt a stab of sadness for all that had once been.

"It's a fine old place," she said quietly.

"Are you a church person? Odd, isn't it, that we have to ask such a question today?"

Kate stopped halfway down the aisle. "I was once."

Thorson smiled indulgently and nodded. "Yes," he agreed, "there are lots of us who find ourselves out of touch with God nowadays. Even ministers, sometimes."

She looked hard at him, but saw no hidden meaning in his expression and no secrets in his eyes.

"In any case," he said, "you're back in a church now, so welcome, and what can I do for you?"

He was completely composed and at ease, as though he had never been hesitant or confused.

Kate was astonished at the change.

"Martin, do you recognize me now?" she asked.

He made a show of studying her closely. "No, I'm sorry to say that I don't."

She didn't know what to say to this man who was her first lover, her first betrayer, and now a stranger even to himself.

"Silly of me, I know," Thorson added, frowning. "I always had a good memory for faces, particularly faces as pretty as yours, but I seem to have lost that somewhere, somehow. I really don't . . . remember?"

"It was a long time ago," she said. "Half a life or more. Do you remember a church called Vinje Lutheran?"

"Of course," Thorson said. "That's down south of here and over toward the coast."

"You were pastor there, fifteen years ago. Don't you remember, Martin?"

"Nonsense," he said. "I've never been inside that church. I know about it. Everyone knows about it. It's one of the oldest in the synod, but I've never set foot in it."

"Are you sure?" she asked, confused at the vehemence of Thorson's denial, wondering if somehow she were mistaken after all.

"Absolutely," he said. "I'd certainly remember being in a church where I was supposed to be a pastor, wouldn't I?"

"I—"

"What did you say your name was?" he interrupted, suddenly suspicious, hawklike in his intensity.

Memories flooded Kate. This was the Thorson she remembered, a man whose eyes compelled attention and whose voice was vibrant with the certainty of God and transcendence. Or, at least, it had seemed like that to her when she was fourteen, fifteen, sixteen.

But she wasn't that young anymore. She was a woman who was trying to answer or heal or ignore or

somehow get past the emotional wounds of her childhood.

"My name is Saarinan," she said distinctly. "My
father was Jarri Saarinan. You conducted his funeral, his
and my mother's."

The name had a surprising effect on Thorson. He
looked away and closed his eyes. "Jarri Saarinan. Jarri.
Jarri. Now there's a name I haven't thought of in years.
Poor man, he and his wife were killed in a car crash."

"Yes, that's right. I'm their daughter."

"No!" Thorson objected. "That's not right. Their
daughter was . . ."

He stopped, suddenly uncertain.

Breath held, Kate waited.

"She . . ." Thorson said. His eyes clouded. For a
moment he looked drawn and haunted. "She . . . I . . .
God took that memory from me, but I know you
couldn't be her. She was only a child, a very talented,
very, very lovely child."

"My parents died fourteen years ago," Kate said. "I'm
no longer a child, Martin."

Thorson focused on Kate, taking her in carefully from
head to toe. His gaze became unmistakably masculine.
He had looked at her the same way the moment before
he kissed her for the first time, seeing her as female.

Then he blinked and his eyes became troubled again.
He looked away, raised his eyes and his hands to the
ceiling.

"Why do you keep calling me 'Martin,' as though we
were old friends? Why are people always trying to confuse
me? What have I done to deserve this state of being where
my mind is neither alive nor yet dead? Am I in hell? How
can I repent what I don't remember? Or is that what hell
is, punishment without reason?"

There was such anguish in Thorson's voice that
Kate's anger withered, overwhelmed by compassion for
the intimate stranger who was trapped in his own mind.

"Pastor Thorson," she said clearly.

He glanced down at her. Surprise flickered over his features, as though he hadn't expected anyone to be in the church but him.

"I didn't mean to upset you," Kate said. "I'm not here to talk about the past. I'm more interested in the present."

Thorson tilted his head as though thinking it over. Then he sighed and nodded. "The present is easier, sometimes. Sometimes it's . . . I forget."

Kate approached him slowly, as though she expected him to flee.

"I'm a violinist," she said carefully. "I live in New York. I came to Langley to play and to instruct young musicians. Maybe you heard about that."

After a moment, Thorson nodded again. "Yes, I do believe I did. It's a good thing, too. Langley can be quite narrow. It needs a breath of the beauty that is its cultural heritage. Especially the children need . . . something?"

He seemed to sway.

Kate remembered his physical frailty. She went to him and held out her hand.

"Come," she said. "Let's sit down."

Thorson let her take his hand and lead him down the single step to the nave, then to the front pew. He sank onto the old wooden seat that had been worn smooth by decades of use. Kate sat beside him, holding his cool, limp hand in hers. He looked twice his age, a confused old man with the curious senile combination of passivity and rage.

"Have you seen the swans?" he asked suddenly.

"Yes. They're beautiful."

He nodded, then frowned. "The beauty of angels, but they always go away. They'll be leaving soon. I can feel it. They always, always go away."

His voice was so bereft that it made Kate's breath catch in her throat.

"Swans are like the seasons," she said. "They go away, but then they always come back."

Thorson thought about that a while.

"I suppose," he said. "I suppose." His tone said he wasn't sure. "They aren't like children. Children never come back, once they're grown."

"Do you have children?" Kate asked.

Thorson took his hand back. He held it in front of him, studying it as though it were an artifact, not something attached to his body. Then he shook his head. "No, I don't have any children," he said. Then he added, "None to speak of, isn't that what they say?"

"You aren't married?" she asked cautiously.

"I was," Thorson said. "Years ago. But she left, poor woman. I guess I wasn't much of a husband to her. Too busy, so full of things for the Lord and the congregation that I had nothing left for her."

The insight sent a chill down Kate's spine. There were huge holes in Thorson's awareness, but some portions of memory were clearly intact.

"Is that why you never had children?" she asked.

"Why do you keep asking about children?" Thorson said, glancing at her irritably.

"Most men want to have them."

He fixed his eye on her. "Are you looking for a husband?"

"No," Kate said with a trace of bitterness. "I'm a modern woman. I don't need a husband. I'm self-sufficient."

"That's right," he said. "You did say you were from New York." He chuckled again. "You should marry a minister, then, if you don't need a man as a husband."

"I'll keep it in mind."

Thorson made a scoffing noise and turned away.

"Don't," he said. "You're too attractive. It would never do for a minister's wife to be pretty. She should be plain, plain and supportive and dutiful. You're none of those things."

"You don't know me very well," Kate said.

Then she realized that he never had. He had seen only the worshipful child-woman, and she had seen only the man who was in touch with God.

Thorson made an angry noise and shook his head. He drew away from her.

"You couldn't love me," he said. "No woman could. Men of God aren't meant to be loved."

The accusation was direct, yet his voice was vague. He wasn't speaking to her but to someone else, someone lost in the demolished hallways of his own mind, where the past and present were the same and nothing had meaning.

Kate drew a swift breath and asked the only question that still mattered.

"Do you know a teenager named Alyssa Corry?"

Nineteen

*T*horson blinked and seemed to come back into focus. He looked up from studying his hands. His dark eyes showed a flicker of reaction, and his face softened.

"Alyssa? Certainly," he said. "She's not a child anymore. She's a very bright young woman. I've watched her grow for, let me see, oh, I don't know. Her whole life? A handful of years? I don't remember. It doesn't matter, does it? She's very talented."

"Really?" Kate asked.

Despite her impatience for answers, she kept her voice very low and calm. Thorson's hold on reality was as fragile as a bubble.

"Talented how?" she asked. "Is she a musician?"

Kate watched his eyes, seeking some kind of reaction, but finding none.

"Not a conventional one," Thorson said, his eyes clear and thoughtful. "That's probably her father's doing. He's an atheist, or at least an agnostic, but a very decent man for all of his blindness."

"Yes," she said quietly. "He told me you two were friends."

Slowly Thorson nodded. "Only a decent man would

have taken on the raising of a girl all alone, after his wife left him."

"Did she?" Kate asked, gently encouraging.

Thorson looked away, thinking, remembering the way the story went, as though he knew it well but hadn't told it in a while.

"Sharon, that's her name," he said after a moment. "Good Lutheran woman, but God didn't see fit to make her fertile no matter how she prayed. God had a better plan for her. A dark-haired little angel girl come to Earth, needing good parents."

Breath held, Kate waited. Thorson didn't say anymore.

"Was Alyssa adopted through the church?" she asked.

"God's ways are often mysterious. Sharon didn't like being a mother. When Corry sold his fishing business, she took half of the million dollars and left. Said she needed to find herself."

At first Kate was too shocked to speak. The anguish of giving up her daughter still haunted her, yet Corry's wife had simply taken the money, walked out, and never looked back.

"When did this happen?" she asked.

Thorson frowned. "Years. Years?" He shrugged. "It doesn't matter, does it? She's gone. Perhaps that was God's true wisdom. Corry has done very well with Alyssa on his own."

"He said you've had a hand, too, in her raising."

Thorson turned his face away from Kate for a few moments. When he looked back, he was wearing a fond, parental smile.

"I'd like to think so," he said. "When you have no children of your own, you sometimes take a special interest in the children of others."

"None to speak of," she corrected him.

He looked at her, confused.

"Isn't that what you said a moment ago?" Kate asked. " 'No children to speak of '?"

"Why would I say that? I never wanted children. They take a man too far from God."

Kate wondered if she looked as pale as she felt. He had said those very words to her fourteen years ago, after her parents' funeral, when she had told him she was pregnant.

"But Alyssa is different," Thorson said. "She is God's child. She sees connections that even adults miss. She's lonely but confident in it."

"She sounds like quite an unusual thirteen-year-old," Kate said.

"She's wiser by far than her years. That's why she's so lonely." He shook his head. "She's begun to develop an interest in boys."

"Really? Sometimes girls of that age get crushes on men much older than they are."

"Yes. That's a danger. Their devout innocence is such a terrible, terrible snare for a man's soul. . . ."

"Perhaps a man's experience is a rather terrible snare for a girl's innocence," Kate said distinctly.

Thorson tilted his head, thinking. "I suppose it could be," he said without interest.

She looked down at her hands, which were laced together so tightly that her knuckles were white. She forced herself to relax her fingers. She had never thought of herself as the mother of a daughter who was ready to pass into womanhood. All the dangers, all the wounds, the probability of despair and the possibility of joy.

My God, she thought. It's a wonder any of us survive it.

"Is Alyssa a member of your congregation?" Kate asked.

"She comes for the music. I don't know if she's a believer. Corry doesn't, either, but she does come. She sings. It's good to see a young face here."

Thorson looked around the old church, imagining it filled with a congregation singing some old Scandinavian hymn. His eyes fell on the hymn board on the wall beside the pulpit. The board was blank. Then he looked toward the organ. For the first time, he seemed to realize the keyboard was no longer there.

His eyes moved around the rest of the church slowly, taking in the demolition.

"Oh, Lord," he groaned. "What in the name of Heaven? Where am I?"

Reflexively, he reached out, seeking human touch as reassurance. When Kate took his thin hand, his fingers closed over hers like talons.

"What have they done to my church?" he said despairingly. "Vandals. Thieves. What have they done? Why does God permit such things to be? *Why does He allow evil in man?*"

When he would have stood up, she restrained him.

"Martin, Pastor Thorson," she said urgently. "It's all right. There's a new church being built. Surely you've been told about it."

"What have they done to the organ?" he wailed. "It was a beautiful organ. It was a beautiful church. Now I've destroyed it."

Tears welled up in his eyes and ran down his sunken cheeks.

"You didn't destroy it," Kate said firmly. "The building is being torn down to make room for a newer, stronger church."

He simply shook his head and wept. Instinctively, she put one arm around his shoulders, consoling him. She felt his bones, frail and birdlike, through the black wool coat he wore.

"It's what I know," he said. "It's all I know, all, and now I'm dying."

Kate remembered what he had told her when he brought the news of her parents' death.

"We're all dying," she said gently. "We must make our peace with it, and God."

"I-I can't." The words came reluctantly. "I can't find the words anymore to pray. I can't find the ideas to think about. If I find them, I can't think about them. It's very, very lonely without God."

A sense of great loss washed over Kate. Thorson's mind had betrayed him and destroyed his faith. Now he was afloat, alone, facing death.

"Martin," she said, taking both his hands and looking him in the eye, "when I was very young, my parents died. I screamed at you that there was no God and you said that was all right. You said God could forgive my doubts."

Thorson looked at her with dawning hope and a total lack of recognition.

"I'm not a church person," she said. "Not anymore. Churches are human institutions and I don't trust them. Yet I've always managed to believe in a good that transcends human limitations. God, if you will."

"You believe?" he asked hesitantly. "You really believe?"

"It's a way of forgiving myself," she said, understanding for the first time. "You should forgive yourself, Martin."

He sighed. "I don't know what I've done. Do you?"

Kate closed her eyes. Nothing that she could say would lift the crushing burden of Thorson's ruined mind.

"It doesn't matter," she said. "It was all a long time ago."

Tears welled up in Thorson's eyes again and he looked away. "I wish I could believe," he said painfully, "but my mind isn't strong enough anymore."

She looked away to the faded colors of the stained-glass window. "If it makes any difference," she said softly, "I forgive you."

"What?"

Kate turned to him. "I forgive you."

"Did I do something to you? I-I don't remember. For a moment, you looked familiar, but I just can't remember."

She released his left hand and laid it gently across his right. Then she covered them both, top and bottom.

"Perhaps that's a blessing from the God neither one of us can touch anymore," she said.

Thorson closed his eyes. When they opened again, they were as empty as the church.

"Do I know you?" he asked.

"No," Kate said. "Come with me, Pastor. Your housekeeper is worried about you."

"Emma?" he asked, standing up stiffly.

"Yes."

"Have the swans gone?"

"I don't know. Shall we see?"

Slowly, matching her steps to Thorson's uncertain ones, Kate led him out of the ruined church and into the field where some of the gravestones were living swans.

Twenty

There were only a few places in Langley to hide, but Bran Corry looked half the morning before he found Kate's car on the greening grass in the churchyard.

The old building was empty, but she had been there. A crumpled, still damp tissue lay on the front pew. Even Corry's nose was keen enough to catch her distinctive scent on it, a cologne that was as clean and wild as a spring wind.

Corry carried the tissue back outside and looked around the churchyard. Then he searched the horizon in all directions and muttered a curse under his breath. Nothing that looked like Kate was in sight.

"Where in the devil would she be, Campbell?"

The collie was investigating the long grass beside the wrought-iron fence. The mention of his name brought him to attention. He cocked his head and looked intently at Corry.

"Kate? You know Kate, right?" he asked, waving the tissue under Campbell's nose.

The collie's tail waved eagerly as he recognized the scent.

"Where is she? Fetch her up."

Those words Campbell knew. The "fetch" was the long run out beyond the woollie ones. It was the most exciting moment of a young dog's life.

But there were no sheep in sight, not even feathered ones. Certainly, Campbell could see a great ocean of white birds out in the field beyond the fence, but he knew from experience that they were geese who would rather fly than be herded.

"Fetch her up," Corry repeated. "Hide-and-seek, Campbell. Find Kate!"

It had been a long time since Campbell had played hide-and-seek with Alyssa, but memory of the game still existed in the canine's intricate, scent-triggered brain. He trotted to the gate and pawed impatiently. The scent of Kate was tantalizing on the grass.

"That way?" Corry asked.

Then he spotted the neat print of a woman's boot in the damp earth at the edge of the field. The track pointed along the fence line, toward the river.

"Fetch her up," Corry ordered, waving at the fence line.

Campbell raced forward, chasing an invisible scent trail. The man followed with long, quick strides. They walked for ten minutes.

Corry missed the spot where Kate slipped under the fence and headed into the field of tulips, but Campbell didn't. He stopped and doubled back the instant the scent of the woman vanished.

He barked once, sharply. Corry turned and came back. The grass between the fence poles had been crushed by a footfall.

"Missed her, did I?" Corry asked when he saw the fainter outlines of footprints in the grass. "Good boy. Hide-and-seek! Fetch her in!"

Campbell wagged his tail and dashed off through the fence. The collie disliked mud, but he loved the game.

Corry vaulted the fence and landed hard on the other

side. He spotted Kate's footprints in the muddy ground between rows of mixed tulips.

A crew of Mexican field hands was harvesting tulips for the cut-flower market, carefully selecting buds that had just begun to show color. They would be bright and crisp for the inhabitants of Manhattan and Los Angeles.

"Have you seen a woman, walking alone?" Corry asked the workers.

Several nodded. One of them pointed over his shoulder toward a dike at the end of the long rows of tulips.

"Twenty, thirty minutes ago," he said with a gold-toothed grin.

"Can I have some of the open flowers?" Corry asked impulsively.

"Sure, they're no good if they've already bloomed," the Mexican said. "Just don't rip out the bulb."

Corry pushed on down the row, snatching off a fully open bloom here and there. By the time he reached the dike, he was carrying a bunch of red, yellow, and orange tulips, along with three beautiful, late-blooming daffodils that had naturalized from a previous year's planting.

A pair of swans conferred nervously at the edge of the muddy field as man and dog passed through a field gate and crossed the gravel road at the base of the dike.

Corry could see a trail in the grass where someone had scrambled up the side of the dike. A bald eagle sat high in a snag across the river, its head and tail glistening like fresh snow in the noontime sun. Red-winged blackbirds sang warnings to one another from the cattails, their epaulets brilliant in breeding colors.

The path at the top of the dike was worn and hard. Corry had to rely on Campbell to keep track of Kate's invisible trail. The dog turned right and trotted along confidently. The man was less confident. They walked a hundred yards before he caught a glimpse of color through the bare trees ahead.

Kate sat perched on a log just below the lip of the dike, watching cold water flow by like time. She was lost in thought when she suddenly felt a delicate touch, Campbell's cool wet nose on her wrist. She looked over, startled but not truly surprised.

Campbell touched her wrist again and wagged his tail eagerly. Tag! Now you're "it."

Corry was ten yards behind, his left hand filled with color.

For an instant, Kate felt an overwhelming sorrow that brought tears to her eyes again. Corry always seemed to find her when her composure was tattered. She looked back at the water, trying to control the sadness she felt for all that couldn't be changed.

"Good morning," Corry said, his voice edged with gruffness. "I've been looking for you."

She couldn't answer, except to smile weakly at him. Then she gestured toward the empty log beside her. Campbell came around the log and sat in front of her on his haunches, demanding a reward for his victory.

"Hello, you clever dog," Kate said softly, taking Campbell's head between her hands and stroking him affectionately. "Are you the one who tracked me here?"

The dog grinned up at her, licked her wrist, and panted happily.

Still carrying the bright bouquet, Corry sat down on the log. After a moment, he held the flowers out to her.

"I was the one who picked up your scent," he said, "but Campbell caught a turn or two or you'd have lost us, sure. We gathered these along the way."

Kate took the flowers without looking at Corry, afraid of what she might do or say.

"Thanks," she said. "I had a long morning. I needed to walk it off."

"Long morning or long night?"

Now she had no choice but to look him right in the eye.

"It was the best night I've ever had," she said simply. "Whatever else happens, don't doubt that."

Relief spread across Corry's face like sunlight.

"I wasn't sure," he said, "not when you were gone this morning without a message." Then he reached over and kissed her lightly on the lips. "Whatever else happens," he said, using her words, "it was the best night I've ever had, too."

Tears threatened to overflow again. She smiled and looked away quickly. The conversation with Thorson had exhausted her, but if she mentioned it there would be too many questions, too many might-have-beens, no answers.

"I had a call this morning," she said in a strained voice. "New York. They need me back there more quickly than I expected. I'm booked on the red-eye tonight. It leaves Seattle at eleven."

Corry felt his breath catch in a chest that was suddenly too small. He cleared his throat and stared at the murky melt water that slid downstream between the banks of the dike.

"You could take an armload of tulips back with you," he said slowly. "I imagine Manhattan could use a touch of color, this time of year."

Kate looked around as though seeing the joyous blaze of colors for the first time. On the other side of the river, beyond the tree where the eagle sat, were more tulip fields, flowers vivid against the wet, rich brown earth. The colors seemed impossibly bright, more vital than all the Van Goghs at the Metropolitan Museum.

Sadness came again, threatening what little composure she had left.

"It's harder to leave than I expected," she whispered. Then she glanced quickly, almost shyly, at Corry. "Even if it were a gray day, it would be hard."

"But you're going anyway."

"This is a very important deal, recording contract,

concert tour, the whole mess. It's worth—" She hesitated, remembering Corry's own million-dollar deal, the one that had cost him his wife. "It's worth the fourteen years I've been working for it."

He reached out and laid his hand on her shoulder, gently testing the flesh beneath her clothing.

"The Strad, right?" he asked.

She nodded. "The Strad."

He grimaced. "That Italian is a tough rival. I don't know what I can offer to compete."

"It's not like—" Kate started to object, but she stopped herself. The pain of the moment was all the more bitter because she couldn't bear to tell Corry the truth.

"Kate," he said, looking at her levelly, "I'm not going to let you go without a fight. All of this has hit us like a squall line on a sunny day, but I know what I want. I want you to stay."

Beneath his fingers, he felt a tremor in the tight, well-defined muscles of her shoulders. Her head dropped forward, as though she suddenly had lost the ability to hold it up.

"I wish it were as simple as that," she said.

"It is."

She closed her eyes, hiding her feelings from Corry. She shook her head emphatically.

"You have no idea how complex things have become, Bran," she said.

"It's still just that simple, too," he said, circling her shoulders with his arm and pulling her close against his side. "I have a feeling it will always be that simple, between you and me."

For a moment, Kate let herself be drawn into the warm circle of his arm. It was so good there, so quiet and serene, so full of promise and hope.

So impossible.

"It will never be that simple," she whispered. "I wish to God in heaven that it could be."

He laid his cheek against the silken softness of her hair and felt the two of them begin to melt together again.

"What do I need to do to convince you?" he asked.

She let herself be comforted for a moment more, as though she could draw from him the strength to send him away.

"It's not you," she said. "It's me and the past and the rest of the world."

He smiled and completed the circle with his other arm, turning her so that she had no choice but to face him.

"I've learned to handle the rest of the world, sweet Kate," he said. "The past is behind us, and I can't imagine there's anything in you that will drive me off."

He kissed her lips with just enough force to show her that he was being restrained. "You're the best thing that's ever happened to me and I'd walk through fire to keep you.

"Hell, I might even think about living in New York, once Alyssa's grown a bit more. I'm not much a part of the town of Langley. I suppose I could learn to live on the fringes of other places, too."

Then he kissed her again, but this time his restraint was gone. She tried at first to resist the power of his kiss and found she couldn't. She just didn't want to. She kissed him back, hard. Then she broke away and laid the palm of her hand on his bearded cheek.

"I will not lie to you," Kate said, looking into his eyes. "So don't ask me why unless you really want to know. Please, just accept my word. There are a thousand reasons to go and only one to stay. Even with those odds, leaving is as hard as dying . . . *but I will be on that plane tonight.*"

Then she lowered her eyes so he couldn't see the tears that filled them.

Corry held her against his chest for a long time, looking out through the barren trees toward the fields of raw color and the white, snow-covered mountains beyond. In the lee of the dike, the sun was springtime warm. He longed to pull her down with him into the dry grass, to lie there together once more, even if just for a moment.

But he knew the ground was still cold from winter. He knew that the coldness would only remind her that she must leave.

"I do love you," he said into the fragrant softness of her hair.

The words seemed to send an electric shock through her. For a moment, he felt her respond to him as she had the first time he kissed her, with a spontaneous desire as honest and direct as her music.

His hands slipped inside her coat and found the tuck of her waist. He spanned her belly with his thumbs and spread his fingers across the smoothness of her back. Then his thumbs slid up and stroked the tips of her breasts.

Kate groaned involuntarily and kissed him until he was dizzy, until they both began to spin out of control. For this moment her body was his and for this moment he belonged to her.

Then she twisted away and collapsed against him, pinning his hands beneath her arms, hiding her mouth from his kisses and shielding her face from his gaze.

"You are a bastard, aren't you," she whispered, her voice husky and her shoulders trembling.

He laughed, deep in his chest, and held her tightly.

"I don't give up, woman," he said. "I can't. It isn't my nature, not when I want something as much as I want you."

She shivered again and slowly regained control of her feelings. Corry felt the desire pass out of her body slowly, like an ebbing tide. He could guess the enormous cost. He wondered where she found the will to deny both of them.

Kate rested her head against his chest for an instant

but said nothing, not trusting her voice. Then she drew another deep breath and eased slowly out of his embrace.

Campbell lay at their feet, head on his paws, waiting patiently for them to sort out the human foolishness so they could move on to the more important things in life, like sheep or swans. Or even another game. Anything that involved him in their attention.

"Your master is a real bastard," Kate said softly to the dog.

Campbell raised his head and looked intent, as though he were confused by the juxtaposition of harsh words and loving tone. After a moment, he whined softly.

"Hush," Corry said quickly, as much to himself as to the dog. "No begging."

The command seemed a gentle joke. Kate would have laughed, but she saw something in Corry's eyes that told her how serious he was beneath the play. For an instant, she realized how tightly the big man had leashed some part of himself. She turned away, a little afraid.

"No more teasing, Bran," she said. "It's not fair to either one of us."

Corry nodded gravely, as though he agreed, if only for the sake of his masculine pride. "I would ask for one favor, though," he added.

"Of course. If I can," Kate amended quickly, afraid that he might ask the question whose answer would leave them with nothing, not even haunting memories of what might have been.

"Alyssa is playing this evening at a local celebration," he said. "It would mean a great deal if you would come and listen."

She started to refuse.

"Afterward," he said quickly, "I'll take you to . . ." He looked away, across the cold river. "I'll drive you to the airport. Don't worry. I'll be sure you make the red-eye to New York."

Kate sat in stunned silence, wondering whether she could hold her end of the bargain she had already made. To see Alyssa again, the pain of certainty and uncertainty both at once. How could she see her?

How could she not?

"Yes," Kate said hoarsely. "I'd love to hear your daughter play."

Twenty-one

The grange hall was alive with light and laughter as Kate arrived. The Skalbeck church loomed in the darkness a hundred yards away. The light from the rising moon was strong enough to pass through stained glass from one side of the building to the other.

As Kate parked her car at the edge of the yard, she caught a glimpse of flickering light in the cemetery. She got out and looked more closely, but still couldn't make out the source.

Kate expected to spend the night in an airline seat, so she wore slacks, a loose sweater, and soft shoes. She carried her purse, but her violin was still in the car. She locked the car from long habit, then smiled. City habits, country towns.

She headed toward the curious light. The closer she came, the more unlikely the scene ahead appeared. A single hunched figure wielded what appeared to be a fiery wand, burning away the grass and melting the frozen ground at the north side of the church. For a second, it looked like some demon burning his way up from hell.

Kate laughed at her own response. There was no God, no demon, no hell, just a grave-digger with a blow-

torch preparing the way for another pioneer who would
spend death even closer to the land than he had been in
life.

The country child in her saw a certain sad memorial.
She suspected that this would be the last grave to be
dug in the old Skalbeck cemetery. She wondered if the
new church would have modern, flat, stones where lawn
mowers ruled and grass was not allowed to run riot and
attract the occasional, tangled swan.

She wondered what kind of minister would replace
Martin Thorson. She hoped it would be a man who
could resist the terrible innocence of girls on the brink
of womanhood.

Better I should hope that girls won't be foolish
enough to mistake their own dawning sexuality for a
religious experience, Kate thought. Better I should hope
that black is white and white is not.

She walked back through the grass toward the grange
hall with her head bare and her coat open to the chill
spring night. The ghostly headstones of Old Skalbeck
seemed like old friends. She felt an odd connection with
them that only comes from family plots and community
burial places, shared lives and deaths. In the cities, death,
like life, was private to the point of anonymity.

The grange was an old frame building that looked as
though it had once been a country schoolhouse. The
sides of the building were lined with windows, each four
panes by four panes. There was the remnant of what
had probably been a small belfry at the end of the roof
opposite the front door.

The light that poured out through the paneled windows was warm and yellow, as though cast by lanterns
instead of electricity. Inside, Kate heard a voice singing
a simple melody, and other voices laughing and talking,
caught up in their deeply rooted communal lives.

For an instant, she felt so much like an outsider she
almost turned and fled. Then the door of the hall

opened up and Corry stepped into the night. She caught a glimpse of sadness in his expression that had not been there before, even when she told him she was leaving.

"Hey, there you are," he said softly. "I was beginning to think you had changed your mind."

"And disappoint Alyssa?"

"I haven't told her yet that you were coming."

Kate felt her cheeks burn with anger or shame. "I keep my word, Bran. I'm here."

The sadness returned to Corry's eyes. "I didn't mean it that way. It's just that she's been pretty upset."

"Performance nerves?"

"No. A friend died this afternoon."

"How awful," she said. "Was it another student?"

Corry shook his head. "It was the minister, Marty Thorson."

Kate's heart stopped beating. For a time, the world slipped out of focus.

Corry saw the expression change on her face and reached out to steady her. "Are you okay?" he asked.

She focused on him slowly, as though coming out of a trance. "Did you say Martin Thorson is dead?"

"Yes," Corry replied. "He died this afternoon. It was very peaceful. Just a nap he never woke up from."

"I saw him today," she said. "In his church. He seemed frail, but not deathly ill."

"Considering the amount of cranial bleeding he suffered after he fell down those icy steps this winter . . ." Corry shrugged. "Death was a blessing."

"Poor Alyssa," Kate whispered.

"It's not the first time she's been around death, but it's the first time she knew someone well."

"Martin told me about her. He thought she was a very special person."

"She thought he was special, too. When she felt out of place everywhere she went, she could always go and play for him."

"I'm sorry," Kate said haltingly. "So very sorry."

Corry looked past her to the church. "The funeral is Monday. I'll put the old church back together as much as I can, and we'll bury Marty in the grave that's being dug right now. I suppose it will give a sense of closure to the place."

He ran his maimed fingers through his beard and for a second, a deep sadness showed in his eyes.

"He was a good friend, wasn't he?" Kate asked.

Corry nodded. "Probably the best I had in this town. I never quite understood why he put up with me, considering my beliefs. He always said we had a lot more in common than I knew."

She drew a deep breath and composed her face to disguise the emotions at war inside her.

"Maybe he was more tolerant than the rest of your neighbors," Kate said. "You are a good man. That's what Martin saw in you and in your daughter, too."

Corry's smile was gentle and genuine. "Sounds like you and he had quite a talk."

Kate felt his hand on her elbow, supporting her and drawing strength from her, as well.

"Martin's—Pastor Thorson's mind," she corrected quickly, "wasn't always clear, but we did manage to connect. I wish I had seen him, say, a year ago. While his mind was intact."

Something in Kate's tone made Corry look at her swiftly. His eyes narrowed. He seemed on the edge of asking something, then backed away.

"Marty was an unusual man," Corry said. "A man of God who understood human frailty to the last full stop. He said it took a sinner to understand a sinner, and only God understood saints."

Kate stumbled, then caught herself on Corry's strength.

She nodded numbly.

"I don't know what sins he committed," Corry said.

"The usual male ones, I suppose. Word was that his wife divorced him over some other, much younger woman."

She stumbled again.

"Watch that pavement," he said. "There's grass growing in every crack."

"Yes," she said through stiff lips.

"Whatever happened," Corry said, "Marty brought more to this community than he took away. We'll be poorer for his loss. He tried to remind people there is a bigger world out there. Only the kids listened, Alyssa in particular. I owe him a lot. So do you."

All Kate could do was stare at him.

"He was determined to get you here for Alyssa. He said it was vital for her development." Corry gave Kate a hooded look. "I think he saw you as her mother in spirit if not in fact."

She felt as though an electrical current had just passed through her body, a fire in her brain, shocking her into clarity.

"Did he say that?" she asked bluntly.

"Not in so many words. It was just in the way he talked about you and Alyssa and God's mysterious ways."

Kate tried to find words to say that wouldn't tear apart too many worlds.

"He followed your career closely," Corry said, watching her. "Every interview, every recording. I'm surprised he never wrote you a letter. Or did he?"

Kate shivered, suddenly frightened. Corry reminded her right now of Campbell, intent on herding a tangled swan.

Does he suspect? she asked desperately. Did Martin tell him or did he simply guess, or is my own fear throwing shadows on everything I see?

Shaman and lover and father. What does he want? What would he do if I told him about my fears, my hopes, Alyssa.

She stared toward the graveyard, now fully illuminated

by moonlight. The night was suddenly alive with spirits, Thorson's included. She wondered if he was laughing at her or at himself or at all of humanity's fragile certainties and relentless hopes.

"You're shivering," Corry said. "Come inside where it isn't cold."

Kate looked from the graveyard to the old community building. The door was open, spilling a rectangle of light across the darkness.

"There are quite a few of Marty's congregation here," Corry said, leading her up the steps, "as well as some of the county's more notorious pagans. He had a way of reaching everyone."

She caught the edge of her shoe on the top step. Corry righted her effortlessly.

"Tonight's performance has become kind of an informal wake now," he said, gently herding her into the crowded grange hall. "I hope Alyssa is up to it. She's pretty young to play a friend's elegy."

They were engulfed in the smell of food and the din of mealtime conversation. Kate recognized the setting instantly from her childhood. A potluck supper, the kind given for weddings, funerals, baptisms, fund-raisers, Fourth of July—any excuse to get together and trade recipes and gossip, personal problems and hopes.

At the far end of the hall, where the teacher's desk would have been in the old school, there was a small stage. The rest of the hall held a dozen scattered card tables and folding chairs. White plastic forks, spoons, and knives had a bonelike sheen in the light. Forty or fifty people were wielding the cutlery as they ate from paper plates.

The meal was almost over. Most of the people looked up when Corry guided Kate into a clear aisle.

"This is Kate Saarinan, the violinist some of you heard the other night," he announced, as though he were introducing a stranger to a family gathering.

"Even though she's supposed to fly back to Manhattan tonight, she's a country girl at heart. It's just taking her time to get used to the idea."

Laughter and applause spattered through the crowd. Kate felt a sudden heat spread across her face. She had stood in front of hundreds of audiences in the past ten years, but there was something intimate and unexpected about this one.

"Come on," Corry said to her, "grab a plate and get some food before the music begins."

"I couldn't," she said.

"People have to eat, even at wakes," he said quietly, "maybe *especially* at wakes."

She tried to demur again, but discovered that her stomach was growling. The smells were familiar and wonderful, making her hungry in a way she hadn't been in days. She let Corry guide her down a long table laden with two dozen hot dishes and plates of salad and bread and vegetables.

Women sprang up from their seats and hurried over to make sure Kate was properly served, particularly with their specialty. Before she reached the end of the table, Corry had to bring her a second plate.

He nudged and gently guided her to a place at a table with five or six other people. He seated her with a small flourish.

"These are all friends," he said, "so I'll let them introduce themselves. I have to go see how Alyssa is doing."

A plump woman named Bethel Kostad took charge of the moment. There were hurried introductions all around, plain names and plain, open faces. Kate nodded and greeted them in turn, then told them all where she had been from before Manhattan. Very quickly she felt entirely at home.

She talked and ate and talked some more, relishing the flavors of homemade Swedish meatballs and scalloped potatoes with hard-cured ham and a Mexican-style

casserole that must have been introduced into country
cuisine in the years since she left the farm. The bread
was yeasty and dense, the Jell-O salad was reliably
bland, and the jellied codfish called lutefisk was just as
repellent as it ever had been.

It was like stepping back several decades in time.
Kate was quietly astonished that such a place still
existed. She had assumed that grange halls and potluck
suppers had gone the way of the passenger pigeon,
physicians' house calls, and childhood.

She looked around the crowded little hall, trying to
understand why she felt so calm and at ease among
these strangers. After a time, it occurred to her that
these people were here because they wanted to be, not
because they felt it was required.

They were not trying to impress their neighbors. They
were not trying to appear cultured or refined. They were
here to enjoy a meal, some music, and their neighbors.
Due to an accident of timing, they were also gathered to
acknowledge the passing of Martin Thorson, who had in
some ways been one of them.

Several times, Kate caught mention of the minister's
name in conversations around her. Tones in the voices
and facial expressions suggested that Thorson had
touched many of the lives in the room.

"The pastor's the only reason my Ronnie ever went to
college," said one woman proudly. "Told my boy that
computers were like logging was in his daddy's time, a
manly way to support a family."

"He was a great comfort when my daddy was dying,"
offered another.

"He talked sense to my Mary when she wouldn't listen to anyone else," said a third.

For all their regret at losing Thorson, no one was
grieving in the way they would have over the death of
someone in the prime of life. The fall had effectively
killed Thorson; it had just taken time for him to die. The

tragedy was in his fall, not in his death. Death was the inevitable end of all life, whether it be that of a man or a field of wheat beneath the reaper.

Something inside Kate eased as she listened to the praise for Thorson's work with the community and the acceptance of his passage from that community. Whether the people believed in God or in natural cycles didn't seem to matter. All accepted the end of life with equal calm.

"You haven't touched your desserts, Miss Saarinan. Or is it Mrs.?"

"Ms.," she said clearly, and took a bite of lemon meringue pie.

After that she dutifully tried each of the six desserts and pronounced them equally splendid, much to the pleasure of the half-dozen women who were watching her.

Corry slipped into the chair beside her and touched the back of her hand, but his expression said he was still concerned about his daughter.

"Trouble?"

"The idea of playing in front of you seemed to worry her."

"Why?" Kate asked, surprised and a little hurt.

"She thinks you won't appreciate what she does."

Puzzled, Kate tried to remember if she had said anything to other student musicians that Alyssa might have overheard. She couldn't think of anything that should have bothered even a teenager's tender ego. Then she remembered that Alyssa had said something about not being up to Mozart.

"Would it be easier if I weren't here?" Kate said.

Corry shook his head. "She'll get over it. That's the thing you learn, raising kids. They usually try to duck the experiences they need the most."

"Adults are like that."

"Only the ones who don't grow up."

Something in his expression made Kate wonder if he might be talking about her, if somehow he sensed that part of her was still caught in the past.

Damned shaman, she thought. What gives him the right to look so deeply into me?

"Don't go away," Corry said. "Promise?"

"I've already promised, remember?"

"Just making sure you did."

He slipped away again into the small back room where the performers had begun to gather.

The rest of the audience began to clear away tables and rearrange chairs for the evening's entertainment. Kate felt a small rush of sympathetic stage nerves race through her. The crowd was kind and the venue unchallenging, but all performers knew exactly how delicate and elusive music could be. She said a small prayer for Alyssa's premiere.

Then Kate moved her chair closer to the stage, where she could see as clearly as possible.

Twenty-two

*A*lyssa came out onto the stage looking pale but composed. She carried a glorious blond fiddle that glistened with clear varnish. Even as Kate thought that the girl's violin looked long for young arms, she remembered that her own violin often looked like that until she put it under her chin; then the length of the instrument proved to be a perfect match for her own limbs.

Standing alone in the center of the stage, Alyssa seemed older than Kate remembered, as though Thorson's death had stripped away some of her childhood. No doubt it had.

At that moment, Kate was glad Alyssa had no idea that Thorson might be her genetic father. She would still face the pain of losing the father she loved, but hopefully it would come at a time in her life when she was better prepared to be orphaned.

Alyssa wore black wool slacks and a black turtleneck, much like the outfit she had worn the night Kate talked to her. Prematurely black, as Corry had said. But tonight she had added a red plaid jacket. Its brightness seemed a gesture of defiance to death, youth whistling past the graveyard they didn't believe would someday be theirs.

The red plaid made Alyssa's pale skin translucent and her eyes darkly alive, thoughtful. She acknowledged the applause from the audience with a grave nod and a small, private smile.

Kate saw Thorson in that smile. He had often taken the pulpit with just that same anticipation, enjoying the first moment of connection with the audience, like meeting an old friend, perhaps even a lover. It was the smile of a natural performer, someone who was exhilarated by standing on a stage and risking the world's judgment.

A bittersweet pleasure went through Kate. Sweet because something of Thorson and herself had been given to the future. Bitter because the worry and joy and sheer satisfaction of guiding Alyssa's growth from a baby's potential to a young adult confident of her own gifts had belonged to another, Bran Corry. It was Corry who had, and deserved, his daughter's love. He was a parent in a way that transcended simple genetics.

"Thank you," Alyssa said softly. Then she remembered she was on a stage. She squared her shoulders, lifted her head, and said more clearly, "Thank you. I'm a little nervous and kind of sad, but you make me feel good about being here."

The applause began again. Alyssa smiled shyly, touched by the affection.

From the doorway into the back room, Corry watched silently and calmly, his eyes gleaming with pride.

"I was going to play something else, something more fun," Alyssa said, "but Mr. Thorson died this afternoon."

A flicker of sorrow passed over her young face like a cloud.

"He was my friend," she said. Then she held up the blond violin. "My dad made this for me. He taught me a lot of what I know about this instrument, and Mr.

Thorson taught me about all kinds of music and even learned to like the kind I play."

The audience laughed, understanding a joke that Kate didn't get. She felt like an outsider all over again.

"I'm going to play a song Pastor Thorson especially liked," Alyssa said. She raised the violin to her chin and adjusted its position. Then she added, "I think he liked it so well because he knew it was one of my favorites."

Kate felt her throat tighten in sympathy for the tears she saw brimming in Alyssa's eyes. Then the emotion was put aside and the girl focused herself on the violin and the music.

In that instant, Kate found herself assessing Alyssa as she would another violinist. Even before the girl touched bow to strings, Kate was inwardly braced for disappointment. The girl held the bow as though she intended to start on an upstroke, with her wrist broken and loose.

What was Martin thinking of? Kate thought, alarmed. He was classically trained. Why did he allow a pupil of his to break such a basic rule?

When Alyssa struck the first note, Kate's alarm turned to dismay. She flinched involuntarily at the flatness of the tone. Then she looked away, unable to watch as the girl lifted her bow from the strings and caught them again the wrong way, on the upstroke, as though she were attempting to start over again.

When Kate could bear to look back, she found Alyssa watching her. The girl's stance was subtly defiant, as though she knew what Kate was thinking. Then Alyssa looked past Kate, ignoring her and playing to the rest of the crowd.

The first phrase of the song was a nightmare for Kate, utterly alien to her ear, flat and slurred and seemingly out of control. She realized that her reaction must have shown on her face, but she was helpless to change it. She could do nothing but listen and pray that the song, whatever it was, would somehow miraculously right itself.

Around her the rest of the audience, too, seemed to be holding its breath. By the time Alyssa moved into the second phrase of the song, the people began to relax. Throughout the audience people exchanged smiles and nods of approval, as though they recognized and understood the jumble of sound.

Frowning, Kate wondered what on Earth the audience was hearing. She listened more closely.

Lying just beneath the surface of Alyssa's seemingly random notes was another musical reality, one that Kate had been entirely unprepared to hear. She had expected Bach or Mozart or Brahms, the classical music that was an integral part of her life. What she was hearing was something entirely different, but nonetheless music with its own tradition and integrity.

Corry materialized out of the shadows off stage carrying a round, flat, leather-headed drum. At first softly, then with more force, he tapped out a complicated, syncopated rhythm with a double-headed drumstick he held easily in his maimed hand.

Watching father and daughter, Kate realized how badly her own expectations had betrayed her. She recognized the drum, a bhodran. It, too, was part of a cultural tradition that predated that of classical music: Celtic music, with its unique, flattened tone scale and idiosyncratic style of play. Scottish fiddling sometimes sounded more like pipe music than strings. Rough, intimate, and melancholy, the sound of violin was like a bagpipe and the drumhead mimicked the rhythm of the human heart.

Within the easy frankness of the music, Kate could hear echoes of country fiddling that was at least as old as Beethoven, if not as well recognized. Celtic music was a musical genre she understood only superficially, probably because she had spent so much of the past fourteen years escaping from her own country roots.

Yet Kate had no doubt she was listening to a talented, disciplined musician. She could have wept for her own narrowness, the cultural insularity that had led her to misunderstand Alyssa's performance.

Then the sinuous melodic line captured Kate, reminding her that mistakes weren't fatal, merely human. As she listened, she understood that Thorson and Corry had both been right. Alyssa was, indeed, gifted beyond her years and her training. She possessed an instinctive understanding of the notes she played and their relationship to the music she felt in her own soul.

The song was dolorous and it lacked intricacy, but it was honest and heartfelt. It was a perfect embodiment of sorrow at the loss of a friend.

Fascinated, Kate watched the way Alyssa and her instrument were one. The girl was not polished in the way that a virtuoso might be; her fingerings were rudimentary and awkward to the classicist's eye. But Alyssa was absolutely certain of what she was doing, and what she was doing was playing a type of music that reached the listeners of the audience at an elemental level.

It was a short, simple piece of music, rather like "Taps" in its intent and effect. As the piece came to an end, Corry held his rhythmic line, gently coaxing Alyssa into playing the song again. This time, she stripped away the flourishes, reducing the quiet melody to a simplicity that was both elegant and elegiac.

If Kate had any doubt about the depth of the bond between father and daughter, their performance would have banished it. Man and girl played in perfect consonance, as though they had played the piece together a thousand times before.

Perhaps they had. There was no question that Corry had made Alyssa's fiddle, and no question that his own vernacular style had influenced her choice of music and her playing.

Yet as Kate watched, she sensed that Corry, for all

his fatherly pride, might not understand how gifted Alyssa was. Only another virtuoso would be able to see the girl's potential.

For an instant, Kate wondered what a good classical teacher might do with a pupil of Alyssa's raw, unshaped talent. Then she realized her own cultural insularity was tripping her up again. Corry had shaped his daughter's talent, and she had entered into that shaping enthusiastically. It wasn't as though Alyssa had never heard classical music before Kate had come from New York.

In the last phrase of the song, Alyssa caught the E string with a strong little finger, doubling the note of the string above in perfect harmony that deepened and enriched the song and clearly surprised her father. He nodded his approval of the embellishment and made the heartbeat of the drum linger, encouraging the audience to savor the unexpected harmony.

When the last whisper of music drained away, he reached out impulsively and hugged Alyssa with a powerful arm. Kate ached with pain and pleasure, for she knew just how wonderful Corry's approving hug could be.

Alyssa closed her eyes, obviously enjoying the feeling of being loved and protected. Then she looked out at the applauding audience with a shy, uncertain smile. She seemed startled that they were even still there. She bowed awkwardly, suddenly a little girl again.

And just before she left the stage, she turned and looked at Kate. The girl's expression mixed triumph and defiance.

See, she seemed to be saying, I may not play music like you do, but I do play music.

For a second, Kate almost wept with sadness at her first, unhappy reaction to Alyssa's music. She closed her eyes against the girl's evident anger. Then she nodded her head slowly, silently acknowledging her own mistake, hoping the girl would understand.

When Kate opened her eyes, the stage was empty. She had the hollow feeling that her apology had been rejected with a haughty hurt that only a teenage girl could muster.

Sighing, Kate bowed her head, looked at her hands, and wondered where Corry had found the strength and patience to handle a girl with Alyssa's talent, intelligence, and volatile temperament. Kate knew just how difficult such a temperament could be.

All she had to do was look in the mirror.

Twenty-three

Corry met Kate at the door to the makeshift dressing room with a worried look on his face.

"Alyssa was supposed to play several more numbers. Now she says she doesn't want to see anybody, especially, uh, outsiders."

The hollow feeling inside Kate grew. Thirteen-year-olds were so wise and so foolish, all at once. They wounded people as easily as they themselves were wounded.

"She's really an exceptional talent," Kate said. "If she'll talk to me, I can explain my reaction."

"What happened?"

"I assumed she was going to play classical music."

Corry laughed out loud. "I'd like to have seen the look on your face when Alyssa started on the upstroke."

"She saw it. She didn't like it at all. To be precise, she was mad as hell at me and I don't blame her a bit. It was stupid of me to assume that all real music is played in the same vernacular."

Corry thought about that for a moment, then shook his head. "Kids. Half smart and a hundred percent vulnerable."

"I would like to talk to Alyssa, just for a minute," Kate repeated. "Then I'd better be going."

"I'll see how she feels about it. I need to tell her I'm taking you to the airport anyway."

He was turning away when Kate put her hand on his arm, stopping him.

"I've been thinking," she said. "I don't want you to come with me to the airport. It will . . ." She paused, trying to control her voice. "It will just be that much harder on both of us. I'll talk to Alyssa and then I'll be gone and the two of you can get on with your lives."

Corry looked at her. He realized that she was wearing the same white down coat she had worn when he first saw her. Her purse was over her shoulder. She was edgy and taut, ready to fly.

Like a tangled swan, he thought. Wild and wary and not understanding why life hurt so much.

"Alyssa is no problem," Corry said. "As for the rest, we'll see."

He opened the door and disappeared into the dressing room before Kate could argue. She waited, her eyes burning and her head aching with the tears she would not let herself shed. She couldn't leave knowing she had hurt Alyssa.

The door opened abruptly.

"She's gone," Corry said. "Went out the back door. I caught a glimpse of her heading over to the church. I think it would be better if we left her alone for a few minutes."

"Did you tell her anything about—about us?"

"Only that I was trying to persuade you to stay a while."

Suddenly, Kate understood how it might have looked to Alyssa. For her whole life, she had had her father to herself; now she was being asked to welcome a woman who disapproved of the very thing Alyssa did best.

Without a word, Kate brushed past Corry. The back door of the dressing room stood ajar, letting a cold draft in from the night outside. She went out onto the little back porch and looked into the night. He was right. His daughter was heading for the church.

Corry appeared beside her. "Wait. I'll go with you."

"It would be better if I did it alone."

"Why?" he asked bluntly. He wasn't used to being challenged where his daughter was concerned. He didn't like it. He also was uneasy about what Kate might tell Alyssa.

"I wouldn't expect you to understand," Kate said. "I don't know if Alyssa will, either, but I need to give her the chance."

"Hold on a minute!" Corry was suddenly intent, almost wary. "What's this all about?"

"Music, that's all. Music and a girl's pride."

"Music and pride. That's all you have to talk about with my daughter?"

The tone of his voice made Kate uneasy. It was as though he suspected the other possible connection between Kate and Alyssa, mother and daughter who had never met.

"What else would we have to talk about besides you?" she asked.

"I was thinking more about Martin Thorson."

"Why would we talk about him?" Kate said sharply.

"You tell me," Corry snapped. "Sometimes I think I'm the one in the dark here."

Kate felt the blood leave her face. "Do you know what you are asking?" she whispered.

Corry stared at her for a long moment, trying to read the secret sources of her pain and fear. But in the end, his anger was undone by the look in her eyes. The look sobered him, made him feel ashamed for whatever he thought. Slowly, he felt his composure return.

"Forget it," he said, his voice as gentle as he could make it. "Go. Talk to Alyssa. Give her what she needs.

"I know you, Kate. I trust you not to hurt my daughter in the name of helping her. A teenager's sense of self is a fragile thing."

Kate started to speak, then turned away and hurried down the wooden steps into the night. Blue-white moonlight bleached all color from the new grass, but she could make out a thin, dark trail through the silvery dew. The way led off to the east, toward the church. She gathered her coat against the chill and walked more quickly.

As she came through the trees into the clearing, the trail veered away from the church and toward the graveyard. Something flashed at the edge of her vision. She turned and looked off to the horizon. A wall of clouds blanked out the starlight and gave the uncertain dance of lightning in return.

Weather change coming, she thought automatically. Enjoy the moonlight while you can. It will rain on you before Seattle. Then you'll be back in Manhattan, where you never pay attention to the weather, one day to the next, unless the snow is so bad the city shuts down.

Once, that kind of freedom from natural forces had seemed like a miracle to her. Now it seemed less benign, as though she might have lost as much as she gained.

So young, she thought. So many choices I can never make again, or unmake, or do anything but live with.

Kate turned and saw Alyssa fifty yards ahead, standing at the grave where Martin Thorson would be buried. She slowed, remembering what she had told Corry: music and pride, that's all.

Suddenly, she wasn't sure if that was all they would talk about. She knew what she intended to say, but she couldn't be sure where those words would take her. She had spent half her life hiding from the world and herself, exercising a kind of exquisite, spiritually exhausting control.

Yet time and again in the past three days, that control had deserted her. Time and again events had surprised her. Corry's honest seduction, Thorson's bleak madness, Alyssa's unexpected music.

Kate had opened a door into her heart and soul for one man; then, without warning, ghosts and strangers came streaming through. She had no idea where it would stop. She had no idea whether she possessed the power to make it stop, or whether she wanted to stop it, even if she did possess that power.

Corry's words echoed in her mind. He trusted her not to hurt his daughter. Kate wouldn't betray that trust; she couldn't. It would be like repeating the past all over again, an adult's need fulfilled at the cost of a child's.

Quietly, she approached Martin Thorson's empty grave. A pile of soil lay heaped near the rectangular black hole among the headstones. Alyssa stood beside the grave, staring down into it as though trying to see what would become of her friend. She carried her blond fiddle in one hand and the bow in the other.

Then she lifted the fiddle and began to play the measured, melancholy song again.

A ripple of pleasure went through Kate. She was thrilled at the precision with which the bow touched and moved over the strings, and at the rich evocation of emotion that resulted. Technical excellence could be taught. Feeling, style, and individuality could not.

Alyssa was not only capable of feeling deep emotions, she was able to express them through her violin. At first the music was dolorous, full of the pain of loss. Then the notes moved faster, more freely, with a kind of subdued gaiety—a celebration of life in the recognition of death.

Kate stood transfixed until the music ended. Then she stepped out into the moonlight.

"Alyssa." She called the name softly.

The girl turned, utterly unsurprised to see her there. "What do you want?"

Kate walked forward slowly, as though approaching a wary, wild creature. "I'd like to talk to you for a minute."

Saying nothing, Alyssa looked away, back to the grave.

Kate came up and stood beside her.

"I'm sorry to intrude," Kate said, "but I have to leave very soon, and I wanted to clear up a misunderstanding."

Alyssa looked up. Her girl's face was calm, as though she had dispelled some of the sorrow she felt through her fiddle.

"You're leaving?" she asked.

Kate nodded. "Didn't your father tell you?"

Alyssa's face changed. Kate couldn't read the new expression in the moonlight.

"He said he was going to try and talk you out of it," Alyssa said. "Dad usually gets what he wants. He has quite a way about him. Just when you're ready to hit him over the head with a pan, he does something wonderful and all you can do is love him."

Now Kate could see a small, private smile of understanding on the girl's face, as though she understood her father as an adult might. She felt a flush of heat on her face and was thankful the moon wasn't the sun.

"I know," she said. "He's very, uh, persuasive, but I'm supposed to be back in New York by noon tomorrow."

Alyssa nodded. If she was relieved, it didn't show in her expression or body language.

"What I wanted to tell you was that I think you are extremely talented," Kate said. "I don't know when I've heard a musician your age play with such exquisite, wrenching emotion. Few musicians of any age are capable of it."

Alyssa looked up, seeking the faintest touch of irony in her words or in her eyes. "It's not Mozart," she said defiantly.

"It doesn't have to be Mozart to be very, very good. I know that, even if I don't know much about Celtic music. That's what you play, isn't it? Celtic music?"

Alyssa nodded, still suspicious.

"What is the name of the piece you just played?" Kate asked.

"'Caledonia's Lament.' It was written in honor of a great Scottish fiddler, Niel Gow, by his son, Nathaniel."

"I've heard of Gow, but I've never played his music. I've been entirely caught up in classical music. That's why I didn't immediately recognize what you were doing when you began to play."

Alyssa stiffened.

"That's why I . . ." Kate smiled in wry apology. "That's why I pulled that awful face. I thought you had blown the opening phrase and I knew how much you must have wanted to play well, tonight of all nights."

The girl watched her defiantly. "You didn't like my playing."

"I didn't understand it. I was expecting apples and you were playing oranges. Once I listened without preconceptions, I realized that you have a great gift of expression."

Alyssa still looked suspicious, as though she couldn't believe what she was hearing. "You looked like someone had stepped on your foot."

"I know and I'm sorry. I was wrong. Adults often are."

The girl looked away. Then she looked at Kate again. "Do you really think I played well?"

"Better than well," Kate said. "You're incredibly talented. You should plan for a career in music, Celtic or classical or Brazilian, whatever. Just don't let your gift go to waste."

Alyssa smiled and swallowed hard. "Thanks," she said softly. "Only two people understood what playing the fiddle means to me, and one of them is dead now. It was . . . hard."

Kate heard the loneliness of a young talent in the girl's voice. It was a loneliness she herself had suffered. In truth, that loneliness was what had made Martin Thorson so attractive. It was the hunger for connection that had seduced her as much as the man. She knew that now, because for the first time in her life she hungered for one man, just one.

She looked at Alyssa, there in the moonlight, and saw herself long ago, poised on the brink of unknowable change, vulnerable to adult praise, adult acceptance.

As she watched the odd, crooked smile on Alyssa's face, Kate realized that this child could be seduced, too. The seduction would be spiritual rather than sexual, and all the more complete for it. She could bind Alyssa to her. A few more words of truthful praise and the vulnerable teenager would become her daughter.

In spirit, if not in fact.

Silently, Kate fought with the impulse to heal the inner wound that had been inflicted when she walked away from her baby daughter.

I have no right to her mind or soul or affection, Kate told herself bleakly. I gave away that right the moment I walked away in order to give my daughter a better life than I could give her. The life she has now is good. It's all I could have wished for her.

Yet the anguish of giving up her daughter had been sharpened rather than dulled by the passage of time.

"Marty, Pastor Thorson, talked to me about making a career in music," Alyssa said. "He made me sit through—uh, that is, he introduced me to—all the women who have made careers in classical music. He played your stuff until I knew it by heart."

Kate smiled past the pain gripping her. "I'll bet you pulled the same kind of face I did tonight."

"Uh, yeah." Alyssa smiled self-consciously. "It took me a while, but it grew on me. When no one else is around, I play Mozart, or try to. That man must have hated fiddlers."

"He pushes you to your limits and then demands more."

"It doesn't take long for me to reach my limit," the

girl admitted. "Some of those notes are so close together it would take a computer to separate them. How do you do it?"

"Practice, more practice, then more practice. And love. You have to love the music itself."

"That's what Marty said. He even told me that someday I wouldn't be able to resist Mozart's challenge. I thought he was crazy." She shrugged. "He was right."

"Did he know?" Kate asked, because it was somehow important to her.

"Yeah. He caught me murdering Mozart one day and showed me how to hold my fingers and the bow. It was a lot easier after that, but it screwed up my Celtic fiddling something awful until I learned to switch back and forth."

Kate smiled even though she wanted to cry. "I'll bet."

"In some ways, he reminded me of Dad. He never rubbed my nose in it when I was wrong. He just praised me when I did right, got exasperated when I was stubborn, and always, always *cared*. Sometimes I feel like I had two fathers, instead of a father and a mother like normal kids," she said.

The yearning in Alyssa's voice was as unmistakable as it was poignant. She wanted a mother, needed one, was hungry for the understanding that only one woman could give another.

Kate shivered in the moonlight. Now she knew precisely how Martin Thorson had felt the moment he had made the decision to lay his hand on her breast and kiss her.

A few words, a sentence, a revelation . . . and Alyssa would have the mother she desperately yearned for without really knowing the consequences of finding what she sought.

The terrible temptation of innocence.

As Kate measured the strength of that temptation, she finally and completely forgave Martin Thorson. She understood exactly how powerful his desire had been, exactly what unwitting role she had played in her own seduction, and in his.

But unlike Thorson, she couldn't feed her own hungers at the cost of a child's, even if the child seemed to encourage it. Terrible or not, innocence was still . . . *innocent*.

Knowing that, she finally and completely forgave herself. A feeling of lightness swept over her, as though she were a bird spreading her wings and stepping into the wind after a long captivity.

"You're very lucky to have had two good parents, no matter what their sex," Kate said distinctly. "And they were very, very lucky to have you. Good-bye, Alyssa. It has been a privilege sharing your music, if only for a night." She hesitated, then couldn't help asking, "Would it be all right if I hugged you?"

Surprised, the girl hugged Kate awkwardly, violin and all.

"Thank you," Alyssa said. "It helps, knowing that someone like you thinks I'm good."

"I don't think it, I know it."

The girl hugged her again very hard, then let go. When Kate stepped back, she saw that Alyssa was shivering.

"You'll catch cold," Kate said. She slipped out of her down coat and draped it around the girl's shoulders. "Here, take this. A gift from one fiddler to another."

"Really?" Alyssa stroked the fabric of the coat and tested the resilience of the down as though she were preening herself. "But won't you be cold?"

"My car is close by."

"Are you sure? It's such a beautiful coat."

"Beautiful coat, beautiful girl. Sounds just right to me."

Kate adjusted the drape of the coat, then kissed Alyssa lightly on the cheek.

"Practice hard and always remember that you're special. Let that carry you through the loneliness and the despair and the frustration. Let your gift carry you to . . ." She paused, smiling. "What would the pinnacle of a Celtic fiddler's success be?"

Alyssa smiled confidently. "Dad made an instrument a couple of years ago for Diane McIntyre. She went on to win the U.S. Women's Scottish Fiddling Championship with it."

"All right, then," Kate said, "let the knowledge that you're special carry you through, not to the women's championship, but to the championship, period."

Alyssa seemed stunned at that prospect. "Do you think I'm good enough for that?"

"I know you are."

"Gosh. Did you hear that, Dad? She thinks I'm good enough to be the best Scottish fiddler in the country."

Kate turned quickly. Corry was standing just beyond reach, smiling at his daughter yet watching Kate.

"You're good enough to win anything you want to work for," Corry say. "Now go on back inside, honey. Your adoring public wants to tell you how much they loved your fiddling."

Alyssa looked suddenly uncertain. "Come with me?"

He hesitated.

"Please? I don't know some of those people."

"Go with her, Bran," Kate said. "She needs you."

"And we need to talk," he said.

"Better hurry," she said to Alyssa. "Audiences have a short attention span."

"Right. C'mon, Dad. You heard her."

Corry gave in to his daughter, but he looked over his shoulder half a dozen times before he disappeared into the building.

Each time he looked back, Kate was standing motionless, staring down at Martin Thorson's empty grave.

Twenty-four

The leading edge of a weather front climbed the sky, edging toward the blue-white disk of the moon. Kate stood beside the grave that waited for the father of her child, watching the sky. She had been freed of the heavy weight of a young woman's mistaken belief in the wrong man.

She felt light, almost giddy, as though she could fly if she truly wished it.

"Martin," she said softly, speaking to the empty grave, "did you know Alyssa was your child, or were you, too, simply healing the wound of the past?"

Whatever he had known or suspected or believed, he had said nothing to Alyssa. This time he had resisted the terrible innocence of her need.

Kate was profoundly grateful for that. It made her past choices less hurtful. Whatever Martin's flaws, there had been goodness in him as well. Whatever her own flaws, there was goodness in her, too.

"Thank you," she said to the night.

Then she turned away from the grave and walked through the old cemetery, gathering strength for her last bittersweet appointment with the past. She found the spot where she and Campbell had first confronted one another, where she had first seen Bran Corry, where she began to fall in love with him.

The irony of it brought tears to her eyes, tears she refused to shed. Corry was the only man in her life she might truly love, but the cost of that love would be a young girl's peace. There was no justice in it.

Or maybe there was too much justice.

She was certain she would never marry, never have another child, never share her life beyond the incomplete communion of the stage.

Polyphony and my music will be enough, she thought. They will have to be. God knows stardom could certainly consume me, if I let it.

She thought she probably would; a last choice, one made in knowledge rather than innocence.

It was time to go, time to give Alyssa and Corry the gift of peace that had eluded Kate for so long. She could hold back from Alyssa's innocence, but Corry's adult complexity could too easily reach past the wall she was trying to build between them.

It's better that we don't talk, she said. I want . . . too much. He'll see that. Damned shaman, knowing too many things. I wish to God that knowledge was enough.

Kate turned and began walking swiftly toward her car, turning away from the human bustle and light of the grange. The instant she moved, an odd, faint drumming sound came from the tree line. The sound was familiar and unknown at the same time.

At the corner of her eye she caught a blur of white and black against the moonlit ground. It was Campbell, streaking toward the cemetery, running fast and low to the ground.

The dog dashed through the headstones as though he were on a long fetch. He passed close enough that Kate could see his head. Twice he flicked his clever eyes in her direction. He knew exactly where she was. He was circling past her.

Then he turned and began pinching in. He came straight at her, slowing as he approached, flattening out close to the ground. When he was ten yards away, he dropped his belly to the ground and stared at her cannily, as though he were trying to hypnotize her. The intensity of his stare touched her on a primitive level. Even though she knew the dog was friendly, she felt like prey.

"Hello, Campbell," she said uneasily. "Did you come here to get your ears scratched one last time?"

The dog inched forward on his belly, then stopped again. All the while, he watched her as though she were an unpredictable, dangerous swan.

In the distance, she heard Bran's keen whistle. She knew it well enough to identify his "return to me" command. But Campbell flattened more closely to the ground and showed no sign of heeding.

"The boss wants you," she told the dog. "I suspect he's not in a good mood. He might make you pay, since he can't control me."

Campbell barked sharply but didn't rise up. Kate took a step backward as an experiment. The dog advanced the same distance.

No doubt about it. He was herding her.

She heard Bran's whistle again.

The dog barked again.

"Let me go, you devil," Kate said. "He can't see me yet. Go home!"

Campbell didn't budge. Kate spun to the side and took two running steps. The dog appeared in front of her. She had no doubt that he would tangle himself in her feet and bring her unceremoniously to the cold ground.

"Go away!" she whispered furiously.

She made another feint. The dog was too quick for her. Before she could try another escape, Corry jogged into sight. He took in the dog and the woman poised for flight. The scowl on his face deepened.

"What do you think you're up to?" he asked.

Kate chose to believe he was talking to his dog. "Ask Campbell," she said. "It's his game, not mine."

"Campbell. Come."

Reluctantly, the dog looked away from Kate. She turned and began walking toward the distant car on a path that would take her away from both man and dog.

Campbell cut her off.

"Come," Corry repeated.

The dog was suddenly deaf.

Corry stepped around a gravestone and spoke directly to Campbell.

"Come!"

The dog flinched uneasily, but didn't take his eyes off Kate.

Corry stopped and looked from the dog to the woman.

"See what I mean?" Kate asked.

"I'm beginning to."

"Watch," she said.

She moved a yard to the left. Campbell matched the distance and direction in one jump. Then she moved two yards back. Campbell advanced toward her.

"Well, I'll be damned," Corry said.

"I thought you had put him up to it."

"I considered it," he admitted. "But I couldn't find him. He had jumped out of the truck and vanished. He's never done that before."

Kate watched Campbell carefully. She no longer felt threatened, just herded. The little dog was as intent in his own way as his master had been in the kitchen the night before.

"Campbell," Corry said firmly.

The dog flinched again but didn't move.

Corry stood ten yards away, rubbing his beard thoughtfully. It was obvious that Campbell, though unhappy at ignoring orders, was nonetheless going to keep on refusing them. Corry looked at the dog and at the direction Kate had been going.

Understanding came. He was tempted to praise the dog but kept his mouth shut. At the moment, he was too angry to trust his voice.

"Do something," Kate said after a minute of silence.

"What do you have in mind? He hasn't refused a command since he was a pup and I caught him stealing strawberries. Animals can be almost as contrary as humans."

She hoped the irritation in Corry's voice was for his dog. Somehow she doubted it. He was looking at her, not at the stubborn collie.

"Let's find the limits of your cage," Corry suggested, amused. "Go to the left."

"I already tried that."

"Right?"

"Tried that," she snapped.

"Backward."

"That, too."

"Then try coming forward," he said gently, "to me."

Kate remembered what Alyssa had said about hitting him over the head with a pan. She spun around and walked directly toward Corry. When she was just beyond arm's reach, she stopped.

Campbell matched her movements, foot for foot. When she stopped, he flattened out again and waited, watching, still on duty.

Corry stepped forward and put his hand on Kate's shoulder. Instantly, Campbell lifted from his crouch. His job done, he trotted off to investigate the rich, fascinating smells of the night.

"The son of a bitch," Kate said with a bitter, fragmented laugh. "Why wouldn't he listen?"

"A good handler learns to trust his dog's instincts, as well as his own," Corry said, drawing her closer. "You'll learn to trust us, too."

When he would have kissed her, she turned her face away and blocked his embrace with her hands against his chest. The warmth and strength of him were a temptation greater than any she had known in her life. She made a helpless, futile sound.

"Can't you see this is more painful for me than for you?" she asked brokenly.

Corry let his lips brush the top of her head, then drew her closer, almost but not quite against her will.

"I can see your pain," he said. "I can feel my own. Why are you running from what we both want?"

For a moment, Kate let herself lean against his hard strength. Just a moment, she told herself, no more.

"Loving you would be so very, very easy," she whispered. "But love based on someone else's pain is too flawed to last."

"Whose pain?"

Kate just shook her head.

"Alyssa?" Corry asked. "Is she the problem? Is the prospect of a daughter so awful that you have to run away?"

The careful wall she had built up broke apart. She stood in his embrace and sobbed in wrenching silence.

Corry felt the tremors in her shoulders, just as he tasted the sweetness of her scent on the night air and felt her tears against his hand. He held her and said nothing, waiting for her to finish grieving for something he didn't fully understand. He only knew that her grief was as real as love.

He watched the clouds lifting against the sky. Distant lightning flickered.

It would be a good night to crawl into bed and listen to the first rain on the roof, he thought. Spring rain, not as warm as Kate's tears but not as cold as winter, either.

A movement in the sky caught his attention. A widening chevron of birds climbed on powerful wings from the saltwater bay where the trumpeter swans spent their nights. In the far distance, he heard the first, faint cries, bugle sounds in the still moonlight as the swans called out the beginning of their inevitable migration north.

The season of the swan was over. He could no more prevent them from flying than he could keep the woman he loved in his arms.

Kate sensed the change in Corry, the weary acceptance. She looked up at him, then turned and followed the direction of his gaze. Now she, too, could hear the swans. Their bell-like voices were a melancholy intermezzo, a bridge between what was and what will be.

"They wait for a good front to push up from the southwest," Corry said. "Apparently they can ride it all the way to their nesting grounds. The lure of it is irresistible. Not one swan will be left by morning."

Kate shivered at the thought. There was magic in this night. She could feel it as surely as she felt Corry's strength.

"See," she said. "They know it's time, even if they can't tell you why."

She kissed him very gently on the lips. Then she moved away from him, trying to open a space between them like the one she had opened between herself and Alyssa.

"I have to go," she said.

Slowly his arms dropped away.

"Remember," he said. "The swans always come back."

Kate's smile trembled with sadness. "Not the black ones. You've got a white one in your nest, though. Doesn't she look good in that coat?"

Corry stood empty-handed, watching Kate. "She was very proud of it, as though she had won a prize."

"You've done a wonderful job with her. And if I can ever help, tell me. I'd like nothing better. I—She—" Kate's voice broke. She swallowed. "You have a great daughter. Anyone would be proud to be her mother or father or—"

She gave up trying to speak and simply fought for self-control.

"Have you ever wanted a child?" Corry asked.

Kate put her hands over her face and tried not to cry out with pain.

He flinched at her pain, yet he kept on going.

"Kate, I love you. I believe you could love me. Isn't that worth fighting for?"

"Not at the cost of your daughter."

Corry hardly recognized Kate's voice. "What do you mean?"

"Damn your dog. Damn the past. Damn Martin for meddling. And damn me for being so weak!"

"He was right, wasn't he?" Corry said. "You gave up a child once."

Kate felt the breath go out of her body. She stared at the rising formations of swans headed north. She thought she had joined them, until Bran Corry shot an arrow through her breast.

"He should know," she said bitterly. "It was his child."

Corry's breath came in with a rushing sound. He watched as the swans passed before a moonlit cloud, their flight so powerful and effortless. Then he looked back at Kate.

"I knew bits and pieces of Marty's life," he said gently, "but I saw no pattern, Kate, not until after you and I started down this road.

"And once we had started, I still didn't figure it all out, not until this moment.

"Is Alyssa yours?"

Kate couldn't speak for a moment. It was a question she had never heard spoken aloud.

"She could be," she admitted. "I don't know. What I do know is that in every way that counts, she's your daughter. I can't get in the way of that."

"What makes you think you will?"

"If she's mine . . ." Kate made a helpless gesture.

"What if she isn't?" Corry asked. "What if Marty was just doing what he said he was, helping out one talented girl because he had betrayed another?"

She looked at him with a longing she couldn't conceal. "Does Alyssa even know she's adopted?"

"Yes."

"Has she ever asked about her mother?"

"No. Neither one of them," he added deliberately.

"Fair enough," Kate whispered. "Both her mothers failed her."

"One of them did; my supposedly adult wife, not the frightened, confused, betrayed teenager who gave her daughter a better chance at life."

Overhead, the first of the swans flew by, so close and low that both people could hear the whistling rush of air through pinions.

"Kate," Corry said. He tilted her face until she had to meet his eyes. "I have a daughter who needs a mother. You're a mother who needs a daughter. Does it really matter so much which mother, which daughter?"

"No."

"Then why are you so intent on flying away?"

"What if Alyssa finds out I'm her mother?"

"What if she finds out you *aren't*. Would you still want to be around her?"

"Of course! What are you talking about?"

"Keeping you here, with me. Do you think you could love me, Kate Saarinan? Loving my daughter wouldn't be enough. She'll fly as certainly as those swans. I wouldn't keep her even if I could. But I would keep you, if you loved me."

Kate listened to the swans flying by in the night, free within the prison of their instincts. And as she listened, she understood what a horrible mistake she had almost made. She turned and looked at Corry.

"Such a strange look," he said. "Is the idea of loving me so alien?"

"Not at all. I'm trying to decide whether you really are a Celtic magician, or simply the best man I've ever met."

"And?"

"I'll get back to you on that," she said, smiling despite the tears in her eyes.

Baffled, Corry watched as Kate reached into her purse and pulled out the cell phone. She turned it on and began punching in numbers.

Kate held the phone so that he could hear. The number rang twice before an answering machine picked up.

"This is the Ethan Farr Agency," a voice said. "We are not in the office at the moment. Please leave a message so that we may get back to you as soon as possible."

The tone sounded, signaling the start of the message tape. Kate put the phone to her ear and spoke.

"Ethan, it's Kate. I'm not coming back tonight, and I won't be there in time to sign the Polyphony contract before Monday morning."

"The Strad?" Corry asked softly.

She nodded, still speaking into the phone. "If the offer is real, it will still be there next week. And if it isn't, so be it. There are other real things in the world. I'm looking at one of them. I'll call you next week and explain."

Smiling, Kate broke the connection and put the phone back in her purse.

Corry stood still for a long moment, watching the dark-haired woman who had stolen his heart. The calls of the swans swirled around them like wild music. He held out his hand. When she took it without hesitation, he kissed her hard and then gently.

"Come on, my Celtic shaman," she said. "I want to sleep with you in your own bed tonight. Oh, damn!"

"What's wrong."

"Alyssa."

Corry laughed. "She'll complicate our lives, but not tonight. She's staying one more night at her friend's house."

Kate looked surprised. "How did you know I wouldn't leave?"

He chuckled deep in his chest and shook his head.

"Tell me," she demanded.

He took her in his arms and held her close for a long, long time. Then he bent and whispered against her lips.

"Even Campbell knows that black swans don't migrate."